EFFECT

ROBERT S. AZAR

Black Rose Writing | Texas

ISBN: 978-1-68433-185-7
PUBLISHED BY BLACK ROSE WRITING
www.blackrosewriting.com

Printed in the United States of America
Suggested Retail Price (SRP) $18.95

Effect is printed in Garamond

Dedicated to my children:
Linda, Alex, Brian and Ryan.
It's never too late to rectify a wrong.

EFFECT

CHAPTER 1
THE PUPPET MASTER

Evil has an obvious identity. It's easily recognizable to the young, old, feeble-minded and literate masses. Old fashion nightly news and ubiquitous forms of social media constantly offer up grotesque images to reinforce the worst forms of human savagery. Kidnap, murder and all forms of tortured victims make us gasp the next day, as they are discussed across the millions of break rooms, while we wonder "how could anyone do such a thing."

There is also evil that is less known. It is camouflaged in high places; in uniforms with shiny medals; in expensive attire and masked with the allusion of power. The worst kind of evil. One that offers a helping hand to society accompanied by a smile, while behind the curtain grand plans map out a destiny that is filled with mass death, debilitating disease and altered expectations for civilization. In short, it's true Evil because these manipulators play God yet have no God except for themselves.

One such illusionist climbing his way to the bottom pretends to be a protector of the motherland. His initiation happened years ago and he is now in the last stages of the transformation aboard an amphibious assault ship that sits in the Indian Ocean off the coast of Somalia.

The ship holds a small elite unit preparing for a special mission on the mainland of Africa. Our Colonel leads the operation.

"Colonel, are your men ready and prepped for Operation Leafcutter?" asked General Fleming.

"Yes sir. My men have trained for weeks and understand the complexities of the mission. They are green for go."

"The last time we did this was a God damn disgrace. I don't want any mishaps this time Colonel."

"Sir, the white coats back home give it a 90% chance of working."

"Those are pretty good odds but what if things go south, then what?"

"Sir, we have contingency plans in that event. Besides, these men are all replaceable."

"Good, the product will be delivered in a smaller cruiser after the mothership. You and your men should not encounter any resistance along the Shebelle River for a few hours at least.

"My men are ready for anything that comes our way General."

"Fine, you'll rendezvous five clicks above the Mogadishu outpost with some friendlies led by Captain Mohammed Daraku. His team will assist from then on."

Colonel Master's team lands in a remote airfield on the coast of Eastern Africa. They gathered their gear and helicoptered to the mouth of the river.

The men of special task force 8 were told tribal chieftain Ali Sakami was attacking merchant ships off the coast for months and needed to be caught or killed. Sakami was also listed on the CIA's target list for a bombing of a U.S. Navy vessel off the port of Alexandria, Egypt.

The team never needed pumping up for their missions but when told Sakami was responsible for American deaths, they were ready for payback.

Bravo team 8 met up with their Somali counterparts at 0730 hours. Captain Daraku led them the rest of the way up the river and to Sakami's base camp. Colonel Masters stays behind in an enclosed floating fortress guarded by several highly paid mercenaries.

As they got closer to their destination, the men of Bravo team glance at schoolchildren walking down the road. Corporal Mackenzie was the first to ask the obvious: "Sir, do we have the right coordinates? It doesn't look like there are any fighters at this village, only women and children."

"Yeh, this is right. I double checked myself," said Sgt. Shavers, a veteran of several Mideast wars and a lifer in the Marines, "but as a precaution, I'll radio back to the Colonel."

"Colonel Masters, the men are questioning the drop zone. It looks like a village and not a base camp for Sakami: only friendlies here, sir."

"Since when are subordinates allowed to question their commanding officer? Where did you get your training from Sergeant? I told you those are the coordinates, now follow your orders."

"You heard the big man. The Colonel says these are the right coordinates and to continue with the operation."

"Well maybe he got it wrong," said Mackenzie. "It is possible for the Marines to make mistakes."

"You wanna be the one to tell the Colonel he's wrong, be my guest."

No one utters a word.

"That's what I thought." Sergeant Shavers then nods to private Kamp, cryptically giving the order: "Let's pollinate. Release the hatch."

With that command, two privates opened the hatch to the cargo. A piercing siren punctured the air as thousands of hornets raced out of their enclosed tomb headed straight for the children, stinging them mercilessly. Some of the hornets sat on the roofs as if they were waiting for others to rescue the children. Their fate would all end in the same manner as the flying predators swooped down and stung everyone in sight.

Instantly, large welts covered their bodies oozing a puss as they feverishly scratched at their wounds. The carnage only lasted a minute as the young and old keeled over holding their stomachs.

There was no sign of the warlord Ali Sakami.

The flying weapons had been doped with a toxin that was transmitted to the "enemy." The special payload was developed by IS&G industries.

"Fall out men. We need to make sure all is accounted for," barked Sgt. Shavers.

"Sir, those hornets are still out there. Won't they attack us?" asked private first class, Dylan Gomes.

"That's why you took your shots back at base camp, remember? Besides, those little zappers are loaded for one trip to unload their payload. They'll be spent by the time you guys encounter them. If anything, you'll get a sting with no real bite to it. Not like those poor bastards in the village," said Shavers, sucking on his cigar.

"Sgt. Shavers, what's all the commotion about? I gave you an order to hit the village and survey the damage. Now get the fuck out there before I court martial your ass."

"Yes sir. I just needed to give some guidance to my team. To be honest Colonel, they're a little spooked about the bugs."

"God damn it Shavers. What kind of outfit are we running here? Sakami could be getting his greasy ass ready to counterattack at any moment; get moving!"

The men of Bravo team landed on the banks of the river and let loose a loud "Ooh Rah" as they ran down the dirt road to the village-armed to the teeth. They were ready to kick ass.

Bravo team met no resistance and found not a single fighter or for that matter Ali Sakami.

"This is bullshit. It's only kids and women here," said Kamp, "This ain't right. What the fuck are we doing here?"

Gomes and Mackenzie echo the same sentiment as the women and children lay on the ground holding their stomachs crying out for relief, but there was no help coming. The hornets buzzed around some still stinging the kids as they tried to swat them away with their tiny hands.

Some of the team tried to help the children but Sgt. Shavers ordered them not to interfere. "They look like civilians but they could be booby-trapped. Stand your ground," he said, incredulously.

The men of Bravo team radioed back to Colonel Masters who was awaiting their report.

"Sir, it looks like only civilians here and they're all messed up with those zappers we sent. I think we should pull back. My men are getting spooked with all the kids screaming for help."

"No, good job Sergeant. Tell your men to be on the alert. I've seen this before. They plant themselves in a friendly village and wait for us to come in. I know you'll find them. Just keep moving. Go up three clicks north and I'll give you further instructions."

"Yes sir."

"The Colonel says to move up river a few clicks and he'll give us further instructions."

"Go up a few more clicks, for what?" asked Mackenzie. "We just unleashed hell and wasted all these people for no reason."

"You'll do as you're told Corporal. That goes for all of you. Get your asses in gear now or you'll all be written up for disobeying orders."

The team moves up a few clicks and awaited new orders.

They never came.

Colonel Masters radioed in coordinates to the village. He uses a secure channel to connect to another ship based off the coast, away from Central

Command and the General. He turned the boat back down river and sped away.

A few minutes later a drone fires a series of missiles roaring across the desert incinerating the village and all the men of Bravo team 8.

•   •   •   •   •

"Colonel Masters, welcome back. I hear the mission was a great success," said General Fleming.

"Yes sir. Everything went as planned. The bees targeted all humans in the area with their payload and returned to the ship after release."

"Did we get Sakami?"

"Sir, we believe he slipped away. We did, however, find a large amount of small arms and bomb-making equipment."

"He's a sneaky son of a bitch but well done Colonel."

"Thank you, sir."

"So, the mission was a success in your opinion?"

"Absolutely sir."

"Is there anything we need to improve on?"

"Well, sir, the bees came back and attacked my men. They killed all of them. Once equipped with the toxin, they need to release all of it. I guess the one drawback is that the toxin is a one shot and done proposition."

"You're right Colonel that is a drawback and it can get pricey. Those bastards at IS&G charge the military a hefty price tag for that shit. My superiors are always looking for ways to reduce costs. Still, once we get this perfected, it will be an awesome killing machine."

"Yes sir. It sure will."

"Well, keep up with the good work Colonel. At this rate, you'll make General in no time."

CHAPTER 2
THE ORDER

Towering over the banks of the Danube River in Vienna, Austria, a medieval structure miraculously kept up for over one thousand years hosts a gathering of the Order.

The guests enter the old stone behemoth under the cloak of darkness. It's rather damp outside, as a blanket of fog hovers around the cars obediently parked outside. The wind is whistling through the different and overgrown trees that line the entrance. The men mingle in the foyer and have drinks brought to them in the great room. No more than thirty are present for the gathering. They then sit around a large mahogany table facing one another.

"Gentlemen, thank you all for coming," said Prince Hans Eckert. "As the leader of the Order in Europe, I summoned you today to discuss the plans from the Central Authority that were agreed upon many years ago and is in its final stages as we speak."

All the men smile and shake their heads in agreement while the Prince continued,

"We are entering turbulent and trying times for the planet. It has been a difficult journey with much mistrust throughout the globe. We have never had consensus before but the Central Authority is confident that we are in the best possible position to make our ultimate objective a reality. We must succeed for the future of the planet."

The men clap and then a scar-faced man with a Hungarian accent raises his left hand. "Brother, at our last meeting we spoke about several methods to meet our needs. Is there one path to achieving our goals or are we still open to employing all options?"

"Thank you, Mr. Prime Minister for the question. Our brethren in North America are convinced the insect approach is the most viable one for their continent. It has proven to have dramatic but mixed results. What can I say; the Americans always have a flair for the dynamics. It is after all the land of Hollywood."

The men all laugh, click their glasses and clap in response.

"Thus, we are gathered today to disclose the plans for the other continents. Tonight is the time to voice a concern, for all will be heard."

The men all look around at each other but no voices or hands are raised.

"For Africa, we will release the virus using the M2240 strain on the population developed by our brothers in Sector 9. This strain must be released locally by a willing participant and then will spread quickly. The Untouchables of the continent are already inoculated. They are not told of our ultimate plans, of course, but realize that a transformation is about to take place."

A person with a thick mustache and failing dark hair raised his left hand and asked, "Do we have enough participants who willingly will carry out this death mission?"

"Our brothers in Hamburg have assured me that they have an ample supply. The number of people unemployed is in the millions and there is no shortage of migrants willing to earn extra money to send back to their home countries. This will be quite painful to watch but those savages have overrun our continent for far too long. They will be repaid soon enough."

A Frenchman then raised his left hand, "Monsieur, I agree with the approach but I hope that in our beloved Europa it will be much cleaner than what is planned in the states."

"My brother, that was the consensus at last year's meeting. 'A gentle death', was the saying as I recall. We agree that the P2040 strain used in North America can easily be sprayed by airplanes to cover the continent. Rest assured that it will be completely dispersed in weeks across our lands without resistance. We have pleaded with the Americans to use this technique but they are fanatic about using this military bug option. In either case, the population will be told this is another pesticide to kill off the bugs destroying the crops."

The men drink and pat the table with their left hands in a show of unanimous support for the technique.

"Of course, you all know we have no agreement on the Eastern block of India, China and Russia, but we will persevere on our own until they come around. As we are all aware, decades of mistrust and wars do not go away quickly."

"Now, this leaves us with South America. Our brothers at IS&G have developed an ingenious strain of wheat over the years and are close to perfection on it. When pollinated, the toxin travels quite far and releases into the air. The problem has always been to pollinate before the crops would fail. The catalyst developed recently in the lab will react to induce pollination and carry the virus across the continent. Once airborne, it has an infectious radius nearly one hundred miles, which should be perfect for our application."

"Monsieur, what happens to the people after the population is infected? Do they die off quickly?"

"The beauty of this technique is that once infected, it lies dormant in the system for months and then transmits sexually to other people. After the incubation period has ended and transmutation has taken place from host to another organism, death comes quite rapidly to both participants, or should I say specimens. The masses will think the virus is another STD and by the time they have discovered the truth, it will be too late to counter the offensive. It will spread from the Amazon to the ocean."

The men all smile proudly at their accomplishment and now are smoking and drinking heavily.

"Well, at least all the poor bastards will go out with a smile on their faces," said a tall blonde haired elderly German. A perfect member of the Aryan race.

The secretive members of the Order laugh uncontrollably, almost feverishly at this point.

The host then said, "We shall in time call this virus Latin Fever."

A rousing, "Perfecto, Bravo" echoes throughout the great room.

After some more drinking and laughing, the men strip off their clothes and change into their new wardrobes. Obedient servants waiting in the halls, who are summoned by a bell, brought robes to them.

They meet twenty minutes later in the rear of the castle. The men including Hans are dressed in all black with just their eyes showing. Hans is holding a golden scepter. It's ice-cold outside while flakes of snow whip around the members gathered around a large fire.

Hans taps the scepter three times and the men recite the oath of the Order. After the oath is recited, a lamb is butchered and its blood is drained into golden chalices where the members enthusiastically drink every last drop of it.

CHAPTER 3
PLANNING

10 Dusseldorf street Hamburg, Germany, houses an abandoned BMW manufacturing facility. Cars stopped strolling off the lines twenty-five years ago. Now, the facility churns out another type of product.

Under the German Intelligence services or BND and affiliated with IS&G Industries, the official title to the building is the Reeducation of the Transient Population (RTP). The men, mainly dark, very dark and black come from Africa and were teenagers during the great migration in the early part of the 21st century. These immigrants never assimilated into Germany or for that matter any part of Europe. Most of them spent time in the prison system. They are middle-aged, unemployed and have no children or spouses: truly dregs of society.

The process of re-education starts with sleep deprivation. Visual and acoustic imagery is an important factor in the conditioning of the selected individuals as well. There are dozens if not hundreds in the large complex. Not everyone will make the final cut. The smarter ones are reintroduced back into the system. The less fortunate are given food and medical "care."

Once adequately deprived and nearly out of their feeble minds, they are conditioned to believe that Europa has been a waste of their lives all these many years. They are not filled with malice, to the contrary, a yearning for their Mother land is drilled into their minds with whatever time they have left on earth. No other goal is to be achieved except in returning "home."

Imagery of an Africa full of sexual desires and heavenly pleasures are reintroduced into their psyche. If they are not compliant enough after several sessions, electrolysis is introduced, involuntarily. The process can take anywhere from a few weeks to several months. The final piece to the puzzle, an assurance that everything will go as planned, is the chip implant, again manufactured by the good people of IS&G. The chip will ensure that no demon of a subconscious raises its ugly head to disrupt the planned emigration back to Africa. It is attached to the base of the brain with one overriding sensation and drive: return to Africa.

Bashir Hamfu hailed from Libya. A small-time dealer in the arms trade and credit card manipulator at the age of seventeen; he learned his trade well as his father pulled him out of school to learn the family business. Hamfu used the prior Mideast wars as cover for his immigration four decades earlier. He paid smugglers ten thousand dollars to take a rickety fishing boat across the Mediterranean. The voyage didn't end with the vessel sinking; however, it did give Hamfu a look at the horrific nature that exists when desperation is the only thing keeping a person alive.

The older men on the vessel routinely raped the young boys escaping, including Hamfu. The ones that refused were thrown overboard. Hamfu did as he was ordered. The vessel landed in Italy where other smugglers had their way with the Africans. The long journey on land culminated three months later in a camp on the Austrian border where Bashir finally applied and received asylum in Germany, as did so many of his other compatriots.

With relatives still in Libya, Bashir has for years sent any money he could spare back home. He was thought to be a prime candidate for the treatment and freely volunteered. After passing the initial stages with no problems, Bashir has second thoughts on continuing.

"Herr Director, I wish no longer to participate in the treatment," said Bashir.

Director Friedrick, manager of the RTP, listens intently as Bashir makes his case. Although middle-aged on paper, his innocent look and trembling hands make him look as if he is twenty- seven.

"Mr. Hamfu, have you not agreed to participate and taken a generous amount of money from the government. Have you not spent and used those funds?" asked Director Friedrick.

"Herr Director, I have sent the money back to Libya to help my sister who is a widow to provide for her children but this facility is making me sick. I want to go back to my house and sleep in my own bed."

"We have medical care, son. Tell me what is ailing you?"

"Herr Director, the treatment is giving me very bad headaches and I am not able to hold down any food."

"Wait here Bashir, I certainly don't want you to do something you are not in agreement with or that is damaging to your health. We will have an answer for you shortly."

Friedrick walks away from Bashir and down the hall with his aide, Herman, whispering to each other.

"Herman, I need willing participants to go along with the process. Why wasn't Hamfu selected out before spending all this time and money on him?"

"Sir, we used various tests including IQ to differentiate the people. Sometimes the process doesn't work and we miss a few. Hamfu looked like the perfect specimen to conduct and continue with the program but perhaps he was deceiving us all along."

"Herman, that's a very long and convoluted answer. Perhaps, you should just say that you screwed up."

"Well, of course sir. You are right."

"Should we expend more effort on him and place him back into the population? I think there is still a chance he will conform."

"Don't be silly young man. We're on a strict timeline. Give him a long sleep and then turn him loose. We'll have enough blood on our hands in a short while. Proceed with the others as planned and try not to make any more mistakes."

"Right away, sir."

The other more obedient inmates came out of the process with a yearning for Africa and a gleam in their eyes. They were as compliant as elementary children in grown-up bodies.

Around the clock, the "men" came off the old BMW assembly line eagerly lining up on the buses headed to the port on the Elbe River a few miles down the road.

Their ships would take them to their original host countries of Nigeria, Somalia, Ethiopia and others, primarily along the coast. They were given passports, money and directions on where to go. Their handlers already equipped with the virus would be waiting for them at a predestined location well within the city centers of their respective capitals. All were given orders to take their special packages to these city centers on April 1 and break the seal.

•   •   •   •   •

Across the Atlantic Ocean on the South American continent, millions of acres of wheat were planted in vast areas of Brazil that were once jungle but now were used for agriculture. Many of the acres are owned by members of the Order. The others are given subsidies to introduce the crops to their farms. Since only one percent of the farms are locally owned, it wasn't hard to convince the large multinationals to go along with the plans emanating out of Europe.

The Order would wait and see if the process in Brazil worked as expected and if so, would introduce the procedure to the rest of the continent. Since Brazil housed one-quarter of a billion people, an effective reduction there would satisfy the goals of the Central Authority and Order.

From the glitzy shores of Rio de Janeiro to the urban sprawl of Sao Paula and in the southern stronghold of Curitiba, the crops flourished and bloomed. It would take a growing season to see if the procedure was a success but the government or more specifically the Order, did not have to worry about the population in revolt, at least not yet.

CHAPTER 4
COMMITTEE OF 300

A sprawling well-kept one hundred-room castle is perched outside of San Francisco's city limits. As long black cars come racing up to the front door, mostly men, but a few women with dark glasses, are escorted with armed men equipped with assault rifles. The guards wait outside while the dignitaries go in.

There are thin, neatly embroidered black notepads covering a long mahogany table in the center of a great room. Jazz music is moving at a frantic pace in the background. On the cover of each pad, are the words Committee of 300 and underneath smaller letters stating, "The Committee of 300 is a charitable organization from around the world engaged in furthering progressive change for humanity."

The guests sit eating light refreshments and then a bearded man in his late eighties with a foreign accent gets up and moves to the head of the table. He taps his glass as the room quietly settles down.

"Brothers and sisters, thank you for coming on such short notice. We are thirty representing three hundred from Europe and North America. At our last meeting, we agreed to enact The NA Reduction program. I am here to report that we have experienced mixed results."

A round of applause echoes throughout the great room.

"I am told the Australians want to see success before they will come on board. Africa is a mess already and will be dealt with accordingly. That of course, leaves us with the Asia and South America. The consensus is that once we get Brazil, the rest of that continent will follow," said the graying old man, as he sipped a glass of water.

"My brother, without Asia, is there any point to this policy?" asked a man with a German accent.

"Asia, has proven to be very obstinate, to be sure. However, we will deal with that when the time comes. Half a glass of water is better than no glass when you are dying of thirst."

The dignitaries nod along and drink from their glasses.

"Please, let us not forget our objective: We have an unsustainable worldwide population of over ten billion people with scare resources. The central authority drafted an agreement to have a ninety percent reduction in all continents to a sustainable one billion overall level," said the elderly dignitary, sipping on brandy this time.

"Is there anyone else who wishes to voice a concern?" No hands are raised.

The graying old man then turned to the American. "We will continue with the program and to its next phase. I'm told by my American friend that we are still using bugs."

"My brother, we have a General who is steadfast in his resolve. He is working with the Secretary of State and they both assure me that the bugs are the quickest way to achieve our goals while preserving the infrastructure. They will not attack the Untouchables."

One of the few women raised her left arm and asked, "My brother, of course I am in agreement with our goals but is there a method other than insects to produce our results? I mean it has proven to cause chaos which is good, but it has unintended consequences. We can't possibly protect our brothers and sisters living in the cities with the masses going wild."

"We represent the Order and they have contingency plans if this scheme doesn't go as planned. We will see how the operation unfolds in America and reconvene at a later date to see if we need to modify our methods. As far as our brothers and sisters in the cities, they were told a long time ago to find alternative living arrangements. The ones that stayed are there on their own free will. They will live or die with that decision."

All the members tap their glasses in a show of agreement.

"Very well, then. Please everyone, enjoy the meal we have prepared."

The members dine on every conceivable type of meat available and wash it down with copious amounts of wine and whiskey.

How often does anyone examine the inside of another person's hands? Even the physical and common act of shaking dozens if not hundreds of hands in a day will not reveal the inside makeup of the hand or if there was a blemish on it.

If one were to examine the hands of the guests representing the charitable organization known as the Committee of 300, they would have discovered something unique to each member. On the inside of every member's left hand, was an oval eye symbol with red dots dripping from it.

Initiates into the Order receive the coveted mark only after they have proven their allegiance and value to the organization. The quickest track into the Order is through a trusted member who selects his or her candidate. A series of tests are given to see if the initiate is ready.

To ensure secrecy, vile acts are performed on the new candidate. This has a two-fold purpose: one, in the event a member strays from the Order and decides to expose the organization, they will blackmail them into silence and two and most likely equally as important, is to satiate the bloodlust of the members, who only understand depravity, control and power.

After dinner, all the guests get up and head to another room. They come back a few minutes later wearing long black robes and masks that cover their faces, only their eyes are visible. They follow each other out to the back of the castle to a wooded area where the man who addressed them earlier is holding some sort of a long golden scepter.

The guests then gather around in a circle with the bearded man holding the scepter in the center. He asked them all to raise their left hands and said, "Please, brothers and sisters, before we pledge our allegiance to the Order, let us show unity with a show of hands. Are we all still in agreement with these goals?"

They all raised their left hands.

"Very well then, let no man or women not of the Order know what was discussed here today. The penalty of course is not a quick death."

He then taps the ground with his scepter three times and the guests recite the following:

"I pledge allegiance to the Order and to the brothers and sisters who stand before me. No ties bind me except the ones of the Order. Until my dying day, I give my blood, heart and soul."

CHAPTER 5
EFFECT

New Year's Eve for Donna and Raymond Brown was a low-key function featuring a bottle of wine and leftovers from the restaurant. Louis and Oliver, their two youngest children, were too old at that point to spend the evening with them and their older children, Allen and Lisa, were away. Therefore, Ray and Donna caught a flick on the tube and awaited the final countdown.

Fifteen minutes before midnight their world changes forever, as Breaking News flashes across their TV screen.

"Oh God, I hope nothing happens down there," said Donna, "There's so many people in one area."

"If something does happen, that would be the perfect place," said Raymond.

"How can you say that Ray? That's horrible."

"Don't pretend you don't know what I'm talking about. With the whole world watching, this would be a golden opportunity for any terrorist to do something."

Raymond sat up to analyze the words coming from the well-groomed anchorperson.

"No way. It can't be."

The picture plastered on their 60-inch flat screen was of their oldest son, Allen. It was a menacing, unflattering picture, taken years ago and barely recognizable to the couple.

The news anchor proceeded to describe how a lone gunman named Allen Brown entered a large multinational corporation outside Washington D.C., shooting several employees, while also attempting to destroy part of the complex with a homemade bomb.

The bomb took out several of the offices and started a fire, which took hours to put out.

Donna only stared at the screen, covering her mouth with her hands.

"Six dead including the gunman," scrolled the words at the bottom of the screen. "No foreign entity is believed to be involved in this crime," said the news anchor. "It is thought that the gunman was a disgruntled employee who was fired last month."

Ray flips the channels to see the same horrid news being repeated about his son.

The crowd at Times Square came back full screen with Allen's picture minimized at the bottom.

"This can't be happening," said Donna.

Raymond frantically dialed Allen's number but only received voice mail.

The words on the screen change to "Domestic Terrorist attacks company killing five and himself."

Donna cried uncontrollably while pacing back and forth. "Aren't you gonna do anything Ray?"

"I don't know what you want me to do. It doesn't make any sense."

"Find out if this is true!"

"Donna, our son's picture is all over the news. Isn't that enough proof for you?"

"This has to be a mistake. My baby would never hurt anyone."

The ball drops as the confetti flickers throughout the artificial lit up air and the masses move their lips to "Auld Lang Syne" pretending that the wind chill doesn't make it feel like it's 18^0.

Lou and Oliver are the first to come home from whatever drunken shit show they were at.

The boys are stoic and sit at the kitchen table, joining their father in shock and awe at the night's announcement.

Lisa comes in a few minutes later, crying, while hugging her mother.

The time is now 1:15 in the New Year.

It's often said that a moment can change your life. That's true, but that change can either be positive or negative. The near miss that could have resulted in your death just may have resulted in someone else's. That perfect job went to someone who was more articulate resulting in their upward mobility and not your children's. The girl or boy of your dreams likes your friend and not you…Fill in the blank for the scars that were left.

For the Brown family, the moment their son walked into that corporation after hours, effectively changed their lives forever.

"Dad, I'm getting all these hits on my phone about Allen. Why'd he do this?" asked Lisa.

The boys are now drinking coffee at the table, years added to their age and yet only minutes of time have passed; the buzz they had earlier clearly faded away as they look up to their dad for guidance, but the reassurance is not there.

Finally, the patriarch for the overburdened family said, "Listen everyone. There's no way to pretend this isn't a tragedy, so I won't even try. It looks like your brother did something horrific and we're just going to deal with it the best we can. I want all of you not to talk to your friends about this. Try and get some rest and we'll deal with it in the morning."

After the last singer swings her hips at 1:30, a special broadcast comes on describing the domestic terrorist who also went by the name "Jack the Beanstalk." The channel repeats some of the more outrageous video podcasts by "Jack" well into the morning.

Ray takes in every syllable with disgust yet morbid curiosity about his son. His thoughts drift from anger to disbelief yet also of embarrassment as to what will become of his carefully maintained name over fifty plus years on the planet.

The "terrorist" made his message loud and clear and it wasn't until much later that his words were prophetic. One of the YouTube clips showed "Jack" professing to have worked for one of the largest food manufacturers at the time but was "let go" because he tried to expose the truth to the American people.

The truth in "Jack's" eyes and plastered on his video posts was that "time was running out for food production and that all modern attempts by government to curtail the inevitable were not going to work."

And what was the inevitable?

"Modern pesticides and genetically modified plants had run their course and the insect population has reached a tipping point. The food you've been eating for years is making you sick and our crops are not sustainable any longer. If you can make it to the hills or the water resources, you still have a chance."

Donna couldn't take any more enlightenment and went to bed. Raymond stayed up another hour to watch a few more revelations about his son.

The genie was out of the bottle but the truth was not so clear.

This was the year 2040. A new era where Millenniums were supposedly all grown up. With information at their fingertips for as long as they could remember and constantly bombarded with many of the lies of the past, they didn't conform nor believe everything told to them. Their parents, the Gen X'rs, were also a cynical bunch but in some respects, were a docile and lost generation with many finding solace in music, fantasy land and prescription drugs.

Helicopters are heard buzzing around in the small, not so close-knit neighborhood of the Brown household. At first, the sound was far off in the distance but the reverberations of the whistling got hauntingly closer.

The couple begrudgingly closed their eyes around 4:30 but then a loud "thump, thump, thump" jarred Raymond and Donna out of bed. Their hearts raced some more as the pounding on the door continued.

6:30 in the morning. Icicles dangle all around the house, formed by the night's frigid breath.

As the weary couple approached their front door, police lights and the chirp of helicopters heard only minutes earlier were now piercing their ears. Ray and Donna held their hands, prayed for the best and opened the door.

"Are you Raymond and Donna Brown, parents of Allen Brown, who had a residence in Washington D.C.?" said a stern-faced agent from the F.B.I., with a foreknowledge of the answer already in his head.

"Yes," the Brown's replied.

"Your son, Allen, is the suspected terrorist who attacked IS&G industries last night and we have a warrant to search the premises."

Donna and Raymond quickly woke Lisa, Oliver and Louis and dragged them to the kitchen. Donna turned the heat up on the stove for coffee as the rest of the family huddled around the table. Each door that opened sent a cringe down Lisa's spine. Raymond thinks of the absurdity that his house is treated as a terrorist stronghold but only folds his arms and hangs his head in shame.

It's still pitch black outside and bone-chillingly cold. The temperature is 16^0 and with a mighty wind channeling its way from Canada, feels like five below. This doesn't deter the neighbors, who gather outside to inspect; however, when told to go back inside by the arsenal of agencies outside their cul-de-sac (Homeland Security, F.B.I., etc.) they quickly retreat.

The couple along with Allen's - A.K.A. "Jack the Beanstalk"- meager belongings are "escorted" to the helicopter.

The world is told for weeks after the event of a "deranged lone wolf" who was suffering from paranoia, delusions of grandeur and was on a host of medications. This was the logic that was sold to a fearful and conditioned population. It was a formula that worked many times before in the annals of human history.

Raymond and Donna are told that their property could be seized if any material for the bomb was in the house. The couple tried their best to explain that Allen was more of a visitor than a son for the past decade in their house. After hours of questioning, the authorities allowed the broken family to go home, convinced there was no foreknowledge or planning on their part.

"Is this real?" asked Donna, as she turned to Raymond, while they pulled away from the lot at Homeland. "I feel like this is a dream and I have to wake up soon."

"More like a nightmare. All night and day all I keep thinking about is the time we bought Allen the chemistry set that one year at Christmas."

"Those are crazy thoughts. Don't torture yourself Ray. Nobody could have predicted this. And Allen is the only one to blame."

"Allen was not a sociopath and would not do a random act like this. I'm sure other parents would say the same about their son if this were to happen but something must have driven Allen to do this and I have to understand why."

"Dad, people lose it sometimes when they get fired," said Lou.

"Yeh dad. He probably had a shitty boss too," said Lisa, sarcastically.

Oliver says nothing and only thinks of the days when his oldest brother would come home and play video games with him or give him a ride on his back.

"Ollie, you ok honey?"

Oliver nods his head.

"Kids, it's going to be tough for the family for a while. You need to promise me that whenever someone asks about Allen, just say we had nothing to do with what happened, which is the truth anyway, OK?"

Lou and Lisa nod their heads without uttering a word.

"Dad, why would Allen do something like this?" asked Oliver.

"I don't know son. It's not logical."

No other words need to be spoken. All was quiet in the backseat during the thirty-minute drive back home.

Allen's bullet-ridden body was sent to Wessler's Funeral home, a few blocks from the Brown household. The viewing and service were held on a Saturday morning. Outside of Raymond's brother and family, no other relatives or friends show up to pay their respects.

CHAPTER 6
TRUTH

Every spare moment Raymond had would go into researching Allen's death and the cause he screamed about on his posts.

"You're taking another day off from school Ray?" asked Donna. "Don't you think that's risky with the situation we're in?"

"The situation we're in is an unresolved disaster for our family. I need to know what triggered Allen to do this."

"No you don't Ray. I'm torn up about this too. You know that, but leave it be."

"I can't."

After school, Ray would surf away for hours, searching for clues. He found some interesting facts about the corporation Allen had worked for: lawsuits for illegal chemical dumping, forced evacuations of various indigenous populations, exploitation of the local farmers and so on.

There was even a paper published by Allen and one of his colleagues that stated crop production was headed for a catastrophic failure due to impotent pesticides and modified plants. As he dug deeper and deeper, other names writing similar reports from other companies surfaced.

Donna felt the need to do research on the death of her son was not beneficial to the family and pleaded with Raymond to "stop his obsession."

"Don't you think we would have known or seen signs that Allen was disturbed over the years, hun?" asked Raymond.

Donna just shook her head. "I know but our family has suffered enough and it's not going to change anything at this point. Please drop it."

"I don't understand how you can just move on with your life without getting to the bottom of this."

"Bottom of what? What choice do we have? We need to move on for the sake of the rest of our family."

"The choice we have is to go quietly into the night and accept the lies put out about our son or find the truth."

"The truth is my baby murdered several people and nothing you find out will change that fact. This isn't some sort of equation for you to solve Ray."

"You're wrong Donna. It is an equation. I know my son and he must have been provoked into doing this. He worked hard for his doctorate and could have found work somewhere else. I need to get to the bottom of this."

•　　　•　　　•　　　•　　　•

Raymond drove to the capital to retrieve personal items that might have been left in Allen's house. He didn't have a key and went to the main office in the hope he would be granted access.

"I'm sorry sir. Allen didn't have you as an authorized agent for the condominium. You cannot go inside," said the receptionist.

Raymond tried to explain that there might be things of real value such as diplomas and pictures in the house and wouldn't leave until he spoke to the property manager. He waited in the lobby for nearly an hour until the property manager came, where he pleaded his case once more in a futile effort.

Dejected, he went back to his car and put on some music that made him feel melancholy. A vicious rainstorm began to pound on the windshield as "Desperado" by the Eagles entered its second haunting verse.

After a short while, his phone started to vibrate. The digital display read, "Meet me at the café around the corner."

"Who's this?" he replied.

"It's about your son, I'm being watched and so are you. Please come quickly. We don't have much time. I'll be wearing a brown hat and glasses. I'm a woman in my mid-fifties."

Raymond's first thought was that it was Homeland spying on him and wanted to entrap him into doing something stupid.

Following his gut instinct, he started to drive home to Pennsylvania but his curiosity got the best of him and he quickly turned around. He parked the car in the back of the café. After a few minutes, he works up the nerve to go inside and sits at a booth ordering a cup of coffee.

The coffee is still hot when a woman came over and introduced herself as Mrs. Rodriguez. "May I sit down?" she asked, gingerly. Her eyes spoke volumes. Raymond knew she couldn't be with the government or police. She was just too broken up- much like him.

"I knew it was you because of the pictures on the news." She opened a bottle of pills and popped a few while glancing with her eyes the need for Raymond's glass of water on the table. He gestured with his hands the acceptance and said, "How did you get my number and why did you text me?"

The woman swallowed the pills and glanced up. Although she makes a conscious effort to control them, her hands are trembling.

"My son kept a diary of names and phone numbers of people he knew. He liked things like that, you know. I didn't know why your name was in it until today. Antonio listed it next to Allen's name and number. Anyway, my son was a partner with Allen. I used to pick him up from that condo sometimes late at night. I drive by it a lot and it makes me feel better, sometimes."

She took another sip of water, fiddled with the pill vial, and then put it back into her purse.

"Mrs. Rodriguez. Are you all right?"

She didn't acknowledge the question and gave no reply.

"Mrs. Rodriguez?"

"I saw you get out of the car this morning going to the apartment office. I knew your face from the TV but didn't know what to say to you. I went home and sat for a while, thinking. I had to call and tell you some things and I'm glad you came to meet me. Antonio was a production worker at the company your son worked at."

Partner? The word that reluctantly stuck out most from what Mrs. Rodriguez said was partner. Raymond thought for a second and in his logical mind, the pieces of Allen's youth fit perfectly in with that word. The minor revelation didn't bother him much for he was content to be learning a bit more about his son. Allen had lived only a few hours from the home he grew up in but it could have been ten thousand miles for he was detached and living in another world.

In either case, he asked, "Why the urgency to meet? What can I do for you?"

She took another sip of water and waved to the waitress not to bring her anything. Her hands slowly stopped trembling.

"My son got sick from the experiments and chemicals in the factory and your son tried to help him. Antonio died of cancer weighing but ninety pounds at the end and Allen was at his side at the hospital."

She reached in her purse for more pills but only fidgets with the vial.

"I just took these didn't I?"

"Maybe you shouldn't take anymore Mrs. Rodriguez."

"You need to know that your boy; he was not a monster. I don't know why all this has happened but wanted you to know Allen tried to help people and was good to my son. I hope that gives you some kind of peace."

She wiped her mouth and said she had to go. Raymond started to grab her arm to stay a bit longer but the woman kept walking.

CHAPTER 7
SLIPPING AWAY

After the attack, the family attempted to move on with their lives. The funeral bought the boys a short reprieve as it kept them out of school for a week. Needing to keep her mind off the horrendous holiday, Donna returns to her customers at the salon.

"I had six appointments today," said Donna, "What happened to all of them?"

"Cancelled, last week. I tried to rebook but they're going elsewhere," said Jennifer, manager of The Beauty Zone. The Zone is where Donna had worked for over nine years, all part-time and no benefits. Donna stayed for years because the hours were great: 10 till 4 Monday through Friday.

Jennifer asked if Donna could change to the evening shift since it was a slower crowd. Donna knew that the real reason was that the regular crowd of high-end perms and facials were in the day and the nighttime clientele consisted of the occasional teenage haircut: dollar tip zone if she was lucky. She had no choice. The looks and the whispering from the regulars during the day were getting her upset, anyway.

"What do they think Ray, I put my son up to killing people."

"No hun. We're guilty by association. It'll blow over in time. You'll see, try not to react if they say anything, that's all."

A week goes by, and then Jen has another stipulation for Donna. She is now told to work Friday and Saturday nights.

"Wow, Jen trusts me to close up the place. I feel honored," said Donna, turning to Brooke, a young graduate of the Atlas Beauty School. Three weeks on the job.

"Well, I'm happy you're here. You mind if I leave a little early tonight?"

"Not at all. I can handle it. I got nothing to look forward to anyway. Enjoy."

Donna cleans up the floor, puts away the tools of the trade and closes out the register. She locks the front door and makes her way to her car.

10:15 PM

A car races down the street, slows down then speeds up again at the intersection. Donna's instinct directs her to walk quickly to the car. She sees the car make a U-turn and rumble back towards her. She's only a few feet from her door handle when a knock and splatter cover her face.

She lets out a scream and cowers to the ground. The first second she's convinced a bullet had hit her face, but on the ground she realizes it was an ugly prank. She pulls the debris and crap from her hair as best as she can and gets into her car. Rotten eggs and real crap, literally, were thrown at her in a half-open brown bag. The windows are pulled down to prevent Donna from gagging as she drives away with tears streaming down her face.

She makes it home pulling slowly into the garage and prays none of her kids or Ray would see the spectacle. In that, she is rewarded. The only person she tells of the incident is to Jennifer on Monday morning. Her thoughts being that Jennifer might somehow feel sorrow for her and ask that she return to day hours. Donna is mistaken, for Jennifer asks if she "could take a leave for a while until things cooled down."

"Sure Jen, but you know I had nothing to do with any of what happened with my son and feel just as bad as everyone else."

"That may be the case, Donna, but I have a business and a family to run as well; I hope you understand."

"I've been working here for almost ten years Jen, and this is how I'm repaid."

Jennifer doesn't respond and Donna didn't feel the need to argue her point any longer. It was clear by the looks of the customers that her services were no longer needed. What broke Donna's heart was her sister, Laura, who stopped coming in for a cut.

Laura and Donna grew up in a household that was in disarray after their mother left. Their parents met while they were both in the Air Force stationed in Kuwait and fought in several of the Middle Eastern wars of the previous century. The courtship moved to marriage when their mother got pregnant.

The young couple and Donna's older sister lived in several different states but eventually settled in New Jersey. Donna was the second child and before she was in kindergarten, their mom had run off with another pilot. This deeply affected their dad who turned inward and left the girls to fend for themselves for most of their upbringing. He was a functioning yet verbally abusive drunk, with little to no motivation constantly reminiscing about the glory days of his time in the service.

Donna called Laura and asked why she missed her appointment for a haircut. "Donna, I wanted to come in but Jim said it wasn't a good idea and I didn't want to upset him."

"What about upsetting me?"

"We plan to come by and see you guys one of these days. I hope you understand."

"I lost a son and a job and the one person I thought I could count on was my sister. You would rather listen to your husband than to help me in a time of crisis. What does he think that his precious reputation will be hurt associating with us?"

Laura cleared her throat. "Jim's a cop, Donna. He's like dad was, stubborn and set in his ways. He needs time to digest all of this. I'm sorry about Allen. I really am. I hope I can bring Edward over to hang out with Oliver at some point in the future."

Laura waited for Donna to reply but only got silence.

•   •   •   •   •

It was the coldest winter the family could remember. The bigger chill was the environment the children had to endure all around them. Oliver and Louis were having a difficult time adjusting to their new reality. They both had idolized their older brother and the thought of him as a terrorist was hard to comprehend. Their daily existence became rather unbearable for both of them as death threats, verbal harassment and being shunned at school became commonplace.

In only a few weeks, years of friendships had turned to a world of avoidance for the brothers, but fortunately they found solace in each other's misery and gravitated towards one another. They never ate lunch at school before the attack but now they both started packing and eating together.

Sometimes the small things in life can get you through tough times: Oliver thanked his lucky stars that he shared the same lunch period as Lou's. Prior to the

New Year, Lou would sit with the obnoxious B-team jock rebels of the school, and only veered over to Oliver in the event he needed money.

Lou found out just how loyal they were when his seat at the table was given to sophomore, Deanna Decker, appropriately nicknamed the "Pecker Recker."

When Lou told her that she was in his seat, she said with confidence, "What you gonna do? Shoot me like your brother." The cackling hyenas at the table were indeed amused at her boldness.

As Lou turned away walking in the direction of Oliver's table, a series of apples are thrown his way, one landing on his back.

"Who threw it!" he screamed, fists clenched.

Only laughter is heard from his table and the rest of the peanut gallery.

For days after being banished from the b-team "cool table," food periodically made its aerial journey over to Oliver and Lou's table. Every time, this caused Lou to search and attempt a scuffle with its owner. The only thing he found was a detention or an in-school suspension for "causing a disturbance" in the cafeteria.

Oliver is content counting the minutes to the next period. He comes late to lunch; bathroom break, and then waits at the end of the food line. This leaves him with sixteen minutes to escape the worst period of the day. He calculates ten minutes for the ogres to eat and another two minutes to send messages to one another before the final four-minute countdown. And oh so long are those two hundred and forty seconds. If shit happens, that's the time.

This is the routine the brothers endure for weeks until Lou abruptly said, "I've had enough of this shit. I'm out of this place…joining the Marines."

With four months to graduation, that idea didn't sit well with Raymond. "You don't owe the government anything and it's not your fault what your brother did. Stand your ground."

"I know dad but we need to redeem our family name."

Raymond then tried the logical approach: "That's fine son but can't you wait a few months longer until after graduation?"

"I can't take it any longer dad. My mind's made up. I'll take the G.E.D. on my own time and go in the summer. Besides, you know school isn't for me anyway. It never was."

• • • • •

Oliver suffered in silence. Never having been a fighter or especially large in stature, he was an easier target for the most aggressive of the hallway miscreants. When a picture of him surfaced stating he was the next terrorist to blow up the school, he decided to speak up. He made an appointment with the Vice Principal after lunch.

Vice Principal Hamon stands over six feet tall and easily tips the scales at two hundred plus. She is considered the smartest of the administrators at the school and Oliver has been in her presence many times but never had any real conversations with her. She hosts the Student of the Month breakfasts for the kids who make high honors, of which, he has never missed.

"Mr. Brown, what brings you to my office this morning?" asked the VP, eating a bagel smothered in cream cheese, clearly in full confidence mode about her stature and demeanor.

"Mrs. Hamon."

Oliver is quickly interrupted, "Miss, young man."

"I'm sorry. Ms. Hamon."

Her face lit up as Oliver is one of the obedient lambs who takes direction well.

"There are kids putting up signs about me being the next terrorist at the school. Can you please do something about this?"

"Do you know who's pulling these pranks on you?"

Oliver tried his hardest not to get irritated by the word 'prank' used by the VP and said, "I have a pretty good idea who they are."

"Well, my advice is that I could intervene but that might things worse for you as they could retaliate. I want you to stand up to them and let me know how it goes."

Oliver quickly realized that he is being told to confront the bullies and let the chips fall wherever they land. He wants to tell her that this is her job and that she should put an end to the harassment but only said, "Ok, Ms. Hamon. I'll try and will let you know."

The Principal notices Oliver's solemn face walking out of the office and asks if he could be of service.

"I don't think anyone can help."

"Well, give me a chance. You might be surprised."

Oliver briefly explained his plight as they stand in the doorway leading out to the hall. This time, he is told in more diplomatic terms to "be sensitive to the fears of others because everyone needs to be on the lookout for potential threats."

Clearly baffled by the doublespeak of the Principal, Oliver nods his head, shakes the Principal's hand and makes his way to the nurse's office where he can lie down in quiet refuge pretending to be physically ill.

CHAPTER 8
CAUSE

Raymond was an indoctrinated robot graduating from a prestigious school with dual degrees. He chose to work in the inner city to start his teaching career but quickly became disillusioned with the tedious bureaucracy. Like so many of his peers, he "got out" and landed a plum-teaching gig in the suburbs where he married Donna and raised a family.

Allen was their oldest son, who always wanted to follow in his father's footsteps but to do one better. He received not only his masters but also his P.H.D. in biochemistry at the university. His interest had always been in the sciences, but also was an environmentalist at heart. When others were working during summer breaks, Allen volunteered to clean up the rivers from generations of neglect and dumping.

In high school, Allen stuck to himself with very few friends. However, at the university he could mingle with other like-minded scientists. He formed a close-knit community of activists who called themselves the "New Millenniums." Their mantra was to "help preserve nature and further society in a progressive manner."

Allen utilized his time effectively at school. Instead of drinking until he got sick on a Saturday afternoon following some sort of a sporting event, he would usually meet with colleagues to discuss current events at the empty library.

The group had seen a documentary claiming that Earth's resources could not sustain the population unless a dramatic change were to occur. Allen was so intrigued by that concept that he was granted a dissertation on that topic by his professor and mentor Dr. Clyde Burrows. His close network of friends wrote similar essays and continued their work in that direction.

Allen tried to stay at the university teaching and doing research but the opportunities were rather slim. There was no shortage of graduates when it was his time to shine.

After working two-part time jobs outside of his field and with over one hundred thousand dollars in student loan debt, Allen's options were limited. He reluctantly accepted a position with the IS&G Corporation, a large multinational company specializing in the manufacture and distribution of grains and seeds as well as a smaller yet profitable chemical division. Allen's background was more biochemistry than manufacturing and logistics but it was a chance for him to get a "start."

The mission of the scientists at IS&G was always to increase production and yield in crops while ostensibly causing the least amount of disruption to the environment. Allen worked in the research and development section of the company in a laboratory sectioned off for the "eggheads." He was paid a low six-figure salary to fulfill their mission and was rewarded with stock options and a guaranteed pension plan sometime in the distant future.

IS&G had been in business for over one hundred and fifty years. Initially, they started as a chemical company and still had a few divisions in that sector, with factories overseas providing revenue to the parent company. Always concerned with their image, the company spent millions on public relations.

Anyone who spent time researching the company would discover it had a dark past: they supplied all warring sides with the nerve agents used in the First World War. Their duplicitous nature extended into the second World War supplying Nazi Germany with the Zyklon B in the camps as well as munition supplies for the Allies. Napalm for the Vietnam War was solely produced by IS&G. Indeed, one cannot overestimate the role the company played in previous world conflicts supplying all sides with munitions, chemicals and logistics.

By the time Allen had joined the corporation, it was one of the largest conglomerates in the world providing agriculture products and pesticides to the market. IS&G had a long history of modifying plants to be more resistant to the dangers (insects, weather) of the environment but only recently had started to enhance the structure in the plants to become larger and produce a "healthier" yield.

The drawback to a bigger crop had always been a decrease in critical nutrients that the organics and smaller plants provided. This is where Allen and his colleagues came in. They were tasked to continue the research in genetically coded seed and crop manipulation that was already in development, and to reduce the side effects.

Allen and his co-scientists worked on a new compound that would enhance the crop yields in certain produce and vegetables while eliminating pests from attacking the plants. They had early success but did notice some side effects from the handlers of the product. It became commonplace to hear production workers complain that their skin felt itchy when they tried to harvest the crops. Days after the exposure, some developed flu-like condition.

In addition to providing nearly all the seeds to the country's farmers, IS&G had the market cornered by working on the back end as well. Their chemical division would supply the pesticides for any critters that proved too resilient for the new batch of seeds. They had been the largest supplier for decades.

The crew in the laboratory made many modifications to their designs over the ensuing years. The results appeared to be impressive and the company wanted to roll out the patent as soon as possible, but Allen and some of his peers suggested more testing to see if the side effects could be reduced or minimized. They protested on many occasions to upper management on the need to wait and conduct further research; however, the most vocal proponent for halting a rollout was always Allen.

"Dr. Brown, we have waited long enough and instituted every protocol your team has introduced," said Mike Krup, district manager at the IS&G corporation, D.C. branch.

"Sir, we need more testing to ensure all the negative effects are removed from our product. We should have the formula perfected fairly soon."

"How soon is fairly? I need a time frame Doc."

"I can't give you an exact date. We're not making widgets here. It's a bit more complicated than that."

"We have waited long enough young man. Every day is costing us millions of dollars."

"I understand the realities of making a profit but our team is not willing to give the go-ahead until we're one hundred percent sure there will be no adverse effect upon the environment and the ecosystem, sir."

"Do you think I give a damn about the ecosystem you jack off. All you eggheads are all the same. Without revenue, there would be no research. Get it?"

"I understand sir but we would surely lose money if we were sued about defective products. That shouldn't be too hard to comprehend, even for you."

"You pompous son of a bitch. Let me tell you the cold hard facts. I don't give a damn about your team and their opinions. And just so you are crystal clear, the F.D.A. is in our back pocket and is giving us the green light."

"I don't know how you can be so callous in regards to the possibility of wreaking havoc upon the environment- all for a few dollars."

"Don't get preachy with me, you young prick. You're working for more than a few dollars too. This is a business. Don't forget. We're paying you for the research and your recommendation. That's it. You don't write policy. We're done here and this conversation is over."

"We won't let you get away with this. The public will find out."

Mr. Krup walked slowly over to Allen. He then put his left arm on Allen's shoulder and said, "Is that a threat Mr. Brown?"

"It's Doctor and no not a threat, it's a fact."

"You're in way over your head Doc. Do as you're told and don't cause me any more grief and I just might forget how much of a pain in the ass you've been to all of us. Don't ever forget, everyone's replaceable."

Their supervisors told them that they were moving forward with or without their approval and if they wanted to continue working, they should keep their opinions to themselves.

Allen went over Krup's head and complained one too many times to the big shots at the main office. The last straw was an internal flyer circulated to the entire staff on the hasty decision to roll out a product not deemed to be safe.

Allen was fired immediately.

CHAPTER 9
BREAKDOWN

The first major report of a farm under distress happened in sunny Palm Beach County, Florida in mid-winter around the time of the Super Bowl. The farm was a rather small one compared to others in the state, but supported several generations of the McCloud family.

Gabe McCloud raised lettuce, cabbage and beets all his life. Gabe's father was the last to use organic farming and implored his son to do the same. He complied with his father's wishes for the first couple of years but when faced with economic pressures, Gabe was forced to switch in order to compete with his competitors and chose to use seeds manufactured by IS&G. He joined over 95% of the farmers who were using readymade seeds from the corporation.

Literally overnight, his entire crop was eaten right down to the root. All that was left was a discolored brown film overlaying rows of the neatly planted produce.

Mr. McCloud's fifteen minutes of unwanted fame arrived when he found himself on the nightly news showing his cabbage and lettuce infested two-hundred-acre farm. When asked if there was any viable crop left, he replied, "Hell no; it's all ruined and so am I. This is the first time in my life to see such a thing. God help us all."

Many parasites, worms and insects have ravaged crops throughout history. Initially, the culprit at the McCloud farm was thought to have been worms. This is important to farmers since knowing the "enemy" is important when you are trying to eradicate them.

Different pesticides work on different species of bugs. In the rush to kill as many types of insects, farmers often try to do a blanket coverage to get the best bang for their buck. Gabe was using such a shotgun approach: spraying with the latest poison to get the greatest yield, which meant more money. His story was relegated to the end of the program: the special interest segment.

One after the other, farms were reporting a major loss in crops due to insect infestations. Prices started to climb for all things produce and it was becoming expensive to be a health-conscious individual in America. Many complained but chalked it up to a fluke of nature for this particular year.

The crop failures were primarily confined to countries in the Western Hemisphere. Ironically, the less developed countries showed little to no sign of crop failures, for they were using organic and pesticide free spraying on their crops. The threat of holding funds from the International Monetary Fund (IMF) to these countries as coercion to try modern farming and pesticides was met with stiff resistance.

As the spring season marched on, more states in the U.S. and Europe began to report significant crop failures and insect infestations. The price hikes continued and rumors of people stocking up supplies were all around.

By the summer, half-filled shelves at major supermarkets were a common scene. If you could afford it, prices for canned processed foods doubled since the beginning of the New Year.

As a young man, Raymond had lived through Y2K or Year 2000. That turn of the century end of the world scam was minor in comparison to what was happening now. Perhaps, because of the ubiquitous construct of the internet or the cynical nature of the millennium population, the "urban myth" of a lack of edible food was certainly in the air. The effect of Allen's attack at IS&G headquarters six months earlier resulted in a population searching for answers.

The media touted the increase in food prices across the board to several causes: a dramatic increase in energy consumption, floods in the Midwest and a prolonged drought in the western part of the country. This was surprising since Raymond researched weather trends with no indication that a drought was in effect at all for the past couple of years. Things weren't adding up and the storyline about his son being a deranged lunatic would not sit well with him or Donna.

"Do you still think there was nothing to investigate regarding Allen's attack," asked Raymond.

"Maybe there was something to what Allen was trying to accomplish Ray, but killing is never right."

"If several die to save thousands or millions, is that not a worthy price?"

"Listen to yourself Ray. I don't know what alerting everyone would have done. There would have been mass panic if people knew what was happening."

"Donna, I think Allen was trying to make a public show of the IS&G plant and the guards just got in the way."

"Well, if that's the case, then why would Allen bring weapons and kill them. Clearly Ray, he went there with a purpose and knew what to expect. And why wouldn't he at least come and talk to us about his frustrations."

"I'm sure there's more to this than IS&G. They might be the vehicle to accomplish the goals but there's some force behind driving the decisions, in my opinion."

"Ray, that kind of conspiracy talk is going to get us all locked up. You need to focus on our family and not stirring up anymore dissent."

"Aren't we locked up now hun? Living every day under a lie and programmed what to eat, who to watch, and where to live. It's all one big prison."

• • • • •

At the start of the second half of the year, the country was experiencing one executive order after the other. The first one rolled out was Executive order 230 (E.O. 230), the abolishment of cash money. It was now illegal to use cash anywhere in the country.

For years, the government and commercial banks have tried to institute a one-chip one-password policy for all users. They finally got their chance to initiate the scheme with E.O. 230. A bank customer would only need to come into the bank one time to get his or her finger implanted with the commerce chip or C^2 chip, whereby, they could use their finger to make purchases and deposits anywhere and anytime.

There was some uproar over E.O. 230 but it was primarily relegated to people who were on the fringes of society.

The second order was a different story. The safety fabric holding much of the poor had been welfare and subsidized housing for nearly one hundred years. All that came to an abrupt and painful end with Executive order 333, rolled out on August 26, 2040. The effect of that decision would have severe ramifications for the country.

Whatever one may think of the government, one cannot question the ability for bureaucrats to plan their next move. The next day E.O. 345 declared the sale or purchase of ammunition to be illegal. That decision made the crazies even crazier as the government simply shut down every firearms dealer in the country.

It was a busy time for agents of the Alcohol, Tobacco and Firearm agency (ATF) as they tracked and collected the millions of guns splattered across the country.

"Is this for real?" Donna asked.

"It's going to get worse," said Raymond. "Let's stock up on as many food items and medical supplies as possible. Time might be running out."

"With what money do you propose we do that with, Ray? I haven't worked all year, which doesn't leave us with much at the end of the month. Besides, no one is accepting paper money anyway and there's a huge line to convert the deposits into the C^2 chip at the bank. By the way, did you get that thing inserted into your hand yet?"

"I did it yesterday after school. The lines aren't that long at that time. Banks are required to stay open until midnight until the conversion is over. Our benevolent government is allowing people the use of their debit cards until the end of the year, but I don't think you should wait until then."

"How in the world could this all be happening?"

"Well it is Donna and we need to adapt quickly to survive. Maybe our son wasn't so crazy after all, huh?"

"What does this have to do with Allen?"

"We'll all find out soon enough, I suspect."

"Let's not connect any dots Ray."

Raymond has his arms folded as if he is looking at student waiting for her to comprehend the situation.

Donna stands at the sink looking out into the backyard. "I just want things to go back to the way they were."

"I know… but change is coming and we need to prepare. Reality is smacking us right in the face."

Oliver and Louis walked into the kitchen and then Louis blurted out, "I'm not going in the Marines after anymore. Something's going on and I need to be here."

Louis clenched his fists while his face contorted and flushed red. "I don't think Allen was crazy, either. I don't agree with what he did but my brother wasn't a terrorist."

Lisa, in the other room overheard the conversation and said, "Lou, you're being a drama queen. Maybe the Marines aren't for you anyway."

"Shut up Lisa. What do you know, anyway? All you do is post and bring people things."

"Well, at least I'm working."

Lisa had recently done some job-hopping and was now commuting thirty minutes for a low paying job because she didn't want anyone to recognize her. The only benefit from working at the restaurant was that she occasionally brought home fresh fruit. The Brown's didn't realize how fortunate that treat would become in the days and weeks to follow.

"We all just need to calm down," said Donna. "Let's go in the living room."

Dinner was a ready-made job brought home by Raymond from Sam's Club. They all sat down, ate the bird and watched the slow-motion destruction of the inner cities, live and in color.

It didn't matter what station was put on since they were all showing the same thing. The riots first started in the largest cities: NYC, Chicago and LA, but quickly spread to all others. Whether it was the food shortage, the C^2 chip, ammunition prohibition or the destruction of welfare, it all proved to be a combustible mixture that made for a memorable end of the summer.

Traditionally, stock markets collapse in October. This time it was the dog days of August. The Dow Jones Industrial average, the proverbial canary in the coalmines for the economy, lost 20% by lunch. The free-fall continued until midafternoon, mercilessly closing early at 2:00pm. The day before its high was 50,000. It was due to open Monday at 31,000.

Going into the weekend, every major indicator was showing the economy in collapse. The Dow futures were all red and into the thousands. Panic selling spilled into all other worldwide indexes. Precious metals and commodities climbed to record highs.

"You know what Donna? I betcha any money they'll outlaw gold and silver next."

"What's the difference Ray. It's not like we have any of that stuff hidden away."

"That's not the point hun. The fact is that all these new policies coming out are making it harder for all of us to move about and be free."

"Free? Who the hell in their right mind thinks about freedom anymore, Ray? It seems like survival is all anyone talks about these days. And I'm sick of all of it."

"I'm talking about survival, Donna."

Lisa came strolling into the room as the conversation ended.

"Can't the both of you just stop arguing? Don't we have enough to deal with?"

"We're not arguing dear," said Raymond.

"You could have fooled me."

The three of them, realizing that a fight was not needed now, went their separate ways in the house.

One would be hard pressed to find a major U.S. supermarket that wasn't cleared of its shelves by sunset. Scenes of people being shot for a loaf of bread were displayed on the evening news with Governors from across the nation encouraging people to stay in their homes.

When asked for a comment on the situation, the U.S. President "urged care and not to overreact to the situation."

The Police initially stood by but when the rioters took to the more middle-class sections on the outskirts of the cities, tear gas and bullets followed. By Sunday, most inner cities were engulfed in flames.

Fearing more riots for the upcoming week and a genuine concern for the sustainability of the economy, martial law was declared across the country in every township, city and municipality. A curfew had been placed at 10:00pm. Only valid employment would allow a citizen to be on the roads.

Although many merchants were hurt by the decision, a state of fear gripped the country and it was palpable for all to taste. To reinforce the gravity of the situation, the National Guard and select units of the army were brought in from reserve status to help with the chaos.

There was no public outcry from most of the country against the infringement of civil liberties. Years of fighting wars and terrorists had made the citizenry a malleable population; one in which it was easy for the de facto electronic police state to manipulate and control.

CHAPTER 10
THE TIMES THEY ARE A CHANGING

The pent-up frustration and rioting in most major cities climaxed on the Sunday before Labor Day. Very few people had ventured to the shores that summer and less so for the end of the season holiday. It was just too risky crossing state lines.

Steven and Susan brought their two children Tina and Thomas over for the barbecue. Unlike the previous year when steaks and fresh fruit were abundant, this year the families had to do with a lighter entrée of hot dogs and chips.

"Hey little bro," said Steven, as he stretched out his overgrown sausage finger hands, "How you making out?"

"I'm all right man. How bout yourself?"

At the same time, Susan kissed Donna on the cheek. "Good to see you again, Sue."

"Always a pleasure, Donna. If we don't come over, we never see you guys anymore."

"Well, it's been a rough year, you know."

"Sure. I understand. I didn't mean anything about it."

Donna forces a smile. "No problem."

Raymond asked his brother, "Are you getting any work in big guy?"

Steve took a deep breath while puffing out his chest. "I tell yah no new houses are going up but people are protecting whatever they got and they're trading me anything they can for guns or ammo. One guy even paid me in medical supplies and food for his new windows. You know I got plenty of that shit bro."

"You're not gonna sell all of it are you?"

"Shit no. I don't got a fancy degree like you but I'm not dumb…selling just enough for us to have supplies to last for a year."

"So you think this whole thing will blow over in a year?"

"I don't know. I'll be ready no matter what."

"Why do you ask, you never shot a gun in your life?"

"Not sure what guns will do if they come and take them away Steve."

"Boys, let's try not to argue and enjoy the day, okay," said Susan.

Steve needs to get the last word in. "Nobody's coming to take my guns away from me, and if they do, they better be ready to kill me."

"I don't think that would be an issue for them."

"Then I guess that's one thing we have in common then, huh bro? We both know that the government is the root of problem and tells one bullshit lie after the other."

Raymond nods in agreement. "No disagreeing with you on that point."

Susan smiled nervously and said, "Wal-Mart laid off half its workers this week but I guess I should be grateful to have a job, even if it is a shitty one."

"I never thought I'd say this Sue, but a lot of people would kill for that job now," said Ray.

"That's what I told her man. Great minds think alike, I guess."

Sue sits at the kitchen table with her hands clasped together. "I just pray things will turn around for all of us shortly. It just has to."

Donna keeps a stern face and walks into the living room.

Tina and Thomas join Oliver and Louis in the pool while Lisa searches online job postings on her phone all the while sipping her Long Island Ice tea on the patio.

"I don't know how we survive as a nation with all that's going on," sighed Susan, "and with the year you had, it must be hard."

Donna manages a reluctant smile. "We're still a family and need to go on. It's been really hard. I won't say it hasn't but we're together and healthy."

The two families ate, drank and pretended all was normal. The "party" lasted for several hours and then Steve rounded up his wife and kids. While they were leaving, Susan turned to Donna saying, "It's too bad Laura couldn't make it. Is everything all right with you guys?"

Donna, wanting to keep a brave face said, "Jim's been real busy these days."

"But your sister could still come over, can't she?"

Donna gives Susan a steely look, daring her to ask another question knowing full well that she knows the true answer.

The women go through the ritual of a kiss goodbye as the kids follow behind.

Another night of a presidential address was scheduled for the country. Would it be more lies or a candid assessment of the new reality facing the country? The Brown family sat and listened to the President deliver his speech.

"My fellow Americans, this has been a troubled season for all of us with restrictions placed on our liberties that were necessary for the safety of everyone. Rest assured, we will get through this together as we have endured trying times in the past and come through a stronger nation and people. I ask for your patience as we use our skills and knowledge to get through this season of sorrow."

Donna prayed he would not mention anything regarding IS&G or Allen. He did not but continued saying, "New rationing would be available for the neediest of our citizens in this time of crisis and change."

Raymond chimed in, "Rationing for what? Now we're going to be monitored for how much food we eat. This is crazy."

With over thirty percent of the country now out of work, it wasn't hard to guess what came next. The President expressed the desire for the nation to persevere but needed "law and order" for that to happen.

A new civil defense force (CDF) was now in order. The CDF oversaw rationing food and preserving "social order" in the land. Community organizing and demonstrations had already been outlawed and if you wanted to survive, it meant standing in long lines for your daily ration.

Oliver started his senior year convinced it had to be better than the previous one but realized that his dreams of escaping to a university and living a normal life were only that: a distant dream.

Lisa, Donna and Louis were all out of work going into October. Because one family member was working- Raymond- the family was not eligible for any rationing by the CDF.

If you were one of the lucky ones to have a job, you ate twice a day instead of the government allotted once. The rations were military equipped frozen meals.

For years, IS&G had worked on developing a new strain of pesticides that would maximize crop yields while prohibiting a negative effect upon the environment.

Popular for many decades, were a class of pesticides commonly referred to as Neonicotinoids or neonics for short. Although effective, many scientists wrote articles about the potential negative effects this class of chemicals was having on the environment.

The industry never acknowledged the dangers emanating from Neonicotinoids but IS&G as well as the other major suppliers moved away from them because of the bad publicity and collectively began working on a new line of "environmentally friendly" pesticides.

The industry called the new chemicals the grenics. The Environmental Protection Agency or (E.P.A.) saluted the new line as it promised to reduce the toxic runoff and other ecological issues that had once plagued its predecessors.

As with everything in life, there is a cause to every effect. Playing with the natural order of the universe leads to unintended consequences.

In less than a decade since the rollout of the grenics on the farmlands of America, stories of farmers contracting weird skin legions and various forms of cancer were all over the internet. When a congressional representative from the Midwest brought the issue up during a subcommittee, he was told that the E.P.A. concluded there was no correlation to pesticides and any public health concern. When he lost his reelection in a landslide due to a lack of campaign contributions, other members who were concerned with this issue did not raise their voices any longer.

There was no single culprit to the crop failures. Depending on the location of the farm, insects such as beetles, locusts and grasshoppers ravaged the countryside. Farmers reported that all types of insects would come out after spraying the crops with the pesticide and "drink up" the poison.

The President directed every major chemical producer to form a Consortium to come up with a solution to the plant crisis and would provide every resource available to them. The industry was primarily led by IS&G and thus the Consortium was IS&G with a new name.

Economists said we were entering unchartered territory and there was nothing in the books to compare the situation to. Some called it a Super Depression. Biblical scholars called it the End times. Whatever it was, the country would never be the same.

Humans, just like every other animal in the zoological order, strive for some sort of normalcy and equilibrium. Rationing, martial law and starvation became this new normal. Historically, autumn is a time to bring in the harvest. This holiday season shaped up to be a lean one for everyone and Thanksgiving was not going to be bountiful; however, the natives endured the hardships the best that they could.

CHAPTER 11
FALLING DOWN

The Consortium had nearly one hundred years of experience developing new compounds for pesticides and had a good track record producing results. They decided to go in a different direction since every known toxin proved ineffective and time was a factor. The country simply could not go through another season with most of its crops dying.

Genetically produced plants had been in existence for many decades and the leader if not the wholesale supplier was IS&G Industries. When other rivals attempted to compete, IS&G would try soft and hard methods to shut them down. The soft was a buyout. The hard method was more covert and the average Joe Shmoe was in the dark.

Because both the genetically modified plants and the few organics still in existence were ravaged by insects, the Consortium had no other choice but to give the green light for IS&G to supply the country with their stock of enhanced seeds. These new and improved smart plants were genetically coded to produce vegetation much like their organics, but now they were modified to release a pheromone that would trick the insects into thinking that a predator was in the plants.

Every conceivable acre of usable land was occupied with this new strain of crops. We had smartphones, smart cars and smart houses, and now the country would have new and improved smart plants, version 2.0, if you will.

On the off-season, America went from one of the largest exporters of food to the world to being the largest importer. The breadbasket of the country, the Great Plains of the Midwest or "fly over country" was now a large brown covered blot of parasites, worms and pests. During the destruction, the farmers planted and prayed.

Militarily, we were a declining empire for years. Overstretched and swimming in debt, the Third World finally got their wish: no nation could evict the U.S.A. from their lands on their own, but the bugs and failed crops brought most of the troops back to Main Street. The Korean peninsula was the only outpost occupied for American service personnel.

The most prevalent jobs for the returning vets were in the CDF. Instead of firing on foreigners in their lands as they tried to end their own occupation, the troops were now tasked with the responsibility to occupy the country they grew up in, and to put down any resistance that was occurring.

The country hunkered down over the next couple of months as Americans settled on their new reality of shortages, bugs and martial law.

A truly different kind of tension was in the air: rumblings from cyberspace told of a planned takedown of the government coupled with a reduction in the food supply. Posts were updated daily with handheld digital reporters depicting people being taken away during the night for exposing the ugly truth.

After several more months go by, the stories turned into reality and the night into day. Resistance to martial law or questioning the official party line to the collapse happening all around them became tantamount to terrorism.

The country was in crisis and as the months dragged on, hungry eyes looked to the government for a solution. The desperation turned to despair as the only resolution comes in the form of total failure for the nation.

The smart plants did not fool dumb bugs with millions of years of evolution. The pheromone released did the complete opposite: instead of prohibiting insects from being attracted to the plants, it made them swarm in greater number.

Like bees to honey, every species flocked to these new plants and devoured them down to the root. The most ravenous of the new flying predators resembled a hornet with red and black stripes. These "hornets" would attack the insects as they ate the plants. They would sting them and then retreat to the trees where their nests were located. The nests were known to be as big as a tire on an 18-wheel truck, with hundreds of Stingers residing inside.

The thinking from the farmers was that these hornets or Stingers were not only killing the insects, which was good for keeping the insect population down, but would also suck their blood, much like a mosquito.

Upon hearing the complete failure of the new smart plants, Raymond asked Donna, "How is it possible for a new species to appear relatively overnight and attack the insects feeding on the plants?"

Donna shook her head, aged well beyond her years now, and truly disconnected from the world. "Why does it matter anymore Ray. Why you so concerned?"

A voice, heretofore marked with trepidation, begins its emergence and has a more coherent answer. "Maybe they've been here for a long time, dad," said Oliver.

Oliver was now in his last year in high school. Unlike his brother Louis, who was extremely athletic but lethargic, Oliver was meticulous in everything he did. He excelled in academia and was hoping to follow Allen's example in college up until that fateful night last December.

Oliver discovered his voice and continued: "I've been reading Allen's writings from when he was at school and work. He used to send me and Lou emails when we were younger explaining the problem with some of the new technologies and pesticides."

Ray looked puzzled yet anxious. "Why didn't you say anything about this earlier? We shouldn't keep things like this a secret from one another. If you knew something was going on, you should have spoken up."

Lou then said, "Dad you don't have a habit of listening to us most of the time and we didn't think you would take us seriously."

"I don't think that's fair to me or your mother. I'm critical most of the time, I'll give you boys that, but if you got something to say, you know I'm all ears."

At that moment, as if the lights just went on, Donna turned to Ray. "You know, this makes complete sense now: remember when Allen was home for the holidays that one time and he mentioned that we should all think about moving north and live off the land with organic farming."

"Donna, don't blame…," but Donna interrupted, "I'm not blaming anyone Ray. Allen reached out to us in his own way and we ignored him. Maybe he and his friends were on to something back then and they were pushed away as being crazy or promoting some sort of a conspiracy theory."

"What do you think I've been trying to figure out this past year hun? After spending all those hours researching, you told me to drop it."

"I just didn't want to believe it Ray. I wanted us to move on and forget the past."

"Well now you know, there's no moving on without understanding the past."

"Well, thank you for the lesson Mr. Teacher."

A cold chill ran down the spine of everyone in the room except for the cynic of the family. "Don't we have enough problems. Let's don't go looking for trouble."

Lisa, the oldest of the children, was smart but also very rebellious. After several unsuccessful attempts at school, she settled on waitressing at the local diner until she could "make her mind up."

"I'm not looking for trouble dear, I just want to know the truth," said her dad.

Raymond, the quintessential scientist himself, wanted concrete answers to the questions. He searched the records and postings from people Allen had known for years. One name that surfaced several times during Raymond's research was Dr. Stuart Blackstone.

Dr. Blackstone retired from teaching at Columbia University ten years ago and was thought to be living in upstate New York. He had a website titled "A Changing World" where he would post articles regarding crop production and pesticides.

Blackstone's followers only numbered in the hundreds but would post passionate articles on issues regarding the government and survival techniques for when the "tipping point would come." One of the articles referenced Allen's name and his company as major contributors to the "coming worldwide collapse" and associated with Allen, was another figure named Michael Pertrowski.

"I know that name. Why does it sound so familiar to me?" asked Ray.

"Because he was at our house a couple of times Ray. Remember the guy who had the punk rock hairdo? You thought he shouldn't be hanging out with Allen."

"Oh yeh, that guy."

"Yeh that guy. When you learned he had a P.H.D. you suddenly were all nice to him."

"OK, so I misjudged or had a bias against someone. I'm not alone in that regards."

"No. But I always liked him. He was very sweet," said Donna with affection.

"Allen brought him home one weekend to attend some kind of conference in Philly at the University of Penn. I think it was on greenhouses or something like that. Allen said he and his friends were part of a club at school and that they needed to do some research with other friends who were in the city."

"Man, you got a good memory Donna. I need to go see that kid and ask a few questions about what he might have known."

"Are you crazy Ray? Why involve another kid in this? What's he gonna tell you anyway- that Allen found out a company was poisoning all of us. And if that's true, is it gonna make you happy?"

"I'm not looking for happiness Donna. I just wanna know if this kid can tell me anything about Ray. I'm not going another day without knowing the truth. I might as well be dead."

•   •   •   •   •

Michael had an address in Parsippany, New Jersey, which was less than a two-hour drive from their house. Raymond called off sick the next day and drove to Michael's house. Traffic was much lighter than it had been in years taking the highway across state lines – a byproduct of millions of people being out of work or who couldn't afford to travel. He arrived around noon and pulled up to a well-kept all brick ranch home.

Ray knocked on the door several times but got no response. He then rang the bell twice and finally a woman around the same age as Raymond's slowly came to the door. "I'm sorry to bother you mam. I'm looking for Michael Pertrowski. My name is Raymond Brown. My son was Allen, who I believe knew your son."

It was the afternoon but the woman was wearing a robe. Her eyes started to tear up when Ray mentioned her son but after a few seconds, she regained her composure.

"Please come in. It's terrible what happened to your son that night and everything that you must be going through."

Ray sat on the sofa. "I make no excuses for my son's actions mam. He was wrong and I feel terrible for what happened."

She sighed for a while and then softly spoke: "I'm in no position to pass judgment on your son. He was a friend of Michael's and I know they worked together from time to time helping such things as the environment. I don't know what went wrong. It's all so tragic and hard to believe."

Ray cleared his throat to regain some confidence. "Mrs. Pertrowski, do you know where I can find Michael?"

Her eyes are glossy and heavy with burden. "What do you need from him?"

"I just want to ask him some questions regarding my son and what was bothering him if that's ok with you?"

Mrs. Pertrowski starts to weep as she reaches for a handkerchief.

"I'm sorry to have disturbed you mam. That wasn't my intention. I'll be going now."

She tugged at his arm and said, "It's nothing you said. I wish I could help you. You would have liked Michael. He was very curious like you are and always questioned how things worked."

In an instant with those two words- have liked- Raymond thought he knew what was coming next. "Michael was shot on his way home from work one night two years ago. The police told me it was a random act of violence. I never believed that. My son was murdered."

Raymond's eyes opened in disbelief. "I'm so sorry Mrs. Pertrowski... But why would do you think someone wanted to murder your son?"

Mrs. Pertrowski, who is standing now and visibly more confident said, "He belonged with a group that wrote about how dangerous some farming or plants were and the stuff, I think, that they spray on them. He would always tell me those were some reasons why there were so many people getting cancer."

"I see. Did he ever tell you people were after him or that he felt unsafe?"

Mrs. Pertrowski grins ever so slightly, reminiscing the moments that must have been spent with her son recounting the unusual events: "We would get calls at night threatening us to stop spreading 'lies.' Michael said it was his duty to speak up."

"Who was doing the threatening? Was it a person or a company?"

"He never said and they never told me who they were; but Michael was fired from his job a couple of months before he was shot, and spent most of his time on the computer. I thought he was looking for work but I guess he was doing other things and posting articles about what was bothering him."

"I know this has been difficult for you but I do appreciate it Mrs. Pertrowski. Thank you for seeing me."

All the pieces started to fall into place for Raymond. A mother's anguish had set him on the path to discovery or at least to the delusions that his son had.

CHAPTER 12
NO TURNING AROUND

Upon hearing the news that the smart plants failed to hinder the insects from attacking them, the Consortium resorted to what they knew the best: toxic chemicals to kill the pests and once again turned to their largest supplier IS&G.

As if the company had anticipated the results, the chairman notified the President's committee that his corporation had ample supplies needed to eradicate the "enemy." The President gives the green light to do whatever the company felt was needed to put an end to the crisis.

Spraying occurred around the clock with some success, especially on fruits. Initial reports were that twenty-five percent of the crops would be salvaged. "Twenty-five is better than zero. This is a partial victory for science," professed Dr. Edwards, chair of the Consortium.

The Stingers that had feasted on the blood of the insects devouring the smart plants were now evolving. No longer content on attacking the dwindling supply of insects anymore, new reports were coming out that they were attacking farmers who tried to harvest the crops.

Some first-hand accounts were noting that the Stingers were growing in size, nearly doubling their capacity in a few months. They laid hundreds of eggs and had a lifespan of three months, which meant they were multiplying quickly.

Almost as if the Stingers were programmed from inception, they began to mutate and mimic characteristics found in bloodborne insects. All across the land, Stingers would attack their victims and then drain an ample supply of blood from them, which then was carried off and transmitted to other humans.

Within days of being stung, a person would develop an itchy red rash that increased over the coming days. This was followed by a high fever, loss of appetite, dehydration and then in most cases death. If the person did not show physical signs of an infection, they were still prone to the debilitating psychological effects that were induced when bitten.

There was no official name given to the mental state of an infected person other than saying they "bugged out." It was advisable to stay clear until sedatives could be administered to the victims, for they would exhibit schizophrenia and road rage for days until they dropped from fatigue.

Panic again hit the public. Signs of the Stingers would drive people to wear masks and coats even while the weather was warm.

With its rich fertile soil and warm climate, Virginia was one of the more Stinger infested states in the country and made for a perfect nesting ground for the bugs. During the first part of the year, approximately one thousand people were stung resulting in six hundred deaths, but no one wanted to take a chance, thus, they limited their outdoor exposure as much as possible.

One of the largest markups at the stores was netting for homes and windows. It was thought that this provided adequate protection from the bugs; ironically, the best advantage the population had was the crops because the Stingers focused most of their attention on them.

The Stingers became even more ravenous eaters of the crops than their insect brethren that feasted on the vegetation. The only difference was that when they became aware of human presence or detected danger, they attacked as if they had been programmed during gestation.

A theory that had a large following on the internet was that the smart plants passed on some sort of a genetic code to the Stingers, which made them bigger and "smarter." Distrust of the government and its new policies were everywhere.

The government operated out of a bunker literally and figuratively at this point, confronting the day-to-day challenges in "normal times" in addition to a new epidemic of a blood born pathogen from the Stingers.

The Consortium captured enough of the Stingers to produce antibodies for a vaccine and immediately tried it on several patients who had been stung. Most would continue to get sick however, some of the patients showed signs of progress. It was a small sign of success in the Bug War.

Veritese, a subsidiary of IS&G was the manufacturer of the vaccine for the Stingers. Their factories ran 24/7 on producing enough product to combat the insect epidemic. The only problem, for the public at least, was that a vaccine was costly and not everyone could be vaccinated in a short time frame.

If you could afford it, you received a vaccination on demand. At five-hundred dollars a pop, it was priced out of reach for millions of people. The government used a lottery system to distribute the remaining batch of vaccines. If your numbers were chosen, you were expected to be at one of the vaccination centers within a day for inoculation.

CHAPTER 13
TRUST

Not everyone was convinced that the vaccines were going to benefit them. If they could afford it, they were forced to purchase the "cure." This didn't sit well with the majority of the population. Although it was the law of the land to get a vaccine shot for others not to get infected, some people would not accept the explanation. Perhaps out of religious conviction, distrust of the government or of big corporations, some forced vaccinations were going to be made at gunpoint.

Steve came over Saturday morning to chat with Raymond. They were never close as brothers growing up but they could count on each other in times of crisis. If there ever was an odd couple, the brothers were it.

Steve went into the Marine Corps after high school. His idea of winning an argument would be to shout and curse at Raymond until he got his way.

"Raymond, did you hear the fucking news. They're forcing people to spend money and get vaccinated for this bug shit."

"I heard."

Steve continued while he searched for something to eat in Donna's refrigerator, "There's no way I'm giving that poison to my kids. Isn't it bad enough what's happening: forcing chip implants and mandatory vaccinations. It's sick. They can arrest me first."

"Where's that gonna leave your kids then, Steve?"

"Maybe with a father that's living, Ray."

"What are you saying? They're poisoning everyone."

"Bingo. That's exactly what I'm saying."

"It seems a bit much and desperate on their part. I'll give you that."

"Damn straight. What are you guys gonna do?"

"I don't know. I'm not comfortable with what's happening either but don't want to put the kids at risk."

Steve sat at the kitchen table drinking his beer. "I heard they're rounding people up if they don't get one and sending them off to some sort of camp."

Raymond tried to say something else but as usual Steve interrupted, "Fuck that bro. It's a labor camp. All for not getting an injection. This isn't Nazi Germany. They've gone too far this time. They're asking for an armed revolution. We're not going to take this."

"What do you mean by that? I agree that forcing injections is unethical but what choice is there? We can't fight the government."

"The hell we can't. Don't they teach anything in that school of yours Ray? We fought our government how many times in history? And the righteous won every time."

"You're right Steve but in those times we had an army. That's not the case anymore."

"Are you shitting me Ray. I betcha there are more guns in this state than the army."

"I don't know if that's true but will take your word on it…but are the people united? That's the important part or else you'll get picked off one by one."

"More than you know, bro."

"I agree with you man, I'm just not sure how to resist. In my job, I get monitored and need to show proof of the vaccination, being around students and all."

"Oh big deal, your job. You should be telling the kids the government has gone too far and people should resist. Tell the truth!"

"I'm not disagreeing with you Steve- just not sure that we can fight back at this this stage or that it would make a difference. Look at everything that's happened this past year. I don't buy the lies either but still have a family to care for."

Steve put his beer down and left out the back saying out loud, "So do I Ray."

Vaccination centers were put up throughout the city and in large retail outlets to make it convenient for everyone to get inoculated.

•　　　•　　　•　　　•　　　•

Susan finishes up her shift at the Walmart and as she walks to her car, her boss approaches her.

"Sue… Did you and Steve get your shots yet?"

"Not yet, Mr. Adams. We might do it next week though. We got a letter to come into the Depot."

"Sue, you can get it over with right here and then you'll be safe. Steve can do it when he gets the chance. So can the kids."

"Well, we're not sure this is the right thing to do…you know."

"Sue, I'm being pressured by my boss to ensure every one of my employees is vaccinated. I would hate to let you go because of this. I hope you make the right decision."

So now I gotta chose between losing my job to a man at work or pissing off a man at home, Susan thinks to herself.

"Mr. Adams. Did you ever think maybe all this stuff is not right? I mean, just because the government is telling people to do it, it could be wrong… you know."

"Sue, come on be reasonable. The government knows what they're doing."

Susan and her boss notice two part-time girls working second shift coming from the exit of the vaccination center. They are both laughing.

"You see Sue; even teenage girls are lining up and getting these shots. It's safe. The only ones causing problems will be the ones who don't get the shots because they'll put all of us at risk."

Susan walks with her boss to the entrance.

They are both knocked to the ground by a large explosion in the building next to Walmart. It was one of the portable depot's stations providing vaccinations. A large piece of metal came flying out of the depot and sliced into the neck of Susan's boss.

Susan lay on the ground whimpering, briefly opening her eyes to see the stunned gaze of Mr. Adams, who had the object lodged in his neck. Black smoke streamed from the building as one of the girls seen earlier comes out, with her hair and clothes on fire. Her screams rip into Susan who still cannot or will not move from the pavement.

The screams finally stop as the young girl falls to the ground.

CHAPTER 14
REACT

Occasionally, the internet is a useful tool, however, most of the time it's filled with unnecessary drivel and garbage. People who did not receive or who could not afford a vaccine were labeled Bottom Dwellers. The ones who could afford it got vaccinated first and were labeled the Untouchables.

The Bottom Dwellers were told to wait their turn and would be serviced at depot stations for mass injections as they became available. It was almost as if the CDF didn't care if they got the injections or not, but most of the Bottom Dwellers were under the belief that they needed to have them in order to survive. They could have been given *anything* in the present climate.

Not all Bottom Dwellers were people without means. Most of them believed in the system, in America, and in apple pie; but a handful of them opted out of vaccines, the cities and truly unplugged from the electronic beehive. An anti-technological fervor started to form underneath the belly of the beast.

The government and CDF had enough to worry about keeping some balance of authority in the country and they weren't going to expend resources trying to bring renegade groups under their thumb. It just wasn't high on their priority list.

A profitable and secure employer for a young person was in the building and maintaining of the Domestic Camps (DC's) of America. The DC's were filled with Bottom Dwellers who fought in the riots protesting martial law and forced vaccinations and anyone else deemed to be an enemy of the state.

The clear majority of Bottom Dwellers simply were not going to be getting vaccinated either because of income or insufficient time and of course, this didn't sit well with them. The earlier riots were over food rations. The new riots were pure anarchy coupled with a resistance to this new form of servitude.

Martial law declared last year prevented the display of weaponry but the CDF didn't go house to house collecting guns. At first, they used incentives such as medical supplies and extra food rations to get the public to turn in their weapons. This had modest results, especially in the inner cities. It proved much more problematic in the suburbs. And although the southern border was secure, there was no shortage of ammunition and guns flowing from either Canada or Mexico.

Steve found a way to augment his collapsing salary: he had contacts whom he had gone hunting within Canada that shipped him small and large arms on a bi-monthly basis. He then would trade them for food and any other supplies he needed.

Some of the depots housing the vaccinations were bombed and shot at. Susan, of course, witnessed that first hand. Within the inner cities, the CDF had more firepower but not enough manpower and most were overrun in days. With no vaccines to distribute to the Bottom Dwellers, an all-out Race war ensued.

Most the inner cities were filled with Bottom Dwellers: people who could not afford the vaccinations. The clear majority of them were people of color and the unemployed. The CDF let the rioters burn and trash their neighborhoods as long as they didn't wander off into other sectors. The real chaos began when the rioters moved into the more affluent areas of the city where the Untouchables were perched in their condominiums and places of business. Helicopters, paratroopers and very accurate snipers were used to protect them, for a while.

Although the largest percentage of Bottom Dwellers were white and poor, the mindset of the underclass was that whites had an opportunity for a vaccine shot and were going to live or at least have a better chance of survival. Even in the midst of the anarchy, shysters would formulate fake vaccines to sell or trade in the underground market. Desperation was the only commodity not in short supply.

The tipping point occurred and the breakdown was inevitable. On the curbs, the trash began to pile up as sanitation workers feared for their lives and refused to go into certain sections of the city. This compounded the problem enormously as not only the stench became repugnant but the vermin were everywhere.

As the bodies of strangers would be shot, no one came to retrieve them. They lay next to the garbage in the streets and on the sidewalk. The only ones happy with this macabre scene were the rats that openly roamed, feasted on the dead and dominated the curbs.

Established and newly formed gangs would kill any rival threatening their turf. The lowest of the low used the opportunity to perform house-to-house gang rapes, murder and worse. People were mugged at gunpoint and the inner-city schools finally found a way to service all their children- they shut down.

The CDF put a perimeter around the worst neighborhoods and let the cities descend into darkness. The guards were arguably no better than some of the rioters. One such guard was new to the block and came from one of the suburbs off the turnpike- Raymond's brother in law, Jim, who lost his job a few months back and took a job with the CDF. The newest members of the CDF got the worst positions and the worst job for a CDF guard was in the inner perimeter zone.

Jim fit in perfectly.

Every day guards had to see people kill one another but their core mission was to prevent people from escaping to another safer zone.

Shifts for the guards were in twelve-hour increments. It was tedious and deliberately grueling work and it was not an uncommon sight to see the guards get sexual relief from a local just to cross the road or to see a relative. Sometimes, they would taunt them with an extra ration for performing a blowjob in the street. It was a dehumanizing environment that often made the guards targets for the resistance that formed. Jim would learn that lesson on his first day.

•   •   •   •   •

As Jim stood guard on the edge of the perimeter for sector B, a girl and boy walked up to him and his partner.

"What do you need?" asked Jim.

"My aunt lives down on the other side. We got her some pills, cause she's sick," said the teenage boy.

The girl only keeps her head down.

"Is this your sister?"

"No, my neighbor."

"She's your bodyguard, huh?"

The boy doesn't say anything nor does he have a facial expression.

"Ok, you have one hour. Do your business and come back this same way."

"Wait a minute newbie. Not so fast. We don't let them through that easily," said his squad leader, Sgt. Bradley Berger.

"She wants to take a tour downtown. Well, she can go downtown on me first."

Berger grabs the girl but she only pushes back. He then slaps her and twists her hair around his hand, which makes her fall to the ground screeching in pain. His gun is in her face and she defiantly looks up at him, daring him to pull the trigger.

"These people still don't get it. Watch and learn newbie. This is how we roll in the hood."

Out in the open, Berger unzips his pants exposing himself to the girl who is motionless but stoic in her resolve. She said nothing as Berger's half-naked body moves closer to her face.

As Berger is inches away from the girl's mouth, she grabs hold of his manhood with her teeth and bites down as hard as she can. Berger tries to yell but doesn't have the energy or ability to make a sound. The girl is holding his legs now so he can't wriggle away. His face is now beet red and a scream finally punctures the stale putrid air of the ghetto.

Jim hesitates and is clearly stunned by this display of bravery yet foolishness. The boy runs down the street away from the guards. Private William Serando aims his gun at close range in the belly of the girl and unloads four shots into her. Remarkably, her teeth are still clenched on Berger's once pride and joy. Jim helps Serando pry apart her mouth as she falls to the ground, part of Berger still with her.

Berger falls to his knees bleeding and is in excruciating agony. He's now sideways holding his genitals in both hands weeping like a baby. As Serando walks over to kick the girl even though she is dead and poses no threat, two shots echo from across the street. Jim doesn't know precisely where the shots came from but Serando could care less at this point, since one of them finds its mark in his right eye.

Serando falls to the ground next to Berger. Jim fires wildly at the building but then realizes he's an open target and retreats behind the makeshift bunker. One more shot lands on Berger, in his back this time. He coughs up some blood and then his eyes go blank.

Serando takes no more incoming and is left with his one eye to contemplate the day's unnecessary destruction.

CHAPTER 15
TRANSITION

"I got a job dad!" said Lisa, while Raymond was cleaning things up in the backyard.

Raymond turned to his daughter and said, "That's great hun. Where at?"

Lisa smiled from ear to ear. He hadn't seen that in her for years. "I'm working for the government at a redistribution center only a mile down the road. I get benefits, a good salary and an extra ration a day. I only register people when they get processed into our system. It's so easy."

Raymond cleaned the grass from his boots. "I think that's great Lisa. I know you'll do well."

While Oliver was finishing up his last quarter at high school, Lou hopped in the car to join his older sister to work. Lisa impressed her superiors so much that they agreed to have a job interview for her brother.

"Look Lou, we need the money. If you embarrass me or say something about the government, they won't hire you."

"I got it Lisa. You don't have to tell me how to act. I can shut my mouth if I want something and I know we need the money, so just chill out."

The camp is a short drive from the Brown's house. The facility flashed its metal roof into the distant sky as the two of them made their way up to the gates. Lisa slowed the car down and then flashed her card into the picture reader at the entrance station.

"Who's with you Ms. Brown?" asked a camp guard, Bill, who Lisa greeted every morning.

"This is my brother, Lou. He has an interview for a processor job and we're a little late." The gates slowly went up as the two of them drove into the compound.

Lisa went off to her cubicle while Lou waited in the reception area.

A busload of new inmates came into the compound as a tall rather unimpressive figure came strolling into the room.

Mr. Evans greeted Lou in the reception area.

"Good morning, Louis. My name is Roger Evans and we'll have a short one on one interview this morning."

"Good morning sir."

"Please, call me Roger."

As they stood there in the lobby, a bus honks its horn and pulls into the front of the compound. New inmates to the facility get off the bus and enter the camp. One of them falls as she exits the bus.

"We don't have any more processor jobs. I had to fill one yesterday. He was a relative of the camp commander. You understand? Don't you?" asked Mr. Evans, with a smirk on his face.

"Yes sir. I do."

As one of the guards went over to the woman who fell, another inmate reached into the guard's holster and pulled his gun out. In an instant, the inmate shot the guard and made a dash for the exit gate. He only made it twenty yards before being shot by one of the snipers in the tower.

"We do, however, have an opening for a guard. Would you be interested young man?" asked Roger, condescendingly.

"No thank you, sir."

"Well, the only thing I have left is an assistant in the kitchen. You interested?"

"Yes. I would be."

"Fine, report Monday with your sister."

It was a low-grade position but Lou was happy to be able to contribute to the family in some way.

•　　　•　　　•　　　•　　　•

"What's become of our family, Ray?" asked Donna, nervously, "We have one child dead and two working at the camps. Oh, and by the way my sister who won't speak to me, has a husband who's a fascist guard in the CDF. Does it get any worse than this?"

Ray looked up from fixing his tie and said calmly, "I know Donna; it's not what anyone wants. I wish I could turn back the hands of time and speak to Allen and change things but that's not reality. Everyone is doing what they think they need to do so they can survive in this changing world."

Ray, ever the calculating and non-reactionary person continued, "When the time's right, we'll do whatever is necessary to survive and protect the kids but for now we need to keep a low profile. I hear every day how people are saying the wrong things in public and getting fired or taken away by Homeland. Hell, I'm teaching a class that's down to 50 % of what it was only a few months ago. It's just a matter of time before I'm out of a job."

Donna turned to Ray and asked if his brother would join them this weekend for Oliver's eighteenth birthday.

"I called him several times this week and left a message with Susan but neither replied back to me. What about your sister, is she coming?"

Donna walked away muttering softly, "She doesn't answer me back either."

CHAPTER 16
DECISIONS

Back in rural America and in the heartland, things went from bad to worse. The few crops that had been harvested were done with great expense. The Stingers were always dangerous and on the lookout for any type of insect to devour. This made harvesting during daylight hours almost impossible.

Most farmers now needed to harvest at night. The bugs rather amazingly, realized their opportunity to feast was greater at nighttime, used the occasion to crawl, buzz and decimate the fields under cover of darkness. It wasn't that the Stingers couldn't see at night, it appeared to be more of an accuracy problem. Their mutation made them bigger but appeared to be hindering their eyesight.

Therefore, overall it was a losing proposition for the farmers once again. They sprayed one night and harvested the following evening, trying to keep one step ahead of the insects and Stingers.

Steve, a professed Christian felt that the vaccinations infringed on his rights and beliefs. His day job consisted of bartering and trading in illegal guns. There was no construction except on high-end shelters of which he was not equipped to provide. Susan was down to part-time status without any benefits. He received a letter requesting his family's presence for the vaccinations at the Central Office Depot located a few miles from his house.

When Steve called to protest on the grounds of his religious convictions, he was told that this was a national security concern and not a religious issue. When he told the woman on the other end of the line what to do with the vaccinations, she calmly told him she would be sending someone over from Homeland to "convince him."

"Sue, we got nothing left in this world to hold on to. Our home will be repossessed soon, there's anarchy in the streets, bugs taking over and attacking. I think we need to consider leaving as quickly as possible."

"This is where I grew up and besides our kids are still in school; what do you mean get away. We're not fugitives."

"I think this is a test from God. If we stay, this vaccine will mean giving in to a government that has controlled and poisoned us. If we leave, we might die but it will be on our terms."

"We have to think about this Steve. Rushing into something like this is gonna be hard on the kids. Let's don't make any rash decisions, please. We may lose the house but we're still living and have our health. I don't see what's the big deal with getting a vaccine. If the government says it's fine, it must be.

"Would you be able to live with yourself if what was injected in our kids made them sick?"

"That's crazy Steve. We've given our kids tons of shots over the years and now you wanna take a stand just when the country's falling apart. Your timing's perfect."

"I know this ain't right Sue. You just have to trust me."

"They're killing innocent people for their beliefs. You know that's what should bother you the most. The government wouldn't be giving people anything that harms them. Everyone says it's fine."

Steve's face is flush red at this point. "Are you kidding me? What do you mean the government says it's fine? They're the cause of all this damn shit going on. I'm not staying to be a robot of theirs. Are you with me or against me?"

"Now you sound like Raymond. He's always blaming the government for what goes wrong. I don't think it's so black and white. Of course, I'm with you but don't pressure me. I need time to think about this."

"Sue, I was just told to report tomorrow for these shots. We don't have time."

"We have kids here and who knows if leaving is gonna makes us any safer. Besides, where will we go?"

Steve described how large groups of people were leaving for the mountains to get away from all the forced vaccinations and civil breakdown.

"I can't believe this is happening. Do you really think the government would make their own people sick?"

"I heard the vaccinations are a way to control the population or make us lose the will to fight back. There's all kinds of militias resisting in the country. I think the government and military have their hands tied with the cities and will leave us be in the mountains."

"It seems like a lot of effort to control the population. What's the point?"

"Sue, open your eyes. Only the strong or rich are going to survive in this world. And I don't know if even money is gonna help too much longer."

"Steve, I think it's a plan and I want to support you. Please make sure it's safe before we pack up and move everything."

An underground barter system developed over the year. Two of the most coveted commodities were organic seeds and bullets. Fortunately, for Steve, he was already ahead of the game and had a system in place with connections. He had an ample supply of ammunition and used that to barter for fuel, canned goods, seeds and other supplies the family needed.

"Once we got everything in order Sue, we'll let the kids know."

"Can't we wait till school lets out. It's only a few days away."

"We'll play it by ear but I think we can hold out. There's gonna come a day when getting up north will be impossible- you'll see."

•   •   •   •   •

Steve and his family head over to Raymond's house to celebrate Oliver's eighteenth birthday.

"Happy birthday Oliver," said Thomas, as he opened the door to Oliver's room.

"Thanks. I'm not sure what to be that happy about except for getting out of school soon," said Oliver, as he put on a shirt and combed his hair for the party.

"Are you going away to school or commuting?"

"I'm going to Penn; besides, I can always commute if the price is too high."

"I heard most of the schools were closed in the city," said Thomas, as he sat on the bed.

"Some are, but I think the privates are all open. They're supposed to be guarded."

"Come on boys, it's cake time," said Donna, as she peeked her head into the room.

"Hey, after the party, I have to show you this blog of a guy talking about Allen," said Thomas.

"Ok."

"The family had a modest meal with small talk before cutting the cake."

The grownups then retreated to the patio while Tom followed Oliver to his room.

The video on the website was titled "Things aren't what they seem" featuring a professor who talked about a government-controlled breakdown and the martial law declared earlier in the year. He explained how the lack of food was planned to have martial law and anarchy on the streets to control the population.

The professor named IS&G as culprits working with the government to cause the catastrophe. He ends the video praising Allen in the highest terms: "Allen Brown was the Paul Revere of our times."

"That doesn't make any sense Tom. Why would the government want to ruin the country?"

"I don't know but he has thousands of people following. They're calling themselves the 'Network'."

"What's that shit about your brother being the 'Paul Revere'?"

"I don't know. Maybe they're trying to say that Allen wanted to warn people about what was coming. Don't you think?"

"Do you think he knew this was coming? Why didn't he tell your parents? He didn't need to blow up the place, did he?"

"He didn't blow up anything… I mean, he tried to blow part of the company he worked at, but maybe they were involved in all of this."

"My dad says that company is the one making the vaccines for all of us and is 'making money hand over fist from the suckers in the white house'."

"I've been reading a lot about Allen's company too. They got a dark past, dude. I'm going to show this tonight to my dad and see what he thinks."

Later that night, Oliver showed his father the video.

CHAPTER 17
NO COMING BACK

"Son, I don't want you focusing on this stuff too much. Your brother was smart and not crazy but did a horrible thing that we can't undo. I want you to concentrate on school and leave this stuff behind. Ok?"

"But dad, don't you wanna know why Allen did that stuff?"

"I do son but I don't want you obsessing with this. That's my job. Your job is school."

Raymond hugged Oliver and continued saying, "The best way to remember your brother is to continue to live and go to school. Your brother was just like you. He studied hard and did well. I don't have the answers to what caused him to do what he did. It's my job to find out and I won't hold anything back from you but the family needs you to focus on moving on. Can you do that?"

"I'll do my best dad."

At Penn Valley High School, the next day, Raymond ate lunch and graded a few homework assignments. He had some time until his next class was due to arrive so he logged onto the web to watch the podcast that Oliver showed him over the weekend.

When he typed in the letters to the site this time, a large screen popped up that read, "Restricted Website. If you continue, your actions will be deemed in violation of the Sedition Acts passed under Executive Order 665."

"What the hell is this shit?" Raymond said aloud. "What's the Sedition Act? We just looked at this the other day."

He ignored the warning and continued to read the blog. It stated, "Something even bigger was about to happen in the coming weeks to all of us and to prepare to resist by any means necessary."

Raymond wanted to continue reading but students from his next block class came in. He quickly shut the computer down and conducted his last lesson for the year.

The next day. Repeat. Same routine for Raymond except that it had a touch of excitement in the air, for the students would be taking their final exams and finishing up the year for him.

"What's up, Mr. B?" said one of Raymond's juniors as he entered the class. "I'm glad I don't have to see you anymore after today."

"Mr. Carpenter, believe it or not, I feel the same way about you, young man."

"You're supposed to like all students and not say things like that."

"I do like students when they act in a civil manner."

Ray continued to hand more students their exams. The rest of the class came streaming in with their hands out grabbing at the papers, spitting their gum into Raymond's wastebasket.

"By the way Mr. Carpenter, you still need to put effort into this exam not to see my pretty face next year."

"Piece of cake Mr. B. This class is a joke anyway."

After all the students were seated, Ray read them brief instructions as they shut off their phones while tucking them away. All was quiet except for the crumpled sounds of erasure marks for nearly an hour.

A phone call breaks the silence in the class as the ambitious test takers were finishing up their exams. Normally, phone calls in the middle of class were to retrieve a student (usually a discipline matter) to the office. However, Raymond knew during a week when students were taking final exams, a phone call was an ominous sign. He walked gingerly over to answer as if he could savor the last few seconds.

"This is Mr. Brown; how may I help you?"

"Mr. Brown, this is Principal Shibled. I need to see you right away. I have someone coming to cover your class as we speak."

"What's the problem?" asked Raymond.

"No problem Mr. Brown. I just need to have a word with you in my office."

A colleague of Raymond's from another department, Mr. Kyle Kessler, strolled into the room as if he owned the building. Ray never liked but rather tolerated his existence. Kyle was one of the thirty percent of teachers who never left high school but continued his glory days in school by bullying other kids and staff. If you weren't talking sports or sex, you simply weren't worthy of a conversation in Kessler's eyes.

"Headed to the big house Mr. Brown?"

"I Guess," said Raymond, with a forced smile. "Thanks for covering. I hope it's short."

Mr. Kessler, sporting his trademark one size too small polo shirt and smirk on his face, sat in Raymond's chair muttering loud enough for all to hear, "I wouldn't bet on it." This brings a chuckle from some of Kessler's loyal admirers.

Principal Shibled or "Shithead" as Ray and his colleagues used to refer to him as, was a social studies teacher many years ago but ended up in administration after a series of "unfortunate events" with some students. It was nothing of the sexual nature but rather badgering and the inability to relate to youngsters was his fault.

He "opted out" but in another way. Shibled was like clockwork in the morning; noted for his five-minute drive by before the morning announcements went off, darting through the halls while the students were in class, clipboard in hand. He cited this on many occasions as his connection to the "pulse" of the school. The typical bullshit artist who rises through the ranks with empty soft sounding phrases that mean nothing.

Ray and his former colleagues shared many laughs contemplating Mr. Shibled's motives in school during their lunch breaks. "Shithead" usually avoided Ray and the smarter clientele at school, focusing his attention on the biggest bang for his buck: the coaches down the hall. They were known for making small sports talk or by displaying their version of harassment by talking about the less important teachers. Sometimes, they would direct their bile at students who didn't shine like the others.

Ray entered the main office with Mr. Shibled staring at him with his hands folded standing in the lobby. The two secretaries who normally greet Ray, even during the past year with his personal tragedy, did not say a word. That was the second indication that things were going to go downhill quickly. Although Raymond had the right to bring a union representative, he chose to go it alone. That was a big mistake.

"Mr. Brown, I'm agent Daniels and this is my partner agent Grisavage from Homeland Security. We need to talk to you about a restricted site that you accessed yesterday," said the older agent.

"Sure," said Raymond in disbelief.

"We need you to come with us," said the younger and more belligerent agent.

"Can't this matter be resolved here?" asked Raymond.

"No it can't and we call the shots now. This isn't your classroom," said Grisavage, as his nostrils widen and the putrid smell of his breath, which must have consisted of stale coffee and tobacco chew, reach Raymond's inner circle.

The agents escorted Raymond out of school and into their van.

On the drive over to Homeland, the only thing Raymond could think of was how far the country had slipped into a police state over the past year.

A large American and Pennsylvania state flag flew out front of the office building housing Homeland Security. In a small heavily lit room, Raymond Brown was interrogated for the second time in his lifetime. This time he wasn't going home.

"You are being charged with a violation of the Sedition Acts passed under Executive Order 665," said special agent Daniels. He then showed Raymond a computer log of his keystrokes to the restricted website.

"Is this a joke? All I did was log onto a website and read a few words. This is ridiculous. I want to speak to my lawyer."

"You don't get a lawyer," said the cocky agent, "We have martial law and people shooting other people for canned beans and your innocent little site that you logged into is inciting revolution. This is a matter of national security. You of all people should be doing whatever the authorities request."

"What do you mean me of all people?"

"You know exactly what I mean…after that stunt was pulled by your son. I guess the apple doesn't fall far from the tree. Does it?"

"I'm not inciting any revolution. I was curious about the site because it mentioned my son. That's it"

"Your terrorist son. Don't you mean?"

"I'm not here to defend the actions my son took but this has nothing to do with him."

"This is a straightforward question: Did you or did you not log onto the website titled, 'Things aren't what they seem' yesterday at approximately 12:05 Eastern Standard time?"

"I did log on to the site but I was only curious as to its origins. This is still America. You have no right to do this!"

"You lost those rights being an enemy of the state," said Daniels.

"How in the world can I be described as an enemy of the state. Have we lost our first amendment rights now?"

"I think we have all that's required. A full confession was just made by our prisoner. Grisavage, take him away."

Ray was stripped of his clothes and dignity and then placed in handcuffs. The agents put him on a bus headed northbound. The bus was loaded with other like-minded revolutionaries going to a special Domestic Camp, DC 10, which specialized in re-education for the educated masses.

The smell of body odor and misery saturated the bus as the young and old American citizens headed to DC 10. After a short drive, yellow lights and a large watchtower were the first things Raymond had noticed pulling into the compound. Two well-armed guards, one in the back of the bus and one in the front, looked anxiously around, almost as if they wanted to shoot at anyone fleeing or trying to make a move off the bus. Next to Raymond, sat a young man who is petrified and shaking like a leaf.

"Don't worry boss. It'll be all right," said Raymond, as he winked at the man.

The young man cannot muster a smile but said, "I don't belong here. I wanna go home."

The sign lit up in majestic neon lights at the entrance to the camp. It reads, "Reform is to Conform."

"Single line, don't make a move," blasted the guard in the front of the bus. Another guard met them on the way out of the bus and guided them to the entrance gates where an older man with a dark black uniform awaited them.

"I'm Colonel Stout and this is DC 10. You will learn to conform to the new reality we are living or will not leave. Your old life is over," said the uniformed man with medals on his shoulders and glasses on his eyes.

The Colonel blasted out a few more choice words, "And what is that new reality? It's a world without wants and doing with less. Think of it as a back to nature thing." He along with the other tin soldiers by his side started to smile.

"The government has spared no expense at setting up these domestic camps for our citizens. Our objective is to take misguided masses like yourselves and help them see the light to re-educate the other less intelligent masses. Consider yourselves the chosen ones. You're all very lucky. There are other camps to be at. Is that clear?"

"Yes sir!" replied every member standing in line, except Raymond.

Colonel Stout, noticing Raymond had not spoken walked over to him, "Do you think you're special or are you just going to be my new pain in the ass, dickhead?"

"I don't think I'm special sir… just unclear why the need for a place like this for American citizens?"

"A place like this is needed to keep the peace, smart ass. Of course, I'm not as smart as you are to figure it all out. I just take orders like a good soldier. Isn't that what you're thinking big man?"

Colonel Stout was only inches away from Raymond's face at this point. Ray wanted to tell him the truth: how a little bit of power does corrupt rational men in dark times like this but giving power to a simpleton like you is reprehensible. His logic prevails and he says nothing.

"And you are branded as a threat to stability and order but for some reason are worthy enough for our government to spend the time and money to get your heads right. Do you understand?"

"Yes sir. I understand."

"Good…Now follow Sergeant Burns over to the receiving line where you will learn to reform and conform."

• • • • •

Donna received a letter from the CDF stating that her husband was in DC 10 for training and would be released as soon as he has his mind right. Every lawyer that Donna called told her there wasn't anything they could do and that it was a matter of national security.

There were rumors on the location of the camps but no civilian would dare drive to the gates. Louis, working at DC 1 with his sister, told their mom it was not a good idea to try and get their father out or drive up to see him. They both had heard and seen stories of people who were killed for similar things.

"Mom, I saw a woman come up with her son to the gates and was arguing with one of the guards for a while. She parked her car and got out of it to speak to the guard. They argued for a while and then few minutes later, one of the guards shot her," said Louis.

"Oh My God. That's horrible. What happened to her son?"

Louis turned to Lisa with anguish in his eyes and finally said, "They took him away in another car mom."

"My gosh kids, what kind of place are you both working at? You need to quit now."

"We're afraid to leave mom and besides we have no money coming in. We have to live," said Lisa.

"You call this living."

Suburbia truly reigned supreme. Earlier in American history, a mass of humanity moved from the farms to the cities for employment. Now, farms and cities were too dangerous, one for the Stingers and the other because of people. If you could afford it, escape to the suburbs was a viable option. For others, it was escape to the mountains or water routes.

CHAPTER 18
URBAN DECAY

In another world, only a few miles down the turnpike, was the locked down city. A better description would be a large open-air prison with different sectors. A daily ritual for the hired hands working under the sadistic CDF guards was painting over the signs resisting martial law and food rationing. Ironically, some of the hired hands who cleaned up the signs during the day were the same one spraying the buildings at night. A circle with a large red painted N in the middle covers the sides of office and commercial buildings throughout upper and lower sections of the city.

Jim and the other guards chased a kid down Canal street who they saw spray painting one of the Network resistance signs. They continued to the end of the road but a large pile of garbage blocked their entrance to the high-rise apartment. They decided not to pursue the kid any further.

"We'll get him later Jimbo. They always come around," said a pimple-faced guard, who couldn't have been more than twenty years old. "They're too quick to chase and probably will lead us into an ambush anyway. Seen it done before, besides, I need to preserve my ammo for the ones shooting back at us."

As they started to walk back, a dog came running across the street towards them. It was small collie with a limp and hair that was dirty as the street corner.

"I think it's hungry," said one of the guards.

"Watch this," said Jim, smiling to the other CDF guards.

"POW, POW," echoed the rounds of his government-issued 9 mm Sig Sauer pistol. The dog lay whimpering by the gutter, bleeding profusely. The guards at first kicked it. Noticing the dog not reacting, then spat on it as they walked back to their guard post.

Jim turned around to see if the animal was still alive.

"Put him out of his misery Jimbo," said a burly middle-aged guard.

Jim then fired his semi-automatic 5.56 mm assault rifle into the head of the dog. A faint whimper was all that was heard. The right side of the dog's head was torn off. Jim walked away with his chest pumped high in the air as if he just shot a terrorist attacking the city.

Things were heating up in the city: electricity, food and water were now scarce and in July, it was nearly unbearable.

It's unbelievable how life continues in such scenarios but children seem to find happiness if given the opportunity.

Jim has moved to an elite unit within the CDF known for ruthless tactics and is despised by everyone. The CDF noticed a group of kids trying to strip a fire hydrant for water. Jim is now the squad leader of the unit and instructs his newest recruit, Riley Cummings, to set an example.

"Show the natives who's in charge Riley," said Jim.

"There's no water coming out of the hydrant sir. Whaddaya want me to do?

"You're in charge man, show em who's boss."

Riley fires his rifle into the air. As if the imbecile didn't recognize the Law of Gravity, the bullet came back down to earth –striking a small child playing on the side of the street. The rest of the kids playing in and around the street all scattered. A few minutes later, the boy's mother came screaming down the street towards her son. When she tried to help the boy, Jim points his rifle at her and shot her point blank in what he hopes is her chest.

Riley is paralyzed with grief. Only a few months out of high school and already with one kill to his name. Jim winked at him and said, "Don't worry about it man. It gets easier the next time around. You'll have plenty of practice."

Jim then walked over to examine the child to verify he was gone. He pays no mind to the woman. As he reached over to see if the boy was alive, the mother grabbed Jim by the arm then took out a knife under her jacket and stabbed him vociferously in the sweet spot of his neck. Jim's last thought was that his aim must have been off for he hit the woman in her shoulder and not the chest. He would have eternity to ponder that mistake.

Every action leads to an equal reaction or if you prefer karma. Jim would have been advised to pay attention to that lesson in science class in his youth instead of making belching noises or picking on kids smaller than him. He lay there bleeding as the other guards shot the mother with about ten more rounds of ammo. They left the boy to fend for himself.

Jim had a state funeral and his CDF guard friends were all there. Out of respect, Donna and her children showed up.

•   •   •   •   •

"I'm very sorry for your loss, Laura," said Donna to her sister.

"Thanks Donna. He was a complicated man but didn't deserve to die like this."

Laura was told her husband died trying to protect a woman from being attacked by snipers who were looting the city.

"I know that I haven't been that good to you or your family when you were all struggling. I'm sorry as well."

"It's ok. You don't owe me any apologies. Why don't you come over tonight and bring Edward? He should be with family."

"I think that's a good idea sis. It's certainly a long time in coming. Thanks."

•   •   •   •   •

Life continued under occupation in the city; forced vaccinations in the suburbs and the occasional strike from the Stingers high above for the remainder of the summer.

Without any fanfare, Oliver moves onto campus in late August. He stays with a roommate that the school picked out for him. His name is Marcus Washington. Despite having economic disadvantages presented to him, Marcus excelled in academia and in sports. He had full rides to both Yale and Penn but chose to be close to home at Penn.

"What's it like behind zone A," asked Oliver.

"Dude, you don't wanna know," said Marcus. "They watch everything you do. People used to jack other people up but now it's all day every day. It's like they want us all to kill ourselves."

"We hear there are sectors all over the city. Can people still get from place to place?"

"You need an ID to move around or leave. The CDF had a list of people before the shit went down last year and they gave special ID's to their people. If you're lucky enough, you know somebody and they let you go to where you want, but those guards are badass and just don't let you be."

"It's nowhere like that where I live except for taking my dad to a DC a few months back."

"What's a DC?"

"It's some kind of labor camp or education center for citizens the government sends people to who they think need help or can help society in the future. Sort of a labor camp like they used to have in some countries for disloyal citizens."

"Wow, what did he do… kill someone important?"

"Nah man, nothing like that. He was a teacher in high school and never hurt a fly. I saw him in the morning one day and then he didn't come home. Nobody would tell us what he did wrong or could help in any way. My mom tried to get him out but he's still in. I never got to say a real goodbye. That's the thing that bothers me the most."

"Man, that's tough. I hope he gets out. My pop died when I was young. It's just been my sister and my mom living in a one-bedroom apartment all my life. Mom had two jobs and did her best. I need to make the most of this for her."

"We'll get through this together," said Oliver. "Do you think it's gonna be the end of the world?"

"We're wasting a lot of money on tuition, if that's the case." The boys both laugh.

"If not the end, then the end of how we live. People think because we're poor and live in the city that we don't know what's going on. I don't believe any of this shit about farms going down."

"What do you mean? We have all these riots because the new rules and food being short? There has to be a reason for it all."

"I don't have all the answers but there's something else going on that we're not being told."

He then pulled out literature and a small pamphlet with a large letter N on the cover. It described how things were going in other parts of the world and provided survival tips in weapons, training and resistance.

"Where'd you get that?" asked Oliver.

"I got it from a dude in the engineering department. I'll let you meet him one of these days."

"Isn't that illegal to have resistance literature?"

That question seemed to bother Marcus a bit because his eyes instantly lit up as he flung his hands in the air: "Dude, isn't it illegal to starve and kill people cause of where they live?"

"Wait..." Oliver tried to speak but Marcus jumped in quickly.

"It's ok man. I know about you and your brother- all that's gone down. I don't like what he did but I'm sure he had his reasons. You should know that your brother opened a lot of eyes to problems that we're facing. I used to search and read everything he wrote about. He was like a cult figure in the hood. Maybe he was branded a terrorist in the suburbs but in the ghetto, we knew something was not right with the story. I think he was set up."

"He was set up? What do you mean?"

"Look man, he was onto something big and wanted to expose it. It's not just about these freaking bugs or farms. It's way more. I think it's happening here as a test for the whole world at some point."

"What are you talking about... a test?"

"Who knows. Maybe a new race of people or some shit like that. We're just guinea pigs in a lab waiting to get probed." Marcus retreated to his bed and opened a book to read.

Oliver thought of the emails he used to get from Allen regarding the dangers facing everyone. He remembered how Allen would sit himself down along with Louis and talk about the need to get away from the cities and be able to sustain yourself in the country. He would also say it's better to question authority than to blindly follow whatever is dictated to them. As little children, it didn't mean much. Now, it had a certain ring to it.

Oliver continued reading the pamphlet on the Network.

CHAPTER 19
SECTOR 9

"Thanks for inviting us over Donna," said Laura. "How've you been?"

"Well, to be honest, not that great. Ray was taken to a camp a short time ago. I'm not allowed to speak or see him."

Donna lit a cigarette and sat down.

"That's not right Donna. Is it because of Allen?"

"No, I don't think so but who knows? Maybe. He was looking into reasons why all this was happening and I guess Homeland got nervous."

"How are the kids?"

"Lou and Lisa are working in another camp helping me pay the bills. They've really stepped up."

Donna took her final drag of the cigarette.

Laura reached over to touch her younger sister's shoulder and said, "What about Oliver?"

"Oh, how silly of me. I guess not everything is bad news. Oliver's at the University of Penn studying chemistry."

"Well, that's a positive for the family. I know he'll do well. He's always been so smart. Maybe he can come up with a cure for all this."

"I hope so Laura. If things don't change quickly, I'm afraid there won't be anything left to fix."

•   •   •   •   •

Steve and Susan came knocking at the door.

When they saw Laura and Edward at the house, they went over to offer their condolences.

Donna then comes over to break the awkward silence.

"Where have you guys been? We've called so many times but get no answer," asked Donna, turning to Susan and Steve.

"We've been away taking care of a few things Donna," said Steve.

Laura and Edward mill around the living room for a minute and then drift off to the backroom.

"Can I talk to you in private Donna?" asked Steve.

"Of course. What's up?"

Steve explained that he was moving his family to the summer home his parents owned up in the mountains along the Appalachian trail, up in Carbon County.

"I think you and the kids should come with us. It's not that big but will protect us. Tina and Thomas are already up there."

"Protect us from the bugs? I thought the countryside was infested with those things too."

"Everywhere is bad but at least there's hunting and fishing and less people to fend off. I think we can make a go of it."

"You mean you pulled Tina and Thomas out of school and sent them up north? What about their future? They're still in school."

"That's all we think about Donna are the kids. Open your eyes. Of all people, you should be skeptical to what's happening."

"Donna, it's not easy for me either but I think it's the best," said Susan.

"Anyway, time is running out. If you change your mind, you know where we'll be. I've stocked up plenty of food for months. I know you'll have a change of heart soon but remember don't tell anyone."

Steve began to leave and turned back saying, "Be careful what you say on your phones. Better yet, get rid of them."

As Jim and Susan were taking the back roads up to the cabin, they saw a swarm of Stingers moving away from the city headed to a large abandoned farm off to the side of the road.

"Keep going Steve. Don't stop," said Susan, anxiously.

"Don't worry. The last thing I plan to do is stop the car. Those poor bastards at that farm are in for a hell of a night."

"Steve, it looks like the Stingers are returning and landing on that roof. What does that mean?"

"I don't know Sue but we shouldn't be here if they change course. I just hope no one goes out while they're up there."

The Stingers, hundreds of thousands perhaps, neatly rested on the top of the metal plated roof, which Jim had called an abandoned farm. The "abandoned farm" rested adjacent to a hill where cars, jeeps and large trailers were seen coming and going.

"Oh My God, those things look like they knew where they were going and have been there before. Don't yah think hun?"

"Babe. I don't know. Let's just get out of this nightmare."

Jim slams his foot to the pedal and takes off, never looking back.

"Batch trial 101 returned to home base without incident sir," said Dr. Bryant, turning his attention to General William Masters.

"Very well, I hope this bunch of Stingers is going to do the job right, this time," said the General. "Billions of dollars in research to have these fuckers attack farmers was not the intention. It's definitely a good byproduct but they should be going into the cities."

Masters lit up a cigar then sat in the doctor's chair putting his feet up on the desk, clearly in charge of the show.

"Sir, we believe they will and are accomplishing their mission. The last batch was unresponsive to the vaccines and less effective. This trial of Stingers is reacting well to the compound. They will target the ones who got them during the last riot," said Dr. Bryant.

"Bunch of mumbo-jumbo gibberish. What about the Untouchables and reserved status folk?" asked the General.

"Sir, there are various vaccines being manufactured. The ones the Untouchables got will protect them from any sting they happen to encounter. We just didn't anticipate the reluctance to getting vaccinated from the general population. However, if I may say so and with all due respect sir, that was the army's job to get the population vaccinated," said Dr. Bryant, meagerly.

General Masters rose from the chair. "Don't tell me my job you little shit. I understand what happened but how do the bugs know who to attack?"

"Sir, the new batch will target the Bottom Dwellers who received the latest vaccine. I assure you."

"I'm not an idiot you little prick, can't you answer a straightforward question. You're as bad as the suits at the Pentagon. Explain to me in basic terms why the bugs will attack the Bottom Dwellers and not the Untouchables."

"Sir, these bugs were coded to be attracted to glucose or sugar which was placed in excessive amounts in the Bottom Dweller vaccine. In addition, the enzyme needed to react with the venom in the Stingers is only in compound Z; this is specifically coded in the general vaccine. The Untouchables vaccine doesn't have a drop of sugar in it and will not attract the Stingers. If I may ask again, what about all the people who don't get a vaccine shot plus all those people running off in the woods. I can't target people without a vaccination?"

"Your job is to do what you're told. I will work on policy. There are always contingency plans. Just have those little demons attack the Bottom Dwellers in the cities who received the vaccine."

"It will work this time General. I assure you."

"It better or I'm feeding you to the batch of Stingers nesting on the roof."

"Yes sir."

The General left from a large metal interior door labeled Sector 9. The outer door to the farm was labeled GRANGERS FARMS AND STABLE.

The General received a call as he was walking out the door.

"General Masters is everything going as planned?" asked Secretary Samuel Hutchinson.

"Yes brother. We have a new batch going out into the world as we speak."

"Good, we need to wrap Operation NA Reduction up by the end of the year."

"I understand. Tell the boss, we are on schedule."

It looked like a large red ribbon cutting across the early morning sky. The swarm of Stingers followed the Delaware River down to their destination, programmed for destruction of the Philadelphia population. If all went well, they would turn north and hit the big prize of New York City afterward.

As the Stingers approached the city, a large cloud of red and yellow lights filled the air. There had been an explosion in one of the factories along the pier. The factory once manufactured sulfur for industrial purposes but was just another abandoned building along the river, most likely headquarters for a gang.

The explosion sent toxic fumes billowing in the air. Clouds of dark yellow and black specks saturated the sky. The Bottom Dwellers and CDF guards in the city were coughing from the fumes but nothing more than a sore throat resulted. As the Stingers began their final approach, the polluted air restricted their arrival and they were diverted away from attacking the city. They headed northwest away from the smoke.

The people on the ground cheered as they watched the Stingers turn the course.

On their approach back to sector 9, the Stingers randomly attacked houses and small farms on their route. Their favorite target appeared to be the bugs feasting on crops. Worms to be exact. After getting their fill, they headed back to Sector 9.

A lab assistant answered the call at Sector 9. It was from their contact monitoring the perimeter of the city informing them that the attack was a failure. The stingers were returning and would arrive shortly.

"The General is going to freak when he hears about this," said Dr. Bryant's assistant, Daniel.

"How could a little bit of sulfur prevent our bugs from performing their duty? They are programmed from inception to be attracted to the compounds we made in the lab. As a fallback, they follow the bloodline in humans not other bugs and worms," said Dr. Bryant, with a puzzled look on his face, "It doesn't make any sense."

"Life has a will of its own doctor. The attraction to live must be greater than the attraction to kill; they must be sensing danger in the city and not the farms," said Daniel.

"That's not logical. They're still just bugs."

"I do find it fascinating though, that their tiny little brains are able to deduce danger and to figure out the path back to the base. It's truly amazing," said Dr. Bryant, looking like a proud father who helped his son get back on his bike after falling.

The General didn't bother with throwing Dr. Bryant and his staff on the roof to be stung. He shook Dr. Bryant's hand and thanked him for his services.

The General made his way out to a private limousine, which included a driver and his loyal servant, Sgt. Duke Mannis.

"Duke, let me ask you a question?"

"Yes sir."

"Do you know the one thing I hate more than anything else in this world?"

"No sir."

"It's not following my natural gut instinct. This time it was gnawing at me for months if not years. I listened to a lot of mumbo-jumbo science crap from that egghead and he got us burned. I knew that bastard was stringing us along for the money to do continued research. He always said things were fine but never gave me one hundred percent of the truth. Now we have a shit storm brewing and risk exposure."

The decorated tin soldiers drove away from Sector 9 and then the General handed Duke a piece of paper.

"Sergeant, target the coordinates on this list. Liquidate immediately."

Sector 9 went up in smoke following a drone strike a few minutes later.

CHAPTER 20
SECRETS

A secret will stay that way when the people who are in the know are few. By the time the Committee of 300 met, Bottom Dwellers (the ninety percent of the population) understood to a large degree that the crisis over the past year was a manufactured one and that they were all targets. Some of the senior members of the CDF even started to abandon their posts.

There was plenty of movement in the cities and the Network was the de facto gang in charge. They set up their own government and shared power with the other gangs by giving each rival faction a seat at their cabinet table. Since they were targets for liquidation, their meetings constantly moved around.

The leader of the Network was voted on several months ago and goes by the name of Gabriel. He is a charismatic figure with auburn hair and dark complexion. He hails from a mixed genealogy and he uses those attributes to relate to all classes and races within the underground.

Gabriel was a graduate student until two years again when his mother fell ill of cancer working at IS&G Industries as a production handler. One of his closest associates is a young man named Marcus- Oliver's roommate.

"It's no secret I ended up with you, Oliver."

Oliver takes his head out of the book he was reading and stares at Marcus. "What do you mean by that?"

"My aunt works on the housing staff and I asked her to change things around so I could be your roommate."

"That's a pretty creepy thing to do dude. You didn't even know me. You mean you just wanted someone from the suburbs who was white to room with you?"

"Man, most kids who come here are white so that's not a surprise. I chose you."

"I don't have a problem with you Marcus but why would you do something like that before knowing me?"

"Because your brother was on to the real reason this is happening. He worked for IS&G and would post articles talking about that company and about how on the surface they produce agro products and what not, but they also have a smaller division that does other things."

"What do you mean other things?"

"You know, the scary shit for the government that we don't hear about on the news. Come on. Use your imagination."

Oliver understood some of the information but still had a puzzled look on his face.

"Hey man, your brother knew they were planning to infect the population and repeated it over and over again on different websites. We were all hip to it in the hood. I'm just surprised he wasn't killed earlier."

"I read some things about my brother too but I didn't hear about infecting the population."

"Dude, he published articles on population control four years ago and exposed his company as the chief supplier to some military lab in the desert called Sector 9. I don't think he knew of everything they were doing but he knew enough. And if your brother knew, how many other people knew? Only your brother understood the real reason he died that night or what else that company had planned. He might have been forced into it or set up with explosives."

"Are you saying my brother was killed. Everyone saw what he did. Do you know what that's done to my family?"

"Maybe I should have told you from the start but I wanted to see what you knew. We all saw what they wanted us to see and I understand how this is all coming out man. I know it's not easy and don't want to mess you up but look around. I'm telling you the way it is. Your brother was a hero not a terrorist. Maybe the way he tried to get everyone to listen was a little bit wacked but he did get people to open their eyes."

"What would be the point to all this. What's the end game?"

"The end game. Yeh, that's the right word for it, a game. I don't know but don't tell me you believe everything you see and read about is the truth? They have everyone looking for enemies of the state but forget to mention their planning on billions to be killed."

"So you think this has all been planned? Where you getting this information from?"

"Look man, let me lay it all out to you in real terms. I think one thing leads to another. Cause and Effect. The plans for population reduction were probably always out there but needed to have an organized group push their plans."

"Are you saying the government pushed the agenda?"

"Maybe not the government. I don't know. One group makes money off pesticides for industry, which kills the crops. Another group makes money off modified plants to keep their workers and Wall Street happy. Military people see the advantages of having programmable bugs to attack other people or countries. On the surface, it looks like one follows the other. Different interests use the different possibilities for their own agendas."

"This thing couldn't have been the government or everyone would have known."

"Yeh, or the government went along or some did in high enough places. When a sinister organization with powerful ties can string everyone along, we have the nightmare we're living."

Oliver started to twitch with the news Marcus just landed on him. He squirmed in his seat while Marcus continued saying, "I planted the bomb at the sulfur plant along the pier to try to stop the Stingers from attacking. I didn't know if it would stop those things from coming or not but we had to try.

"Do you think I ever thought of being able to make a bomb? No! But one thing led to another. I'm sick of seeing inner-city kids get killed for food. We're targets because we're poor. I think they have a world planned that includes people with money, power and what's left will be a slave populace. They certainly don't need millions or billions to be workers anymore."

"So you're saying a company working with the government and military was planning this?"

"Dude, you're not listening. I'm saying the government is reacting to events the best they can. If you question too much, you're called a conspiracy theorist or worse, you end up dead. I don't know if they're in on all of it but some must know. The others just follow orders. Know what I mean?"

He turned to Oliver hoping he would put the pieces together.

"Does everything need to be programmed? Aren't some things just random acts of nature?"

"This could be and we all might be full of shit. Who knows. There's just too many dots that are connected for this to be random and happening all at once. And if it's all environmental why not in all countries at the same time? Why just here? Think of it this way. Does every kid in a class of thirty realize what the lesson is for the day?"

"Probably not."

"Right, the same is true for this. All you need is a few people in high places pulling the strings and the rest of the machinery and people just react to the events just like they were programmed to do."

"What kind of organization is powerful enough to get the government to go along or react with all this?"

"I don't know that dude. Hell, I live in the ghetto. Did you forget that? Am I supposed to have all the answers? I just know things aren't what they seem and it was too scripted to be natural and whatever the true goal is, we'll all find out soon enough. This thing is too far along now to be stopped. It's amazing nobody opened their mouths up about this before it went down. It's hard to keep a secret. Whoever or whatever is behind this must be real tight with each other."

"What are we supposed to do about it or can we do anything at all. I mean if they're that powerful, what chance does anyone have?"

"Sometimes just knowing is powerful enough. If things keep going this way, we won't be in school too much longer and we'll all have to make even tougher decisions. Can I count on you?"

Marcus held out his hand as a gesture to fist bump.

"Yeh man of course you can." Oliver bumped his fist.

CHAPTER 21
IT BEGINS

The demonstrations in Europe were not nearly at the level they were occurring in America. Nevertheless, the major cities, especially the capitals staged weekly protests, primarily in reaction to the price hikes that caused a one hundred percent spike in inflation for just about everything.

The population of Europe was convinced because of daily broadcasts and embedded disinformation outlets on the internet, that the crops were being overrun by insects and needed an adequate pesticide. The prime ministers from the largest countries such as Italy, Germany and France along with their neighbors, went on the nightly news channels explaining the need to eradicate the "enemy" with spraying from airplanes.

The people wanted results and eagerly anticipated the arrival of a solution. They didn't have to wait too long.

Morning after morning across Europe, citizens of the Old World would awaken to shiny purple specks on their lawns. Although most of the spraying occurred in the farmland, wind would pollinate the rest of the country as expected. Most of the insects ate the toxin. The others avoided it.

The humans on the other hand, absorbed it through the air and skin. The effect it would have on their health would take a while to manifest. The one advantage of an effective inoculation program is that intravenous or vaccinations are a direct approach. Spraying has many unintended variables that reduce the effectiveness. The tradeoff is public awareness versus immediate gratification and results.

The Americans chose a strategy somewhat in the middle. Waiting for every Stinger to infect three hundred million people, was just not feasible, not to mention the accuracy was always an issue for the little bastards. To speed up the process, their scientists would deploy spraying and direct infections. This had the added benefit of a scared populace giving the local defense forces and extreme advantage with their martial law tactics and domestic camps.

The rural areas of Europe noticed the first effects of the P2040 toxin in a few weeks. Much like the cases in the States, where the production workers started with rashes on their bodies working at IS&G, so it was with the farmers in the countryside. When stories of mass graves were reported, the Europeans understood that the government was now either the real enemy or inept at handling the bug and pesticide issue.

As was the case in America, the riots started and continued for the remainder of the spring season.

With Easter right around the corner, the dark-skinned sacrificial lambs met their handlers on March 30 who gave them small canister sized vials of the M2240 virus. The handlers wearing silk suits departed for unknown destinations that same night. The lambs were programmed to enter the city center and open their vials.

They performed as expected; thousands marched into their respective town halls and sat down as if they were on their lunch break. They opened the vials and released the future onto the continent.

The effect of the M2240 virus was much quicker than their South American or European models. Almost instantly, people started to cough, a rather uncontrollable and violent cough. Moreover, with every airborne particulate, the virus was launched further and further into the cities and hamlets of the continent. The elderly and young were no match for the virus as they were the first ones to succumb to the stranglehold. As with every other plague that ripped through the continent, sub-Sahara, mainly because of the congested population centers, quickly spread the virus like a rushing river after a violent storm.

The Security Council at the United Nations was convened for a special assembly of the African delegation.

Ambassador Amunu Aquimba of Tanzania addressed the delegation of members present: "My fellow members of this renowned hall. The country and for that matter, the continent that I hail from and I would venture to guess ten percent of this hall is comprised, has been overrun with an unknown virus that we can't explain nor eradicate. I don't think a wall will protect anyone in this chamber but you should realize that this contagion will not be confined to the shores of the Mediterranean. And I fear without much financial and logistical aid, the continent will slip into the abyss."

The Secretary-General of the United Nations, also a member of one of the African client states, addressed the ambassador, "My fellow citizen of the world, I wish there was better news I could give you. In this, the richest of nations, they are experiencing severe hardships brought on with their own disaster. Europe is having its difficulties as well. The Eastern Alliance is bracing for the worst and there just aren't any funds left to help a member country. We wish we could help but we just do not have the means. I'm very sorry."

The ambassador tried one last effort before a hall that is usually filled but was a quarter the size on that day, "I understand the realities of funds and the issues facing different countries throughout the world. I am asking medical personnel to come in from around the world to assist in helping to treat the casualties we are accumulating at an alarming rate. We need the people more than the money."

"My fellow ambassador, we have neither the money nor the personnel to help. I'm afraid Africa is on its own as are the other member states. In addition, Europe and Asia have sealed off the borders because of the health crisis. May God help you and the rest of the continent."

Most of the members did not stay for any other speeches and left the city and country.

Was there a point when the returning Africans realized that they were opening a plague onto their home country? The pandemic resembled earlier Swine, Bird and Spanish Flu that to this day exists in society. The M2240 virus worked quicker than its earlier counterparts did, and had the distinct advantage of staying dormant with the host for days, spreading from person to person.

Of all the planned reduction programs, the M2240 African model worked the best. It could have been released through planes as was being concocted in Europe; however, this technique proved to be much more diabolical and more of a lethal weapon by having the advantage of not pointing a finger at any organization, country or government.

In a few short weeks, if the virus did not kill you, there was a good chance that a roaming mob would have their way with you. The Untouchables were already out of the continent or shortly would be. Only the fortified, wealthy and armed stood a chance.

The legions of the so-called "Manchurian Africans" as described by the brainiacs in Hamburg, had performed exactly as programmed and served the exact dictates of the Order. Africa was locked down and diving deeper and deeper into the heart of darkness with every passing minute.

If it were one hundred years earlier, the quick and savage death that gripped Africa would have been reported in the newspapers days after the event. However, it was the modern era and even the poorest of the poor, counterparts to the Bottom Dwellers living in America, were equipped with phones that televised the horrific nature of humans striving to get over on their neighbors for however long they had left in their meager existence.

It was like watching a slow-motion horror show that foretold of an event coming soon to a town near you. However, this time, one could not just click the remote but was forced to watch man's inhumanity to one another all brought on by an organization that pretended to offer a global solution to economic and natural resource issues.

Did the ends justify the means? To the millions who lay pot boiled and stripped of their dignities or raped at gunpoint, it did not make a difference. Only a quick death would bring absolution.

CHAPTER 22
TURN THE PAGE

It was late Spring of 2042 and Brazil was on the brink of collapse. The fields were in bloom and the crops had performed beautifully. The infected numbered only one percent of the population but the disease was quickly spreading.

Latin Fever as the media outlets were proclaiming was a "deadly pathogen" transmitted by sexual and casual contact from person to person. Rumors spread that the indigenous population of South Americans originated the virus because of their poor hygiene. This led to ethnic cleansing on a mass scale. The natives tried escaping to Bolivia and Columbia but the borders were closed. Mass suicides of people not even infected ran through the country like a wildfire.

Social norms changed almost overnight with only the bravest venturing out onto the clubs and bars. Brazil's economy collapsed in the second quarter of the year. Much like their neighbors thousands of miles up north, the government declared martial law and a host of draconian measures were put in place to "protect" the society from further erosion.

Two continents separated by the Atlantic Ocean were facing a contagion not seen since the Dark Ages. What was important, or perhaps not even relevant any longer, was that the silent hand behind the destruction was not labeled as the culprit initiating the diabolic plan.

In America, it was a different story. It wasn't that the people were smarter than the Europeans or Brazilians but there had always been a long history of government mistrust going back to the founding of the country. Within the cities, especially the northeast, the Network was fighting not only the CDF but aggressively forming their own government and militias.

"My brothers and sisters, look at what's become of not only our cities, not only our country but of the continents of Africa, Europe and South America.

Do y'all still think this is a natural phenomenon?" screamed Gabriel, as he stood in front of a packed and armed crowd, at the First Baptist Church on Girard Avenue in Philadelphia.

The crowd cheered and asked him to continue preaching. No CDF or local police were anywhere in the vicinity. They evacuated a long time ago.

"I say once again my brothers and sisters. Do not be fooled into thinking that God has brought this calamity onto the nations. There are sinister people. That's right, I say sinister people with pure evil in their hearts. Oh, they may look snazzy in their thousand dollar suits and their fancy titles but they are as evil as the Father of Lies himself- Lucifer. They will say that their intentions are pure. That their intentions are for the good of the planet. Look around you. Do you like what those intentions have brought onto you?"

The crowd went wild with clapping and shouts of "preach on" and "that's right, tell it like it is, Gabriel," as he brought the people to a standing ovation.

"Once more I say to y'all. I am a peaceful person. We are a peaceful people but when you plan to kill me, and when you plan to eradicate me, when you concoct a plan to stamp us out like cockroaches, we will fight back with any and all means necessary!"

The crowd cheered and clapped, while stomping their feet. The reverberations of the stomping echoed through the hall.

"I leave y'all with this thought my brothers and sisters. My days may not be long on this earth but I say to each and every one of you, open your eyes to the truth. Do not be deceived by the evil doers with expensive suits and high ranking titles, for what is written in the good book shall surely come true: that the righteous shall and will inherit the earth."

The speech was recorded and sent out to leaders and members of the Network throughout the city and country.

•   •   •   •   •

Firepower was certainly in the hands of the CDF but by the time Gabriel's latest speech was delivered, half the posts had been abandoned by the guards. Only the most violent and sadistic operated their posts. There were reports that some of the more violent sociopaths who had been incarcerated were now being released and recruited for the CDF in the cities. They were an easy target for the Network.

"Watch and learn Oliver. This isn't rocket science but if you mess up, you'll get yourself killed or worse my man, get me killed," said Marcus, as he loaded a magazine into his semi-automatic Bulgarian replica of an AK-47.

Oliver, like his father, was a stranger to guns and only wanted to provide support to Marcus. He had no real intention of hurting anyone.

The two of them had been uploading videos of Gabriel and spreading them throughout the net and printing out posters of the Network throughout the city. They spotted one of the most notorious guards who had terrorized the block of Marcus's old neighborhood. He was patrolling the block with one other guard fresh off the recruiting station of the CDF.

Marcus took aim and struck the guard between the eyes. "A perfect shot, man," he said, as he playfully punched Oliver in the arm.

The guard's friend came over to offer resistance but quickly realized he was dead. "Quick Oliver, before he calls for backup, take him out," pleaded Marcus.

Oliver took aim but hesitated. He had never shot nor killed even a spider before and the thought of taking down another human being, albeit a sadist asshole, was abhorrent to him. He froze.

The guard began to radio in but Marcus quickly got off another shot and killed the other guard.

Oliver put his head down in despair. "I'm sorry dude. I just couldn't do it."

"It's all right man. Not everyone is a killer. This is my neighborhood and I need to defend it. Schools will be closed soon and they probably won't open back in the fall. I think you should find your way back home and help the cause in another way," said Marcus, holding out his hand for a shake.

"I'm sure you understand Oliver. The resistance that you were a part of at school, will continue, even though you aren't here."

"Don't worry your secrets are safe with me. You're protecting your family. I get it. My brother was doing the same thing in his way too, I suppose."

The two of them shook hands and parted ways. Oliver made one last tour of the University he aspired to attend since being in seventh grade and gathered up the few possessions he had.

Marcus packed his belongings and traversed his way through the sectors to rendezvous with Gabriel on the west side of the city.

CHAPTER 23
CONTAGION

By the summer of 2042, the P2040 sprayed from the skies above the old world of Europe had taken full effect. What took days to incubate and transmit throughout Africa and weeks in South America took two months in Europe.

The rashes were the first mark that a person was infected. The virus would transmit through blood, saliva and then went airborne when a person coughed. The boils and bumps, much like smallpox, last seen in India nearly eighty years earlier were prevalent throughout southern and northern Europe now.

In fact, health care practitioners at a loss to describe the phenomenon, treated the victims with the smallpox vaccine. The reaction produced interesting but horrifying results. It kept a person alive however, that's a loose translation of what being alive is.

The infected, having received the smallpox vaccine produced a zombie-like transformation where the patient would walk around in an isolated stupor mumbling to him or herself.

Naturally, the population not infected pointed fingers at the government for spraying the pesticide throughout Europe causing the outbreak. The cause didn't matter to the rioters, whether through negligence, ignorance or ineptness, the rioters wanted heads to roll.

A people's tribunal was set up for crimes against humanity and listed the prime ministers of all the major countries in Europe. The problem was that nearly every prime minister fell victim to the virus and never stood trial. In fact, German President, Helga Schmidt addressed the parliament and nation and before her speech concluded, she died of the virus.

The wealthier nations of Europe, who are initially able to afford the tremendous costs associated with caring for the infected, can only hold on for so long. The poorer nations are on their knees. Without assistance, some local officials resorted to openly killing the infected. And anyone harboring a diseased person, was deemed to be an enemy of the state.

Fear gripped the population, as rumor spread that insects could feast on the dead bodies further spreading the contagion. The slaughterhouse factories that churned out processed pig products were converted into incendiary warehouses for the dead. Miles and miles of new arrivals came one after the other. Ancient fire was the process to convert bodies to ash, which saturated the atmosphere and cleansed the countryside.

People who were suspected of being infected but who showed no visible physical or mental signs, were not afforded a reprieve. At gunpoint, they were placed in detention and holding camps, much like their American counterparts.

When the numbers became too great, Greece offered up its island of Crete to be used as a housing station, not only for their citizens but also for the wealthier European countries. In return, their financial debts were absolved.

This continued for several weeks until the island exceeded its capacity. Before the catastrophe, the island had a population of under one million people. The quarantine zone, broken down into several sectors, reaches nearly ten times that number - arguably, the most densely populated space on earth.

When not even the destitute would take a job on the island, for fear of "catching" the contagion, the government sealed off the border and let the inhabitants fend for themselves.

The camps featured cholera, dysentery and typhoid fever for the residents to choose from. The more rambunctious availed themselves to murder, rape and other forms of savagery.

Hamfu, who managed to make his way from Germany to a camp in Italy wins the unlucky lottery of not only infection but a seat boarded for Crete.

"Bashir, do you think we'll be safe on the island?" said Ali, a friend of Hamfu's, who he met while in Italy.

"I'm just happy to be leaving Europe. I spent my life there and now I am lost between two worlds: One that despises me and the other I only recall in my dreams."

"The news from Africa is not good, my friend. I hear the contagion has spread from the south to all countries in the continent."

"Then we should be with our own kind. Don't you think?"

"Yes, but we are going to Crete?"

"We'll be much closer to Libya when we get to the island."

"But why would Africa take us in if we are infected?"

"They will have no choice."

"But how do we manage to get there if we're on the island?"

"I made it here on a little raft many years ago, Ali. I'm sure I can do it again going home this time. Once established, we can try and get a small vessel to cross the sea."

Hamfu's boat is the last to leave the ports of Italy bound for Crete.

The boat is tightly packed and Hamfu questions whether it will sink before they make it to Crete.

"They put too many people on this ship. We'll be lucky to even make it."

"Maybe that was their plan along, my friend. If we are in the last boats to leave, they'll just sink us all."

"That's nonsense Ali. They aren't above killing us. That I know is correct, but they wouldn't want to lose the investment in these ships. Don't worry we'll make it."

A large explosion is heard from a distance as Hamfu and the others on board of their ship are knocked from side to side by the shockwave.

"Dear God, what is that?" asked Ali.

The men glaze up to the sky to see a bright flash brighten the horizon and then slowly go dark.

Unbeknownst to Hamfu and his colleagues, the European leaders decided that they would be proactive and merciful in dealing with the infected on the island. The French unleashed a ten-megaton nuclear bomb on the tiny island, effectively killing every creature on it.

"Is that the island we were going to?"

"It was."

A ferocious wind sweeps through the sea smacking every member on the ship. Two guards fall to the ground, which is the window of opportunity needed for the crew.

Hamfu grabs one of the rifles and shoots the other guard next to him.

"Quick Ali. Grab the rifle and cover me when the other guards come to assist."

Ali waits behind the door as two more guards race up the side of the ship.

Ali takes aim and shoots at the both of them, which gives Hamfu time to sneak up on them as they are reloading. Other members of the crew join in on the mutiny and bash the guards in the head with their own rifles until they are unconscious.

The crew leave the captain alive and instruct him to continue south to Africa.

CHAPTER 24
RUS

Noticing that mother Russia and for that matter much of Asia was not infected with the virus, the blame shifted to countries in China and Russia as having a hidden hand in the destruction of not only Europe but three other continents. Without any proof of involvement, some members of the European Union, most notably Germany, France and England, were asking for war against the giant powers to the east.

The ambassador for the European Union addresses the United Nations General Assembly by Skype, for the UN building in New York City stopped functioning months ago. A transitional General Assembly is set up in Cyprus housing the permanent members of the Security Council. It is optional for the other members to attend.

"Fellow members of the Security Council and members worldwide. By now, you are all aware of the calamity gripping our continents and the despair we are facing. It is unlike any other enemy ever encountered in the history of the human race. I make no accusations to member states that are not afflicted with this virus. Whether it was started by insects, pesticides or other methods of delivery, we aim to put an end to the crisis. We ask and need the assistance of everyone to help and especially call on our members in Asia to come to our rescue," pleaded Jean Bertoffi, ambassador to the European Union.

There were no remnants left in Russia from the last great war almost one hundred years ago but anti-German sentiment still ran through the bones of millions of Russians. After all, over twenty million of their citizens were butchered in that catastrophe.

"Mr. President, we may never have an opportunity again in our lifetime. Please consider deploying Operation One Europe," asked General Victor

Abromovich, as he turned to Prime President Vladimar Slavig of the Russian Federation.

"Are you crazy, the countryside is infected with those creatures and the virus is at our gates. Why would I send my legions to attack Germany? You're risking another world war and for what purpose?" said Slavig.

"Sir, we would tell the Americans that this is to reduce the possibility of any infected coming into our lands. It is a preemptive move to protect the motherland. They have used many preemptive wars in their past and would understand."

Slavig poured a drink and thought about the discussion being contemplated.

Abromovich senses that the leader is favoring the idea and goes in for the kill, "The old alliances that Germany once had with their European counterparts and America have long been abandoned. We would be able to gain the heartland and industrial wealth of that county and once again bring back Poland and the Baltics back in line."

"I am not saying no or yes but a decision of this nature needs to be approved by everyone. A misstep will have me working in the Siberian gulags."

"Sir, we would stop short of France and deal with her at a later point. Germany doesn't possess any nuclear arms and will not be able to deter the attack."

"Are you convinced that England and France will not come to their aid?"

"Our contacts assure us that there will be no military assistance. We have been meeting for weeks and I see no signs of an overt or covert alliance."

"Convene a meeting of our Supreme Council and let's see what they think."

"Yes, Mr. President."

The old men of the Russian Supreme council spent little time debating the question to invade or not. It was unanimous: strike first while Europe was on its knees.

•   •   •   •   •

The first motorized tank division of the Russian army broke through the northern border of Estonia without a shot being fired. The attack came in three waves. The second and most pivotal roaming mass of Russians came through Belarus. Led by General Alexander Puchniko, a former KGB operative as a youth in the Soviet Union, he smashed through the defenses and was nearing Poland with an estimated arrival of two days.

The last movement of troops came through Ukraine and was led by all non-Russians. The state of Ukraine voted long ago to become a satellite state of the Russian Federation and was obliged by the Armistice Pact of 2035 to defend the borders of Russia. All three armies formed a pincer attack formation headed to Berlin.

German President Helmut Schmidt makes a desperate call to D.C. and asks for the Americans to honor their NATO agreement. The Americans call for an emergency meeting of the permanent members of the security council.

The council agreed that Russia had a right to protect its borders from the virus being spread in Europe but saw no vital interest to continue the advance any further. The Russians and Chinese vetoed the resolution. They stopped on the Oder River a few miles outside of Frankfurt, Germany.

"We should continue with the operation Mr. President. Any further delay and the plans will be useless," said Abromovich.

"You are not a good chess player Victor. You need to know when the game is a stalemate. Going further will only invite the British and Americans to counter-attack."

"But sir, we have not achieved our primary objective. Why stop now?"

"We have achieved our goals General but perhaps not yours. We have the Baltics and can await the further collapse of the continent. At that point, we will move in but we need to be diplomatic about these things. No need to rush."

"Sir, the time is now ---"

"That will be all General. I have heard enough."

"Yes sir."

Five hundred thousand Russian troops camped along the river mingling with the native population.

Movement is life. And to every action there is an equal and opposite reaction said Sir Isaac Newton. How right he was.

The large army could not help but resist mingling with the population but also taking full advantage of their power over them and the natural descent of depravity that follows.

Thousands of innocent Polish girls were used for the amusement of the Russians.

The only defense the Polish had were the infection rates of the P2040 virus.

Indeed, many of the Russian troops would see a purple tint in the Oder River that must have been a remnant from the spraying done months earlier. The saturation within the soil caused a runoff into the river and sea. The Russians would get a taste of the virus through direct contact with the natives but also in the vegetation and water that surrounded them.

Colonel Danov of the 1st mechanized Russian army updates Central Command at Stalingrad. "My men are catching the disease from the natives and it's not safe to be here any longer. We need to pull back."

"Colonel, the only thing you need to pull back are the pants on your men. Of course there will be an infection among the troops if they mingle with the locals. Have them do exercises and stay within their barracks," said Defense Secretary, Boris Mucah.

"Mr. Secretary, the disease is spreading and not just from the women. It's all around us sir. I implore you. We need to retreat before I have a mass desertion."

"We do not retreat Colonel. You have orders to stay and deal with the infected in any manner you desire."

The troops proceeded no further. They are stopped by an invisible yet deadly force. Their invasion was brief and futile and the only booty brought home to the motherland was the virus.

CHAPTER 25
PURPLE HAZE

"It's good to see you again General Masters," said the Chairman of the Board of IS&G Industries, Robert Burkman. The two men greeted each other in the lobby of the corporation's headquarters in Armonk, NY.

I hope you brought your appetite Will. I have a catered lunch for us in my office.

"Sounds good Bob, we have much to discuss."

Burkman pours a brandy for the General and himself.

"It looks like all is going well overseas. Wouldn't you say, General?"

"We shouldn't get ahead of ourselves Robert. These things have a way of turning around quickly if we make one wrong move."

"I should be the pessimist here. Learn to enjoy the small things General."

"I am enjoying the success but also need to be cautious. Don't forget all roads lead back here."

They sat and drank while making small talk and then Masters turns to Burkman and said, "I need to know if you're on board with the committee's recommendation for the domestic plan enacted last year Bob."

"Of course, I am."

"Great. Were you fully briefed by those knuckleheads at Sector 9 regarding the operation and requirements for a contingency?"

"Yes, General. We have ample supplies of what is needed in our facilities."

"Ok, what about delivering it to those freaking bugs. Will it take?"

"General, we were first to have developed the compound to be administered to the bugs. We have been in development for over a decade on this product. Those bugs will suck it up. They do so now in our labs."

"But can they release the shit and will it be airborne?"

"Stop worrying. Look what happened in Europe and Africa. It'll work. Besides, we have the added assurance of the vaccines to enhance the effect. Europe only had the toxin and look how well that turned out."

"I'm naturally a cautious person and you shouldn't take my hesitation as questioning you Bob- just our process. I've had mixed results with those freaking bugs. Sometimes they have a mind of their own."

"Will, we have known each other for more years than I can remember. Don't ever forget I'm the one who recruited you and I'm not in the business of lying to another brother of the Order. Nobody can guarantee success in science but I have every confidence that we are ready for the task."

"I know. I know. I'm not questioning your loyalty to the Order or myself but you do know we'll only get one shot at this."

"It's gonna work Will, relax."

"I'll relax once the Order can reign supreme."

"So, your only concern is the use of bugs to disperse the toxin?"

"No. The insects have always been our primary use of delivery. I just need to make sure they'll strike on command."

"William I need to ask, why the insistence on using these bugs to fulfill our mission. We have other methods at our disposal that would meet the objectives."

"Brother, you're right, we could achieve our goal without the insects but there is another effect that we're going for as well. You wouldn't get it because you're not a military man, but nothing terrifies the public more than the fear of the unknown. And with poisonous insects, you get both unknown and creatures that people hate anyway. Imagine, being afraid to go outside because of not only the virus but of something looking to sting and kill you. People will be asking us for protection – I mean the ones that are left. It's beautiful."

"You got issues William. Were you not loved as a child?"

"As much as you were Bobby."

"Besides, the goons in Washington think they're so smart. They won't know what's hitting them when the skies are filled with these Stingers. No bullet, missile or bomb will do anything. They'll soon know who the true masters of the earth are."

"Are there any signs that we're risking exposure to the Order?"

"We have a small window of opportunity, that's for sure my brother but in a few more months, it won't matter anymore. There will be too much chaos for anyone to make the connections."

The men finish their lunch, shake their left hands and hug each other.

"I'll see you on the other side," said the General.

They both raise their left hands and simultaneously said, "Long live the Order."

· · · · ·

In the Mohave Desert, two hours north of Los Angeles housed one of IS&G's largest research and development facilities. Hundreds of acres of barren land surrounded the long aluminum cases in the hot California sun. The tops of the aluminum buildings had fist-sized holes in them. The Stingers, smaller in size than their east coast counterparts were seen coming and going from the holes. These Stingers didn't seem to be as aggressive as the ones afflicting the east coast. No civilian enters the compound, ever: only lab rats and military muscle.

Inside, Dr. Kraft, chewing on his fingernails, paces up and down the aisle asking his subordinates if they could account for the entire species of Stingers.

"Dr. Kraft, the Stingers do not veer far from this facility. They travel a twenty-minute radius but always return," said his young lab assistant.

Dr. Kraft looked over a confidential memo from Mr. Burkman. It read to have the species ready as we were entering the final phase of the operation. Major supplies of P2040 were on route and should be given immediately to the bugs.

Outside Mobile, Alabama the south coast laboratory of IS&G industries, received a similar directive from their CEO.

Their northernmost facility in Oshkosh, Wisconsin, received the last directive.

All three sectors of the country were poised and ready to enact the next phase of the operation.

The go-ahead was given at 0600 hundred hours on July 4, 2042.

From all across America, millions of Stingers formed a wave of pestilence only imagined in books written for the end of humanity. They flew over population centers of every state in the continental USA. Halfway through their flight, they started to emit a purple mist that left a haze in the air.

The smog centers of Los Angeles, Houston, Baltimore and others, held the purple toxin up in the sky for hours until the density of the compound released it slowly onto the inhabitants.

Early morning news outlets claimed it was a mass migration of bees from South America searching for a new source of food and crops to pollinate with. The story lost all its validity when other creatures of the air, such as birds, moths, butterflies, etc., fell from the sky, after the mist was released.

Although the story was run constantly that morning, only the feeblest of idiots believed it. As in a futile effort to stop the spraying, there were reports of people shooting shotgun shells in the air to kill the Stingers. A few fell from the sky, however, many more pellets rained back down than the insects.

As the purple toxin fell to the ground, it landed and mixed with the water and quickly dissipated on the vegetation. All that was left was a faint purple stain on clothing if one did venture out to see the purple rain.

After the Stingers had unloaded their payload, they returned to camp making sure to sting anyone who ventured out. Unlike the less concentrated form released in the air that would take weeks to go into effect, if you were stung on the spot, your future would be measured in hours.

CHAPTER 26
TAKE THE LONG WAY HOME

An emergency curfew is raised across the country after the purple rains fell. No trains, planes or buses are leaving the city but Oliver meets up with Brittany, a girl he knows from his psychology class. She's taking summer classes to make up for too much partying during the spring semester. She's also very desperate to get home but is fearful of the travel. She's outside the campus when Oliver notices her.

"Where the hell have you been Ollie?"

"Hi Brit. Good to see you too. I was Downtown if you must know."

"I guess it's possible to be crazy and smart at the same time."

Oliver smiles at the backhanded praise dished out.

"Looks like you were in a war. It's not safe downtown. Is it?"

"It's not safe anywhere."

"I know. All classes are canceled. Can you believe it?"

"That's probably the least of our worries. Don't you think?"

"Ollie, you live only a few miles from my parents…Wanna ride home?"

Oliver is surprised by the advance but realizes it would only be offered in this the strangest of times.

"There's a curfew Brit. No one should be traveling."

"Don't you think I know that but I need to get out of here today. I can't stand it any longer."

"If we get stopped, we might end up in jail."

"Do you wanna go or not? You can drive my beamer."

Oliver contemplates his options for getting home without the car, which was slim at best. "Yeh, let's get out of here."

The turnpike is closed but interstate 309 is open. The temperature hovers around 95⁰ and Brittany's fancy car has lost its air conditioning.

Oliver is already worn out from the outing with Marcus downtown and only thinks of getting back home. A sweltering heat is a necessary tradeoff to get out of the hellhole.

"Do you think we'll be back in the fall, Ollie?"

"I doubt it."

"We've been watching all day how those things were spraying in the sky. Where do you think they came from?"

"I don't know."

"Wow, are you gonna be like this all the way home?"

Brittany looks at him, waiting for a response.

"Brit, you should keep your eyes on the road."

"Why, there's barely any cars out?"

The light blue canvas coloring the atmosphere turned darker as Oliver peeks his head out of the window.

"Shit, do you think it'll rain Ollie?"

"Why…don't your wipers work either?"

"Yes, smart ass. They work."

The sky is now dark as millions of Stingers blacken the sky.

"Quick. Roll your windows up Brittany."

"No way, we'll suffocate in this heat."

"Would you rather be stung by those flying hornets in the air above?"

"Oh my GOD. We should turn back."

"It's too late, keep going."

Purple diamonds glowing in the midsummer heat fall gracefully to the ground. Brittany's windshield begins to fill up with fresh powder from the toxin. She uses the wiper to get her vision straight but in the process inadvertently causes some of the flakes to reenter the window and cover her hair and arms. She finally rolls up her window gagging on some of the P2040 released as she rubs the flakes from her hair.

"Brittany that stuff is all over your hair and arms."

"I need to pull over."

"I think we should keep moving."

"Fuck you, Oliver. I can't breathe and the stuff is itching at my skin."

Brittany is swerving back and forth on the road while coughing up what appears to be particulates of blood. Oliver's head is banging on the window and the roof of the car at this point.

"Pull over Brit."

The car slides off the road and into a field. Oliver tries to peek out of the window to survey the sky for Stingers but also to get some relief from the entrapment of the beamer with no air conditioning.

Brittany's skin is extremely blotchy now as she begins to mumbling in circles.

"The sky and plants are coming tomorrow if not I'm going back home."

"Brittany, I think you should lie down. You don't make any sense. I'll get you some water in the back."

Brittany lays on the grass with newly laid purple P2040 toxin surrounding her. She starts to go into convulsions and foams from the mouth. Oliver has retrieved the bottle of water from the trunk but doesn't attempt to deliver it to Brittany. She continued to twitch and wriggle in pain until she drew her last breath.

The sky is clear and the countryside serene. Brittany lays out in the field as Oliver grabs the keys from her hands and jumps back into the car for one last push home.

CHAPTER 27
HOME

"Welcome home Oliver," said Donna as he walked into the house. She gave him a hug while Lisa and Lou got up to greet their brother.

"What's the deal bro. We hear Philly's in the toilet," said Lou.

"I don't think I'm returning in the fall. It's so bad. More than half the people I started with, went back home months ago. There's talk that all the universities are shutting down."

"Well, it might be for the better anyway, Ollie. We're barely getting by as it is," said Louis, as his mother gingerly slaps him in the arm.

"Why? Isn't dad home yet?"

"No, they don't even let us see or write to him. All for getting on a restricted website. It's not fair. They should be putting criminals in there not dad," said Lisa.

"Me and Lisa are working at one of the camps dad got sent to. It's supposed to be different than the one he's at though. We work at one that takes people who are resisting the vaccines and causing riots."

"Louis and Lisa have been a big help since your dad got taken away Oliver. I'm not sure what I would have done without them."

"Mom, this is going to sound strange but my roommate told me this whole thing was planned. He used to read and research a lot of what Allen wrote. He said it was more about causing the whole system to break down to control all of us."

"I don't wanna hear any more of that kind of talk from you or anyone. Understand?"

"But mom…"

"No. You sound like your dad now. I don't care what the reasons are behind this whole thing or if there is some kind of conspiracy to control or reduce the population. It doesn't really matter at this point, does it?"

"If you would just hear me out ---"

Donna gives him a look that he remembers all too well from his youth.

"Planned or not, it's all too real and we need to pray your dad gets out and then I think we should join uncle Steve up in the mountains."

"What do you mean join Uncle Steve in the mountains?"

"Oliver, you've seen the worst in the city and this shouldn't come as a surprise to you. Now there's a virus going 'round. It's not safe here from either people or from those things flying around, is it?"

"No, I suppose not but that's what I'm trying to tell you."

All eyes turn to Oliver.

"I saw the bugs and purple fields driving up here from the city. I think something more than the government is spraying and controlling them."

"Nobody's sure dude. At first, we saw them too. They said they were spraying for the bugs but it looked like the bugs were the ones spraying. Those freaking things then started to sting people and then all of a sudden, they left. It's so strange," said Lou.

"I wonder where they came from?" asked Lisa.

"Hell," replied their mother.

Unlike other countries, the P2040 that was released into the population was much more specialized. The earlier vaccines that were supposed to protect the population, specifically the Bottom Dwellers did not do a thing. In fact, early cases of the sickness were prevalent in almost everyone who had a vaccine shot except for the Untouchables who were given a different strain of the vaccine. They were not affected. In addition, the so-called Bottom Dwellers that refused the vaccines shots also showed no signs of the virus.

Most people were living off the residuals of stored up food they had from the winter. Remarkably, the water still flowed, as did the garbage, TV, internet and mail, but nobody was shopping, going out or dining. Even if you did possess tradable or precious metals to buy with, the stores were wiped out of goods to buy them with. It was as if a giant magnifying glass was put over the population daring people to go out into the open where they could get burned. In this case, getting burned was a Stinger, a virus or a roaming mob searching for food or another victim with or without a gun.

The barter system truly took hold in full force now. If you had bullets, you could trade for practically anything. However, what most people wanted were the basics: canned foods, milk, rice, bread, toilet paper and medical supplies. Paper money outlawed a long time ago is now being used as kindling to burn in bonfires to dissuade any of the Stingers from attacking houses.

The President issued a statement to remain inside until the insects had run their course. There were no presidential televised broadcasts as had been made so many times in the past two years- even he knew by this stage that there was no controlling events any further. He called his cabinet for an emergency briefing.

Two hundred feet below the capital resides an elaborate bunker, more of an underground fortress really, for the transitional government in times of an emergency or nuclear attack.

The cabinet members sit around a well-lit room drinking coffee staring at a daily briefing with their phones on vibrate next to their laptops. Real-time drone footage of the Stingers spraying their purple death over the country has them all in despair.

The President is the first to speak, "Who or what authorized these demons onto the public? Is it the Chinese?"

"Mr. President. There are reports that they are organic," said Blake Jennings, the President's Chief of Staff.

"What the hell does that mean?"

"I'll defer to Henry for that one Mr. President."

"Sir, the origin per the footage is from facilities within the United States," said General Henry Richardson, Chairman of the Military Joint Chiefs of Staff.

"Are you telling me that these things are being raised here in America under our noses. That can't be."

"Sir the footage is undeniable. It's not a foreign source."

"Have they been infecting people all along and who the hell gave the green light for this?"

"Sir, by all indications the Stingers were initially thought to have been a genetic outgrowth of some kind due to the pesticides. It is now our belief that they are used as a weapon of some sort," said Richardson.

"A weapon of some sort? What kind of shit have you guys been up to out there? Don't tell me this is one of our operations gone bad because I'll start chopping heads right now."

The cabinet members are reticent in their resolve and sit motionlessly.

"You're pretty quiet over there Mike. How come the C.I.A. is unaware of this shit. Don't tell me this was a black op planned under the previous administration. I suppose another lovely piece of bullshit that got thrown in my lap."

"No sir. We have been knowledgeable on the operational stages of using insects as weapons for quite some time. We worked in conjunction with the armed forces for covert missions and the development has always been in the states."

"Then why am I hearing about this now?"

"Sir, we did brief you on operation Leafcutter and similar projects under development and active in the field, nearly three years ago. And as I recall, you were quite impressed with the results. The staging ground was housed in several locations, most notably in Sector 9. General Masters, I believe, is still running the show over there," said C.I.A. Director, Michael Beiman.

"Don't try and get me to assume responsibility for some crazy bullshit you guys came up with and now is out of control. It's one thing to do a hit on a foreign dirtbag but quite another to let loose on our own front lawn. I recall a two- minute overview and shook my head to continue development for overseas not here in our own backyard!"

"But sir..."

"Don't interrupt. It sounds like you have a rogue member of the echelon doing his or own thing and now it's coming back to bite us all in the ass or worse take the country down. I'm the President damn it. I should be in the loop. I want the individual or group responsible for this shit to be strung up by their balls and you geniuses need to come up with an answer to these flying things all around the country!"

"Sir, I have never been insubordinate but please understand there are forces that have a hand in this that we don't control. Even as President, you might not even be able to stop or have a say in it. I mean no disrespect," said Beiman.

"Mike, I like you but don't confuse like for being soft. If I find out others knew and allowed this in my administration, they're finished. I might be out of the loop but don't tell me I have no say. I still have the allegiance of the armed forces. Whatever kind of hidden hand started this thing will find out just how hard we could hit back. Get Masters on the line or better yet bring that son of a bitch down here to answer to me directly."

CHAPTER 28
CORE

"Clay, get General James Hackman down here asap," said the President, as he turned to Clay Braun, his National Security Advisor.

The war room in the President's bunker is filled with a few military men and women but mostly politicians. By the time Hackman arrives, they are all asked to depart leaving Braun, the President, Hackman and his right-hand man, Colonel Dylan Cummings.

All eyes turn to the President. "General, how long have we known each other?"

"Sir, I guess close to fifty years now."

"I have full confidence in Clay and yourself. Is your Colonel to be trusted?"

"Sir, I would give my life for Colonel Cummings and I'm sure he would for me as well. He's a true patriot."

"When I took this job, I was briefed on many things. Some made my sick and a few gave me comfort. I understand you took an oath to not only the country but to the Core as well?"

"Sir, we all took an oath to the Marine Corps way back when," said Hackman.

"I'm not talking about the military but the unit that's been around since the founding days, before the first President took office. The one that vows to protect this office if an internal threat is presented." Hackman and Cummings looked stunned but say nothing.

"Yeh, that's right Jim, the agency does a good job believe it or not. We know about the Core. And who gets into your organization. You recruit at the academies swearing allegiance to each other. You provide financial assistance to each other and if one of you gets into trouble, you bail them out, by any means."

"Sir, it's more of a fraternity than a cult, if that's what you're driving at."

"Look, I don't care what kind of secret handshakes, private parties or even blood rituals your group does, but I'm told you take care of the President's problems and make them go away. Is that correct?"

"Sir, our pact is to aid in whatever the President deems as necessary to defend this office. We have never left a President dangle in the wind. What can we do for you?"

"I read the files. You do a good job. You understand quite well what has been happening on the surface to the country with this virus, crops and bugs?"

The two men look at each other and then nod their heads.

"Well, we believe this started from a foreign source and it's not that easy to just target someone or some country for annihilation. The problem is that we have traitors working for this government whose allegiance is to another organization."

"What type of organization would unleash this type of madness?"

"If you think your group is secretive, it's nothing compared to these maniacs. They take the cake- under our noses all along."

"Why go through all this effort? What's their objective?"

"General, it looks like their goal is to bring the whole damn system to its knees. They're purists, internationalists and deranged lunatics. We don't have the complete list but can give you one name. You should interrogate him first to find out who else is in the operation before taking care of our problem. His name is General Masters over at Central Command in the western district."

"I know Masters. He's a hardcore son of a bitch. He runs the special weapons division out of different sectors throughout the country. I could definitely see him going nuclear but a traitor is hard to believe," said the Colonel.

"Be that as it may, he ran all those divisions where those fucking things came out of. I know he's been doing this thing in other countries for a while. Someone got to him to use those things here and who knows what else was planned- probably this crop thing as well. Anyway, you have a private line to Mr. Braun. He can provide any intelligence you need, use whatever methods and resources for this. Make it happen and be discrete. I would like to know who else is involved in this but if that's not possible, take care of business."

The two men left, leaving the President and his National Security Advisor in the war room.

"You know this will mean a low-level civil war Mr. President. Masters has plenty of resources," said Braun.

"I think I have a bit more tools at the ready than some General."

"Sir, my advice is to wait for all the facts to come in before acting in a hasty manner."

"Are you kidding me? I'm not going to be the President who let the country go down the toilet without a fight."

The two men go back to their rooms.

Braun sends a text message to someone.

•   •   •   •   •

Near Indian Springs, Nevada, sits the Creech joint military base. It was built during the Cold War era, fully equipped with stealth bombers, conventional and nuclear-tipped cargo. The facility holds one thousand troops, aviators and support staff. There is no dispute who is running the show. Masters is seen at a distance with a telescopic lens relaxed in his easy chair smoking his cigar. Members of the Core survey his movements from outside the gates.

"It's suicide going in," said Sgt. Dixon, one of the younger Core members.

"He has to leave sometime," replied Major McMannamon.

A dozen men wait hours and then a black car holding Masters leaves the gate.

The entire operation is recorded in real time for the President in the War Room.

Two cars holding the Core members followed them for miles outside the compound until they are on a remote desert road in the cold Nevada night. The car holding Masters realizes that something is up and starts to race away. The dust covers the windshield of the cars following them.

McMannamon gives the order for one of the cars to catch up to Masters. He stays in the second car that follows behind the General. He then gives the order to take out the General's car with the Core members veering their heads out, shooting high-powered rounds at Masters. Nobody shoots back and the car slides off the side of the road.

All three cars are now off the road sitting in the pitch-black desert. There's no movement only the howling of a coyote off in the distance punctures the air. Then, three men jump out of Master's car shooting with automatic rifles at both cars that drove them off the road. The members of the Core quickly drop them without any one of them being hit.

McMannamon cautiously creeps up to the car.

"We need to talk to the General. Come out and no one else gets killed."

There's was no reply. Masters sits in the back seat with a smile on his face. "Poor dumb bastards following orders from their empirical attack dog."

The other Core members join McMannamon alongside the car.

A faint humming is in the air. It gets closer and louder.

The car Masters is in goes up in smoke just as the members of the Core are at the door. A drone targeted the car killing everyone within twenty feet of the car.

"What the hell happened!" screamed the President.

"The order wasn't given to blow up the car. I need to talk to Masters."

Secretary Braun, who left the War Room mysteriously for a while, came back into the War Room. "Sir, Masters and the team we sent were hit by a drone."

"How the hell could that happen? He doesn't have those kinds of resources. We're the only ones who knew they were being sent. Damn it. Now what the hell are we gonna do?"

"Sir, we really should consider evacuating the country and go north."

"What the fuck are you talking about. Move the country north. Don't you think a virus or bugs can travel north? That's the dumbest thing I've ever heard. Go back to your office and come up with another plan. I'll deal with you in short order."

The President called in his chief bodyguard and quietly whispered in his ear. "Braun's a traitor to our country, I don't want him taking another breath. Take care of it immediately."

The President was spared a murder on his watch. Braun, remarkably, did the honorable thing. As the guards opened the door to Braun's office they saw him sitting on his sofa with blood dripping from both arms. He used some of the blood to write "The Order" on the wall next to him.

CHAPTER 29
SUBURBIA

Civil servants were now being paid in rations and their frozen meal bags weren't cutting it for the masses. The treasury was depleted and the CDF administration was forced to reduce the workforce by 75%. Lisa and Lou were shown their walking papers on a Friday after lunch. They were "given" the rest of the afternoon off for a good job to the CDF. Lou was able to bribe a guard at the camp before being let go. He traded hundreds of pills that were confiscated from one of the "inmates" for a Beretta 9 mm pistol and sixty rounds of ammo to the head chef in the kitchen.

There was no school in the fall. Most industry and businesses operated with a skeleton crew. The only stable sectors of the economy were security, energy and shipping. The might of the military still allowed America to coerce a few nations to import perishable goods into the country.

"Shouldn't we wait until it gets warmer to head up north?" asked Lisa, looking to her mother for assurance.

"There's no point in waiting any longer. Both you and your brother aren't working anymore and Oliver is out of the city. Besides, I don't know if your father will ever get out. We need to go up to the cabin where uncle Steve and his family are. I think we have a better chance up there."

"Let's give it until after the holiday, please mom. Maybe dad will be back by then," pleaded Lisa.

Always a softy for their oldest child, Donna gives in immediately.

"Ok, but after the New Year we need to go."

Candlelight lit the living room as the family huddles around the table. They have peanut butter and marshmallow sandwiches for dinner chased down with tap water. Lou tells a joke about a time when he was a freshman and he and a friend of his plastered a wall of their science class with a peanut butter sandwich.

"You should have seen Mr. Smith when he finally noticed the sandwich," chuckled Lou. Donna gave a faint smile as well.

"We were taking bets on how long it would take him to notice. I won, twenty minutes if you can believe it. It wasn't until he went over to the wall with metamorphic rock symbols or some kind of crap like that did he finally notice it. And when he did, he stood there turning his head analyzing it and then said, 'I bet this would stay for a week without falling.' It was priceless, the whole class cracked up."

The family laughed at the story- even Donna. It had been a while since the family sat and laughed together. A rarity indeed.

There were no decorative lights or manger scenes outside their windows for this holiday season.

Is it just too expensive to put out anymore? Donna thought to herself, *or would it reveal that a family had extra spending money or other things to trade with.*

Donna recalled earlier footage on TV where roaming gangs would terrorize less fortunate parts of the cities and suburbs. She never thought that those issues would reach her doorsteps, until it did.

The neighbor's dog, who rarely barked unless provoked, was the first sound to be heard. After a few seconds of intense barking only a whimper in his voice was noticed. Then another dog barking. Finally, a shot and another two shots. A loud thud follows. Next, a series of firecracker sounds that needed to come from an assault rifle. However, the critically important question was if it was an assault rifle from a friendly, a CDF rogue member or worse? The sound echoed and bounced across the cookie cutter houses like an old-time pinball machine.

The sound came from the worst. The family wanted not to look but their curiosity got the best of them. Three houses down, two men in the front and two in the backyard, taunting Mrs. Baker and her two daughters to come out. Mrs. Baker screamed bloody murder as Mr. Baker shot his last gun moments ago. His last day in suburbia came when one of the four men unloaded three rounds of their AR-15 into him.

Mr. Baker was a friend of Raymond's when the world was predictable, sometimes even making it to his front lawn to talk about an election or another current event. Mrs. Baker in an attempt at vengeance but futility, fired five shots wildly, with her 357-magnum revolver and then there was silence.

The cul-de-sac didn't have to wait in suspense for too much longer for the next scene. Relentless screams were heard for nearly an hour. Each one cutting through the psyche of the families listening in the neighborhood, ripping apart Lisa who held her hands over her ears.

Lou thought for a moment to go down with his 9mm but quickly came to his senses. He liked the girls and saw them every day when he went to school but if he went down there now and got killed, there would be nobody to protect his family.

"Couldn't they just do their business and let those poor girls be? Animals take what they want and leave, why humiliate like this?" asked Donna.

"Because they can mom, that's why," said Lou.

Donna, unbelievably prayed to God to end it quickly so the tormented sounds would stop. Louis knew enough to picture the inside of their living room, which probably looked like theirs: featuring the girls to go first while Mrs. Baker was forced to watch. And he was right, Mrs. Baker, pillar of the country club and Parent Teacher Organization president, howled the last scream of the household.

"Can we leave right now mom? Please---," begged Lisa.

"They'll see us take off and chase us down. Let's just sit quietly until they go."

When the screams and anguished moans had stopped, all four men came stumbling out of the house. The site of the Cadillac in the driveway seemed to enrage them a bit more as they all felt the need to urinate on it. One had a bottle of cognac in his hand, which in short order found its way through the windshield of the tormented family's status symbol.

They then went to the next house and hit the door with their guns shouting for the residents to let them in for "teatime" but nobody replied. Perhaps too drunk and exhausted from their mayhem, they left the house after a few minutes and hobbled their way across the street, knocking on Donna's door.

Lisa's heart almost came out of her chest. She started to sweat and her mother needed to cover her mouth not to make any sounds. The family huddled together but would not go to the door. Some more knocking and a few more taunts continued from the unwelcome visitors. Lou pulled out his 9 mm.

"What if they break the door down and come in?" Oliver whispered.

"Shhhh, don't make a sound." Donna grabbed Lisa closer to her chest.

"If I shoot at the door, maybe they'll leave."

"Lou, if you shoot, you'll invite them to stay longer and shoot back. Just sit there quietly, please."

The men went around back and kicked the door with their rifle butt. Lou cocked his gun while Oliver shook his head, imploring him not to act.

The men didn't bust the door in. One of them whistled to the others and they were gone. A black truck pulled up and the four of them jumped in.

Lisa began to cry and nervously laugh, sweating profusely now.

The family slept in one room. Lou had his 9mm Beretta at the ready. Only the sounds of a few dogs barking were heard from that moment on.

On and off, Dona's eyes struggled to stay open. She also had her knife by her side. She convinced herself that if they could make it to sunrise, they would be fine. Next to that awful night of interrogations at Homeland and thoughts of Allen's last moments, it was the hardest night she ever had.

The sun rose and the family shook themselves from their last night in suburbia.

Dogs again started to bark but it was the familiar ones that woke neighbors up in the morning. "Go to the bathroom, enjoy the shower and grab anything that's valuable to you. I'll get the essentials," said Donna, hastily.

The trailer had already been hitched to the Jeep. It was now a matter of loading it up with whatever possessions deemed essential to accompany them on this new kind of family adventure.

"We'll leave a note here in case dad comes out and sees it," said Lisa.

Oliver grabs a handful of books packed into a cardboard box.

"Leave that shit bro," said Lou, "Books aren't important anymore, school's over. Haven't you heard? Only the strong survive now."

"I understand about the strong surviving Lou. Haven't you heard: It's not the strongest of us or the smartest that survives, but the ones most apt to change."

"Wow, that's deep Ollie. If our lives and the world ever get back to the way it was, you can make money off that saying," said Lisa.

"I can't. It's already taken. I was quoting Charles Darwin."

Most of their neighbors peered out at them eerily while they loaded up their few precious belongings. No one came out to say anything to them. A tear ran down Donna's cheek as she thought about the past twenty-five years living in this suburban wilderness. She got what she wanted all right, all those years ago, finally detached from the tightly packed neighbors in the city who knew her every action.

They're no different out here too, she thought to herself, *they just go about their day and gossip in another way*.

CHAPTER 30
MOVING ON

"I wanna go by my sisters and say goodbye to her and Edward before getting on the turnpike," said Donna.

"I don't think that's a good idea mom. Stingers are all still around and who knows what effect that purple stuff has caused. It could be a toxin or pesticide or worse," said Oliver.

"Excuse me young man, but college life doesn't give you the right to tell me what to do. I might never see your aunt again. It's on the way and we're going."

The family made their way through the upscale neighborhood of Laura's. A guard stood at the gated entry. He stopped the vehicle and nonchalantly questioned where they were going. Donna showed him her government issued ID and he waved them through.

They saw familiar cars in the driveway and left their car running as they got out slowly and walked cautiously to the front porch. Edward answered the doorbell.

"Hi Eddie. Is your mother home?" asked Donna.

"She's in bed Aunt Donna."

"In bed at this hour? She's usually up at 5:00. Is the hospital closed or is she off?"

"She's been out of work for some time now."

"Did she get laid off?"

Edward's face was grim. He shook his head and then gestured for them to follow him as they made their way back to Laura's room.

The smell of bleach couldn't mask the smell of misery and disease hiding in the bedroom.

The moans and gasps came from behind a door that was halfway open. Laura lay in bed looking like she was ninety years old, pale, coughing and with her hair falling out.

"My God, Laura, what happened?" asked Donna.

Laura managed a faint smile and said, "By the looks on your faces, I guess I don't look that hot anymore."

"You're always beautiful, sis, but why didn't you tell me you were ill. We should get you to the hospital."

Laura coughs up some blood into a handkerchief next to her bed. "That won't be necessary. There's no point."

"Did you catch the virus from a patient at the hospital?"

"I don't think so. I was out doing some cleaning up in the backyard when those flying things came by. The purple flakes landed on me."

She takes another deep breath and a drink of water. The last sentence cost Laura a precious amount of energy. Edwards comes over and holds her hand.

"I thought it was a pesticide for the crops at first. It seemed harmless enough, only making a stain. I thought it was to protect us."

Edward wiped away tears from his eyes.

"Maybe we should go with Aunt Donna to the hospital mom."

Laura dismisses the suggestion and manages another grin, "I learned something through this experience Donna."

Laura stopped to gather enough energy for another sentence.

"I now know that we're the pests they've been spraying for."

Edward wipes his mother's forehead with a clean washcloth as more tears cannot help but run down his face.

"Laura, we're going up north to get away from all of this. I want you and Eddie to come with us."

"Donna, look at me. I won't make it through the day. I have no right to ask but will you look after Edward and give him a chance?"

"Of course I will Laura. It's the least we can do."

"Mom, I'm not going anywhere."

"Do me one last favor sweetheart. Listen to your aunt and leave here today before you get sick. Please go. And take some of dad's guns and whatever else you'll need for the road. Be careful. I love you."

"No mom. I'm not leaving you."

"If you truly love me, you won't make me say it again. Please go."

Jim's closet had rifles, ammunition and revolvers. Edward thinks they would be better off if they take similar guns to conserve ammunition.

Three .38 revolvers on the top shelf beg to be taken. Donna, Oliver and Edward each took one. Edward also picked out his favorite long gun in the collection used many times when he and his dad went hunting: A Remington .30/06 bolt action. They kissed their aunt goodbye and packed the guns and supplies into the back of the jeep.

And so, it goes. The virus that spread through Africa, Europe and South America had arrived in America with a vengeance from the friendly skies, compliments of IS&G.

CHAPTER 31
GABRIEL

A transformation is happening within the cities. People are moving from block to block without much harassment from the guards. As long as the population stayed within their sectors, the CDF would not interfere.

Marcus made his way to Gabriel's hangout on Henry Avenue. After going through a series of checks to get in, Marcus is greeted by Gabriel.

"My brother, always good to see you, young buck."

"Thanks man. Good to see you too. What's up?"

"Well, the hits keep getting better my friend. The shit that those flying bees sprayed is making people sick. I mean real sick. It's in the air now."

"I thought people were vaccinated against those things."

"It's not the bites, the purple shit they dumped is making everyone drop. They get dehydrated, bad stomach pains and then die. Well, at least most of them do. It's all over the place, even on the hill."

"What do you mean even on the hill?"

"Man, the rich folk aren't getting sick from what I see or hear. I mean I ain't having a beer with any of them, but seems to me that the only ones not getting sick are the ones who had the first vaccines, remember the ones that cost so much."

"What about people who didn't get the shots, are they gonna be ok?"

"People are dropping everywhere man but if you got a vaccination from the CDF way back when, your time is up a whole lot quicker."

"Did you get a shot?"

"Hell no. I didn't put that poison in me. I knew it was no good. Probably mixing in some way with the shit those bugs sprayed and making people drop like flies. Part of the plan, I suppose. I'm not saying I'm immune but I gotta better chance without the shot and so do you."

Marcus nods his head in agreement and shakes Gabriel's hand a second time.

"Listen my man, I got an important job for you."

"Anything Gabriel. You know I'll do whatever for the cause."

"I know you will my man. There's this radio station on City Avenue. It was guarded until last week. CDF abandoned it but it still has juice and is being run by these two psychos."

Marcus smiles a bit. "What do you mean by that?"

"They were DJ's on the night shift. I think they got sick but in the wrong way sick. You know…in the head."

Marcus nods his head. "I've heard that. The poison is having different effects on people."

"Yeh man. Some are dying and some are going apeshit. Here's the thing: these two fools are broadcasting night and day telling people to keep their lights on. And if they got red bulbs, to put them in place of the white ones."

"Red bulbs?"

"Yeh man. Red bulbs. I think red light is attracting those Stingers and these two fools are telling people to put them in their houses."

"Why would they want to attract more of those things?"

"Didn't I say these idiots were sick in the head. They say the stuff they're spraying is making them stronger and we should all get the 'purple into our lives.' They been playing Purple Haze by Hendrix over and over. All day long."

"You want me to pay em a visit?"

"Look man. It's dangerous. No shitting yah. I lost two men three days ago trying to get them to stop broadcasting. Some people are listening. I saw two houses on the hill all lit up in red. People are desperate for answers and they don't know who to believe. If enough listen and put red lights up, we'll be overrun with those flying demons in no time."

"So, you want me to stop them from broadcasting…by any means, right?"

"I wanna give it one more try. You're my best shot. Take Tyler and James with you. They're damn good too. Put an end to em. Can you do that my brother?"

"You got it. Gabriel."

The urban trio made their way down to the station using one of Gabriel's jeeps taken from the armory. They met no resistance on the way to the station and stopped one hundred yards short of the entrance.

The station sits on a hill in a glass enclosure. It's daytime but the faint red light is all around the building. And resting on top of the building are thousands of Stingers.

"Damn man. We don't stand a chance with those things all around. Let's get out of here," said Tyler.

"Yeh dude," said James, "We could tell Gabriel we gave it a shot and those things attacked us. That's all."

"Haven't we been lied to enough all these years? I'm not about telling another one to Gabriel," said Marcus.

The trio sits in the jeep calculating their next move to get inside the station but realize it's a suicide mission with the Stingers above their heads.

"I got an idea," said Marcus, "We don't need to go in. If we can break the windows. I betcha those things will go in and attack them inside."

"It's a good plan," said Tyler, "except what if those things come after us instead of going in?"

"We gotta try and see if this'll work. Gabriel wouldn't send us if he didn't think it was the right thing to do. I trust him with my life."

The three of them take aim at the building and fire a series of rounds at it. At first, only a hole or two is noticed but after they unload their magazines, the front façade cracks and falls apart. The nighttime duo of "Mike and Ike" came running over to witness the damage. They peek their heads through the opening and are introduced to their purple people eaters, who they so anxiously yearned for. The Stingers, were not bothered by the shots fired from the urban trio, but instead filled the station with their black mass.

No signal came from the station from that moment any longer, although the red lights still flickered at WKPA.

CHAPTER 32
PLAGUE

As Donna and the kids make their way through the last turn before jumping on the highway, they noticed a girl, half-naked, sitting next to a dog under an apple tree.

"What the…," said Lou.

"We should stop and see if that little girl needs help," said Donna.

The kids aren't so sure that stopping is wise. Donna looks at their sullen faces stating without words that they have their own problems, and should move on but Donna cannot continue.

"I can't leave a girl who is hurt. Where's your humanity kids?" She slowly pulls alongside the curb and rolls the window down.

"Honey, are you ok?"

No response is made but upon closer inspection the family can all see that the girl has been physically and most likely sexually abused. Black and purple bruises are on her shoulder and neck. Her hair is cut in a lopsided manner and she is barefoot. Drops of fresh blood adorn her ripped blouse. She says not a word but pets the dog and does not look up.

Donna makes her way out of the car, trying her best not to make a sound to startle the little girl.

"Who did this to you dear?"

There's no reply from the girl and Donna repeats her question.

The girl then slowly mutters, "Ralphy tried to stop it but he beat him too."

"Can we take you home sweetie? I won't hurt you."

The little girl tenses at the suggestion of going home.

Donna asks again and this time the little girls mumbles, "It's not safe there."

Without another word, Donna realizes this was done to her by someone close.

"Daddy ate too many apples last night."

"Did your dad hurt you little girl?"

The girl shrugged her bruised shoulders and continued to pet the dog.

"What's your name?"

"Angela."

"That's such a pretty name. My name is Donna. I have a daughter too. Her name's Lisa."

Lisa waves at Angela from the car.

"Is there somewhere else I can take you, Angela?"

"Daddy ate too many apples."

Donna looks up at the apples above her head. She picks one.

"No!" Angela yelled out, "They're no good."

Donna holds one of the apples in her hands and notices purple flakes slightly discoloring the exterior.

A scrawny middle-aged man comes running feverishly out of the house.

"You want some apples too?" asked the man.

Angela doesn't look up. As if she could bring Ralphy back to life, she continued to slowly pet him.

"Sir, what have you done to your daughter?"

He laughs. "Nothing, she's fine. She just needs more apples. Can't you see?"

"You're crazy. I'm going to the police to report this at once."

"Her mother only had two apples. She didn't have enough. You have to have the right balance. I know… It's all I eat now. Once Angela understands, she'll be fine."

"You're out of your mind dude," said Ed.

"Get off my property before I kill y'all."

The man reaches for his daughter and pulls her by the arm. Angela starts to cry and pulls away. "I don't wanna go daddy. Stop it."

"Get your hands off her! Haven't you done enough to this poor girl," said Donna.

"She just needs more apples, damn it."

As the man drags his daughter back to the house, a large Doberman comes out from behind the house and lunges at him.

Angela breaks free and runs towards the car whereupon Lisa opens the door for her.

"Drive mom!" screamed Lisa.

Other animals come out from their respective backyards, some are frosting at the mouth while others run aimlessly around in circles.

Angela's dad makes a feeble effort to ward off the Doberman but to no avail. He lies on the ground covering his head as the dog rips into his neck.

"What the hell's going on mom?" said Lou.

"I don't know but I don't think we should stick around to find out."

"Maybe it's the stuff that was being sprayed by the bugs. And whatever it falls on, will make people sick," said Oliver.

Oh God, it's probably making the fruits and vegetables toxic too- nothing's safe, Donna thought to herself.

"Kids, give Angela something to eat and try not to think about what happened.

"How long will it take till we get up there mom?" asked Lisa.

"It could be a couple of hours. I don't really know. Try to relax."

Donna makes a U-turn to get back on the main road. Before she can put the jeep into drive, a woman plunges herself onto the rear of the car.

"Mommy!" screamed Angela.

Donna, realizing the woman must be Angela's mother, puts the car in park.

"Give me back my daughter!"

"I'm sorry mam. We saw your daughter and thought she needed help. We mean you no harm."

Angela races out of the back to hug her mom.

"I don't think it's safe for the both of you to be here. We could take you and your daughter to somewhere safer if you want," said Donna.

"There's no place that's safe anymore. After that purple stuff fell from the sky, everything has been a nightmare. It was supposed to kill the bugs but it was the bugs that did this. It's killing the plants and everything else."

"What do you mean?"

"We have well water. Use it for everything. It's in the ground, in the plants, all around."

"What happened to your husband?"

"It's not just James. Others are infected and not just getting sick. They're going mad. He had me locked up in the basement-eating bugs. When I refused to eat the apples because they tasted like bleach, he went crazy. I tried to protect Angela but he was too strong."

"Please come with us. You and Angela have suffered enough. Your daughter should at least see a doctor. We could take you to the hospital or wherever else you need to go."

The woman bites her fingernails with one hand and in the other holds Angela's.

"Aunt Donna, they're coming this way!"

The hounds must have had their fill of Angela's father for they now turned their attention on the rest of the family and started to charge at Angela and her mother."

"Please, get in. Think of your daughter…There's no time."

In a last-second bout of sanity, the woman grabs Angela and jumps into the back seat of Donna's car. Several dogs leap onto the rear of the car gnarling and banging their heads on the glass.

Donna drives faster than she ever has as the hounds slither off.

"Thank you for saving us."

"It's the least we could do. And I'm sorry about your husband."

The woman doesn't reply back but gives Donna a look that implies he was a savage and got what he deserved, but Angela has seen and heard enough for the day and she lets it be.

"I'm Sandra Ladue. This is Angela."

Angela tugs on her mother's blouse. "How come you didn't say it mommy?"

"It's not the right time dear."

Angela pouts a bit more. "But you always say it to a new person we meet."

Donna looks back at Mrs. Ladue questioning why she doesn't entertain whatever game her daughter clearly wants her to play.

"Ok, Ok Angela. I'm Sandra Ladue. How do you do?"

Angela chuckles at the rhyme while her mother tries to cover her bloodied blouse with her own skirt.

"I know a place where we can go. I'd like to go there before heading to the hospital. It's only a few miles up the interstate."

"Is it a clinic?"

"No. It's a house."

"Sure, we'd be happy to take you and Angela but we can't stay long."

"I understand."

"What's the address?"

"It's my mother's place. Only about two miles from exit 29."

"Sure, that's not a problem."

"James sold our car last week. He said we had everything we needed in our own backyard, with those damn rotten apples."

Mrs. Ladue sheds a tear gazing out the side window.

"Are we going to Grammy Darlene's?"

"Yeh baby."

After a few miles traversing the back roads, the family makes it to the interstate.

"If you take the next exit and then a right onto River Road, that'll get us there. It's then two miles on your right: 2100 River Rd. It's got a huge American flag out front. You can't miss it."

"Ok."

"Mom remarried a few years back. Daniel's a retired officer from the army. They have a small farm; although we haven't been there in six months, so I don't know what's become of it. James and Daniel never got along that well."

Donna veers off the interstate onto exit 29 and then pulls right onto River Road.

After a few minutes, she sees the American flag out front of a Victorian style house. The home rests on top of a hill with acres separating it from the other houses along the road.

As Donna pulls into the quarter-mile dirt driveway, the family stairs off at the fields to their right. In their heyday, rows of corn lined both sides of the house up and down the hill. There was no corn on the fields or any other crops on this day. A large film of what appeared to be red paste smothered the fields.

The car slowly pulls to the rear of the house.

"Why are the fields red mommy?"

"I don't know dear. We'll ask Grammy when we see her."

"Something's not right mom," said Lisa.

"Just relax. Let's just wait and see if they have people here and then we'll be on our way."

An old woman is sitting on a porch, busy knitting.

"Look, there's grandma."

A loud grinding is heard from the barn a few hundred feet down the driveway.

Angela is the first one out of the car, running to the woman on the porch. She hugs her grandma as the others come walking up to the porch.

"Hi mom."

"Well, hello stranger. It's good to see you and my grandchild. I thought I wouldn't see you before I die."

"Mother –"

"Are you dying grandma?"

"Not today sweetheart."

Mrs. Ladue has her arms folded but doesn't embrace her mother.

"Well, what happened to you? Don't tell me James?"

The old woman on the porch gives Mrs. Ladue the death stare.

"He got sick mother and couldn't help it."

"Is that always been his excuse?"

"We don't have to worry about it anymore. He's gone."

The woman rocks back and forth with Angela in her arms.

"Hi mam. My name's Donna and these are my children and nephew."

The woman continues rocking, "Pleased to meet you."

The grinding is getting louder.

"What's that noise mother?"

"It's Daniel in the barn. He's prepping the fields."

"What kind of fertilizer is he using? The fields are all red."

"Oh, we're not planting anymore. We're making an offering."

"What do you mean an offering?"

The grinding continues for a few seconds and then stops.

An old man with a haircut that belongs on a teenager comes strolling out of the barn. He walks with a limp, is drooped in overalls covered with blood and has a fat grin on his face.

He notices the guests at his farm and waves at everyone.

"Why's Daniel all covered in blood. Is he butchering the animals?"

"We need to make an offering dear, so the bugs don't attack us."

"What?"

"We haven't had an attack in weeks because of the offerings. Before, they would come every night. Daniel sprays to keep the fields ready for them to feast. That keeps them from coming to the house and the neighbor's too. It's not that hard to understand is it?"

"Where's all the animals grandma?"

"They're gone dear. We had to make room for the offering you see. It's better now. They were sick anyway."

Donna looks at her kids who are all rolling their eyes and moving their heads in the direction of the car.

Sandra has gone from one household led by a lunatic to another. Her stepfather has butchered all his animals to be churned into some sort of a medieval blood offering for their aerial masters.

"When Daniel gets cleaned up, we'll go inside and have some cookies and tea. How's that sound dear?"

"Yummy, grandma."

"Thank you mam but we need to be on our way."

"No please stay," said Sandra.

"I'm sorry, we have to get going."

Donna wanted no part in meeting Daniel and told Sandra she would take her to the hospital to treat her daughter but needed to go.

"We just got here. Can't you stay for a few minutes?"

"We'll wait in the car ten minutes and then we're gone."

Before Daniel had a chance to see his stepdaughter, a ferocious sound came rumbling across the hill.

Donna noticed at once that it was a slew of Stingers headed straight for the house, only this time they spotted Daniel and his blood-drenched overalls as an appetizer.

"Quick kids. Get in the car!"

The old woman gets off the porch and heads down to warn Daniel.

Donna cracked the window and yelled, "Sandy come with us!"

Sandra nudges her daughter to get in the jeep but lingers on the porch to see if her mom would turn back in time. She doesn't and has to watch as thousands of Stingers ravage mom and Daniel.

Sandra screams and turns to the car, sprinting as fast as she can down the porch. She trips on the last set of stairs but valiantly tries to pick herself up in time to reach the jeep. Half of the Stingers notice the injured victim and head towards her before she can get to the door. She's too late. Sandra is saturated with the little flying devils as the family is paralyzed, watching the freak show from the safety of their 4x4.

Donna gasps but doesn't want Angela to see her mother. She covers her eyes and pulls out as quickly as she can. The others turn their heads in disgust. The Stingers are pre-occupied with Mrs. Ladue to make chase.

Off again onto the interstate with Angela crying for mommy.

CHAPTER 33
DC 10

The inmates do morning calisthenics for thirty minutes upon rising for the day. That's followed by an open shower with the other inmates at the camp. That too, is thirty minutes and you were expected to include bathroom time in there as well. Everything regimented and timed to a tee. Breakfast was usually meat and water. Fruit is out of the question. Some of the guests, as the guards so euphemistically called them, have some sort of duty for the day. A few are selected for classes. Ray was one of them.

Raymond sat in class listening to the government official drone on about the new era for America once the countryside was cleansed of enemies of the state and the cities were free from radicals.

"When your mind's right, anything is possible," said Professor Delong of the CDF. Delong was brought on board to the CDF after his for-profit technical college went belly up. Before the technical school, Delong was a paratrooper in the U.S. Army. The lecture continues with Delong highlighting the virtues of the new society and how the inmates were all going to be essential leaders, as long as they conformed and pulled their weight.

"You were chosen because you're enlightened. You could see the wizard from behind the curtain. A special gift indeed."

After fifty-five minutes, the class broke for recreation time. Ray milled around the perimeter fence wondering what had become of his family. He never associated with anyone since his arrival at the camp, but on this day, a stranger in his late sixties approached him.

"When or should I say, if we get out, what's going to be our function in this new society?" the man asked Raymond.

"I don't know. Whatever they tell us it'll be, I suppose."

"They make it sound as if we're the lucky ones to be alive and useful in the future. After my past, I still think I'll rot here."

"You're past. What's so bad about your past?"

"I was accused of corrupting the minds of the youth without authorization."

"What the hell does that mean. Were you a pervert?"

"I don't think perverts would end up here. They would get a quicker treatment, in my opinion. No, I taught Environmental Science at the collegiate level. Some of my students took everything I said literally. Others took it to another level. One happens to be rather infamous."

Raymond's heart raced. *It can't be*, he thought to himself.

The man held out his hand to shake. "I'm Clyde Burrows."

Instinctively, Ray puts out his hand but finds the words a bit difficult to say or come out of his mouth.

Finally: "I'm Raymond Brown."

"I know. I taught your son about a decade ago. I've since retired but was brought here last month. I've seen you out in the yard many times and thought it was time to introduce myself."

"Are they accusing you of implanting ideas into Allen's head?"

"From what I gather, they rounded up any previous associates to see what they knew. Some didn't make it out of the interrogation. I told them everything I knew: that your son was smart, kind and a pure environmentalist. He never spoke of violence to me. I'm not sure if they believe me or not, but it's the truth."

"Don't you think this is a little excessive for being an associate of my son?"

"Yes, I do, but that was a pretense to lock us up. I know you don't talk with too many people in here but more than a few at this camp are corporate types."

"Why would they get put here?"

"A dirty word around here is IS&G. Hundreds of their people and competitors wound up in here and other camps. This thing is definitely related to that company. I'm convinced they're a major contributor to the events."

"In what way?"

"I'm not sure but your son was on to something very big. His method for uncovering it was a bit extreme but a seeker of truth he was."

"Why these camps?"

"Your son and his friends discovered more than I ever knew. My focus was on science and the environment with limited resources. Whatever my private thoughts and cynicism I felt for the government, I never shared that information with my students in class nor in private conversations."

"Well, Allen picked up this stuff from somewhere and your name was mentioned in several of his papers."

"I'm not trying to be coy with you Mr. Brown. It's a little late for doing that. Of course, I did do a lesson or two on the hypothetical effect of a break in our food supply and what might be the causes leading to it. I guess Allen and his friends took it to heart and looked more into it than I thought."

"That's an understatement."

"Mr. Brown, I never had any contact with your son after school. He was one of my best students. I know that he cited my name more than once on some of his video posts, which is probably why I'm here. I don't know the reason for the camps. I think they were most likely set up years ago for radicals or terrorists. Now they can put anyone in here who's accused of a being a subversive."

"What's the point of these classes. Are we supposed to go out and actually retrain people how to think? That's crazy."

"Who knows. From what I gather with all this, we're being used for something and it can't be elimination or that would have happened already. It's definitely some sort of indoctrination: part of the New World Order, I guess."

"At first, I thought it was the government leading the way but now I'm convinced they're riding this effect of the breakdown for their own purposes."

"That could be Mr. Brown. I don't really know."

The roof of the compound is still covered with the P2040 purple toxin dropped a few months earlier. Nobody thinks twice about it or even tries to clean it up. Some of the guards even take turns pissing on the purple dust to see the pretty colors that are made.

At the camp, dinnertime is 5:00 sharp. The inmates form a regimented line and proceed to the dining hall. Classical music plays in the background as some kind of paste is offered up as the main entrée on the trays. Ray and Clyde sit together at the center of the hall.

"What do you know about IS&G?" asked Raymond.

"They have a bad rep despite millions to cover up their past. I would usually get a paper each semester from a kid that would analyze the effects of some of the modified seeds and plants that they have a monopoly over."

"What effects did they write about?"

"I never got any raw data but students would make a correlation with rising breast cancer in women over the past thirty years and the genetically modified plants and hormones used in agriculture."

"Did you ever consider looking into that?"

"Kids always look for conspiracies by corporations and the government. I'm not an obedient little soldier but sometimes you can't just think the worst. I never acted because I never got concrete proof on any of the hypotheses presented."

"In other words, you looked the other way."

"If you want to draw that conclusion of me Ray, be my guest. I only open the possibilities to my students. I don't tell them what to think. And yes, I was comfortable in my ivory tower without lifting a finger to expose anything of real substance. For that, I am guilty."

One of the guards watching over the camp high up in his tower is seen coughing feverishly. He starts to tremble and his face contorts. Other inmates notice the spectacle and this causes a stir in the dining hall. The guard rocks back and forth and then bends himself over the side of the railing as if he is going to puke.

"Look over there Ray," said Clyde, "That guard's gonna hurl."

"Great, that's all I need to go with this crappy lunch."

The guard didn't release any of his lunch but instead drops his rifle over the edge. It falls to the ground as the inmates of DC 10 look up at him. He then lets out a loud screeching noise and then throws himself off the tower. He lies on the ground, broken and with limbs pointing unnaturally in different directions. Other guards rush over to see what happened and point their rifles at the inmates to move back.

A shot is heard from the rear of the camp. More guards rush over to see what's happening. Dozens of men are slowly approaching the camp. They're not walking quickly nor are they armed. They sway from side to side in a zombie-like trance and approach the compound. The guards yell at them to get back or they will be "liquidated."

They continue to push forward to the gates of the compound. Another warning from the lead guard to stop coming forward is made but they continue, anyway.

The lead guard gives the nod and then a dozen subordinates fire round after round into the crowd of "zombies" mowing them down one by one. They lay in a huddled mass outside the gate.

"I guess I gotta go clean this shit up now," said one of the newest guards. Several of the veteran guards go out to insect the lump of humanity. Their real motive is to have a clean path to get home once their shift ends. A few of the semi-dead corpses reaches up to grab the arms and legs of the guards.

"God damn it," yelled the guard. He unloads his revolver into the bloodied intruder lying there reaching up at him. Another man lies there trying to speak, oozing with blood and puss from his face. He receives another dose of help from the guard.

"Playtime's over ladies," said the lead guard to the inmates of DC 10.

"Go back to your cells, now."

"What was that all about?" asked Raymond.

"I don't know. Unwelcome guests to the camp. Those bastards can shoot at anyone or do anything they please. They have been ever since martial law's been declared. Anyone deemed a threat is dealt with by whatever these sadistic assholes want to do."

A few moments later a siren is heard. All the guards look up to the sky. It was a beautiful blue sky day but suddenly turned darker. A loud humming resonates throughout the camp.

"It's those fucking things in the air again," said the lead guard. The Stingers target on this day wasn't releasing their payload onto any city or countryside. They swooped down and stung anyone standing outside. At first, they went for the intruders at the gates but then turned their attention to the inmates of DC 10, who all ran into the compound as quickly as they could, but the Stingers were too fast. They stung nearly everyone, including the guards.

Then, as suddenly as they came, the Stingers departed.

"You ok Ray?"

"Yeh… You?"

"I'll live."

"What the hell were those things?"

"I don't know but they looked they were communicating with one another and attacked."

"I wonder if it's those insects that were eating the crops and attacking the other insects that were infesting the farmland a while back."

"Maybe."

Wounded and demoralized, guards and inmates retreated to their offices and cells for the night.

Night passes peacefully for the residents of DC 10.

"Wake up ladies and get in line," yelled Dylan, second in command to the lead guard. Dylan wanted to be a cop back in the day but didn't make the cut, since he dabbled in heroin as a youth and sometimes as an adult. He found a good career at the camp where he could let out his frustrations on the ones who once told him what to do.

The inmates stood in line rattling off their assigned numbers to the camp. Cellblock F was short three inmates.

"Where the hell are they?" barked Dylan.

"Still in their cells," replied the guard for cellblock F.

"Well get those scumbags up. They're holding up my block and we got shit to do."

"They're lying in their cots. I think they might be sick or dead," said the guard for cell block F.

"What the Fuck is with these lazy assholes," said Dylan, as he runs down the corridor to cellblock F.

Dylan goes in to inspect one of the inmates lying there. "Dude you better have a good reason for holding up my line."

The inmate says nothing just a faint moan.

Dylan continues to berate the inmate: "Get your ass up and back in line now you piece of shit."

Still no response, which causes Dylan to club the man with two blows from his nightstick. Dylan then reaches over to pull the cover off the inmate.

The wounded man reaches up at Dylan from his cot and scratches at his eyes. Dylan lets out a high-pitched scream of pain while the other guards come in to smack the inmate down with their clubs. The wounded man won't be doing anymore scratching but Dylan isn't fairing that well either.

It's not just tears coming down Dylan's face but puss much like the intruders the day before. Another guard and a medic come over to treat Dylan. He goes into a convulsion reaching for his stomach and keels over. Another guard follows this pattern.

"They look like they caught some kind of virus that's spreading through the camp," said the medic, "We need to call this in."

"I'm not calling shit in man. I'm out," said one of the guards next to the medic. Others ran out of the camp, leaving a skeleton crew to watch over one thousand enlightened individuals of the New World Order.

Inmate after inmate start to buckle over grabbing at their stomachs. The few guards remaining went back to their offices and locked themselves in.

Clyde looked down the hall and saw Raymond. Ray ran over to him and said, "Now's our chance Clyde, let's make a run for it."

"What do you mean run for it. They'll shoot us before we hit the gates."

"Are you kidding? They're too busy saving themselves. It's survival mode now and they'll be more afraid of us now than we are of them. Let's just go."

"How the hell are we going to survive with those things out there?"

"Look, you can stay if you want, there's a contagion happening now and I'm not staying to get infected. I'll take my chances out there. If I have to die, I'll die outside trying to be free not in here caged like some sort of a trained monkey."

With the cells open, it didn't take long for everyone to flee and empty out DC 10. Raymond was the first to get to a guard's vehicle. It was Dylan's truck, with his keys hanging arrogantly enough in the ignition. Raymond remembered Dylan bragging about it nearly every morning to the other guards. "My truck's the only thing that doesn't let me down, not like some bitch," grunted Dylan on many morning walks with the other guards.

It was a blue pickup truck with stickers across the back depicting various popular culture sayings such as "If you're going to ride my ass, you should pull my hair." That was one of the better ones. The others were less obtrusive: either a kid peeing or some sports reference.

Ray jumped in and pulled the visor down where Dylan's keys dropped onto his lap. A sigh of relief gripped Ray for the first time in more months than he could remember. Burrows tried to get into the passenger side but another infected inmate grabbed his arm and pulled him down.

Burrows cried out in agony, "Just go Ray, save yourself."

Raymond went around the car and tried to pull the infected inmate off Clyde but then it started to lunge at him.

"Ray, don't be a hero. Don't let Allen's death be in vain. Get out and expose the truth of what's happening. Save your family. Run to the hills."

And so, Raymond did. He drove out of DC 10 on a bright cold Monday morning with hordes of infected inmates streaming out of the camp into the countryside.

Cause and effect, Raymond thought to himself, as he drove Dylan's truck to the place he once found sanctuary in. *What the hell happened to those things at the camp*, his thoughts rattling again in his mind.

Raymond spent the next hour meandering through the backcountry. Without anyone telling him what to do for a change, he finally had time to think.

CHAPTER 34
DETOUR

Ray's self-reflection about the events over the past year didn't last for long. It only took a few miles up from DC10 for the stolen Jeep to halt his progress, apparently out of juice.

That jackass. Couldn't even fill the tank before coming to work, he thinks to himself.

The events of the past day leave Ray tired and thirsty, but he knows staying in the vehicle will only invite scavengers hungry to take anything of value. He leaves the truck and starts to walk up the highway.

Hugging the interstate, desperate to get home, Ray sticks his thumb in the air hoping to cop a ride. He's never done it before but after seeing this particular strategy employed on TV a gazillion times, thinks maybe it would work.

Normally, hundreds of cars pass by every minute on this stretch of the interstate but with the world in the toilet, only a trickle pass by - some beep, others yell obscenities.

A late model Dodge Charger races in front of Ray and then abruptly comes to a stop. The color of the vehicle must have been black for the underside shows the original paint, but most of the sidewalls and hood are purple. And not a good job of laying the coat, almost spray painted on. The tires are extra wide, which adds a menacing yet cool look to the car.

A lanky arm dangles from the driver's side covered in tattoos. Some are crosses and a few are strange symbols. Music is initially loud and unrecognizable but then gets lower as Ray gets closer.

Ray comes around the other side and walks up to the car. His better instinct advises against getting in but his thirst and need to get off the highway are greater.

"Where you headed to partner?" asked a man in his early twenties, with a large set of bug eyes and stringy hair.

"Up the line about fifteen miles."

The bug-eyed man nods his head for Ray to enter.

"Much appreciated...name's Ray."

"Max."

"Thanks for the ride."

"No problem... looks like you were caged up for a while dude?"

"I was in one of the camps down the road."

"You escaped, huh?"

"The place kinda fell apart. You know...bugs attacked."

Max smiles a bit and turns up the volume on the radio. The music takes Ray back many years as he recalls hearing it played by one of his burnt out college neighbors, many moons ago: "Teach You How to Sing the Blues" by Motorhead.

Max is banging his hands on the steering wheel, singing along with the tune.

"Too loud for yah?"

Ray shakes his head, "No man. It's fine."

Before the song finishes, Max turned the knob counterclockwise and said, "Do you see that dude?"

Max is looking at the woods to the right with his head over the steering wheel trying to get a good view.

"What is it?"

"That big oak in the middle. Can't you see. It was chosen."

There was a large oak tree, more than ninety feet high with glowing green and purple leaves off to the side. Max makes a hard right off the interstate and onto the fields darting for the tree.

"Where you going man? You need to slow down."

The Charger roars onto the grass, sliding sideways, as Ray bangs his head on the windshield.

"Can't you see those flying Stingers chose to spray that tree. Of all the trees, they nested there."

"Hey man, I'm just trying to get home. I don't need to see a tree."

"It's special you dumb shit. You'll see."

Ray realizes that his better instinct was correct and it should have prevented him from entering the car but he's stuck in Mad Max's thrill fest now. He knows Max is clearly insane but doesn't want to antagonize him any more than he already is.

"If they sprayed, it means it's been saturated with concentrated toxin Max. We should be going in the opposite direction of anything that has that shit on it."

"What the hell you talking about?"

"The tree is poisoned man. Whatever polluted it, bees or bugs with the toxin, you should stay away."

The car slides a few feet from the gigantic oak.

"Come on and earn your ride. Help me collect."

Max grabs a bag from the back of the car and runs over to the tree waving his arm for Ray to assist.

Ray reluctantly opens the door and thinks about running into the woods but is unsure if Max will follow him on foot or worse, in the car. He decides to assist and play along in this strange endeavor.

"Why are we collecting leaves from this tree Max?"

"It's not any tree dude. Can't you see it's chosen. Of all the trees in the woods, those Stingers chose this one."

"That just means they nested here. Max…Don't you think it's wise not to be here when and if they come back?"

"Stop whining. I think we got enough anyway."

Max's bag is full and he starts to lick one of the leaves with a heavy concentration of the purple toxin sprayed by the Stingers. As if he is a kid unwrapping the golden ticket, his eyes light up with every lick. "Try some. It's a little tangy but the after effect is great."

"I'm good man. Knock yourself out."

"You don't know what you're missing dude."

"I think I do. Can we go now?"

"Just a minute —"

"Max, people are dying from that stuff. Why would you eat it?"

"That's not always true. Some are dying but others are getting stronger from it. You have to be chosen for the gift and I'm one of the few that can handle it. I've been eating it for weeks now and I feel great…better than I ever have in my whole rotten life."

Max gestures for Ray to try some but Ray is not buying the lunacy or flawed logic.

"Before the purple rains came, I was nothing: nobody ever listened to me but I always kept trying to fit in. I was just a joke to everyone. Now that I've been chosen, I take what I want and others listen to me."

"You think that's helping you Max but it could be temporary, and you'll feel the negative effects later. It can't possibly be good for you."

"You're wrong. I feel like a million bucks. Look at my car. How sweet it is. I took it off Bill Richards. He was the big man in town. Not so much anymore."

"You took his car?"

"Damn straight I took his car, his house and everything else. I would never have tried that before. I feel alive for the first time in my life. Sick? You're the one who's sick."

"So you killed him for the car?"

"I killed him and anyone who stands in my way. I told you I was chosen."

Max gestures for Ray to eat some of the leaves but Ray shakes his head, "No thanks. I don't think I was chosen."

"Suit yourself dude. Only the strong survive now and if you can't adapt to the new world, you'll die."

"Wow Max, I used to paraphrase that very quote to my students at school but it didn't consist of eating toxins to survive."

They walk to the back of the car as Max uses the remote to open the trunk.

The musky dead air causes Ray to gag as the trunk opens up.

"What the hell you got in there man?"

Max smiles. "I know how to use it. I seen em drop but I'm gonna make it. You gotta know how to use it."

"Use what? What the hell you talking about?"

A squirrel's head peeks out of the trunk of Max's car. It tries to jump out but must have been injured in some way for it makes one more futile effort before sliding back down. Another critter follows suit in a vain attempt to escape the caged misery but finds itself back down in the gallows.

Ray's curiosity cannot resist, although he knows it will make him ill when he gets a full frontal view of what this wack job has in the trunk. His heart is racing faster again and is unsure if having Max in back of him is a smart idea. He waits for Max to catch up to him before proceeding any further.

As the both of them approach the trunk, they see dozens of squirrels, rabbits and chipmunks lining the inside of the Charger. They lay on top of purple leaves. Some are bloodied but most lie dormant. The music must have been loud enough earlier that Ray didn't hear any of the animals whimpering.

"You see dude. I'm saving them. They would have died without me but I rescued them. I feed them only purple leaves. They'll get better and then I'll eat them too."

Max unloaded the collected leaves on top of the poor creatures and slammed the trunk shut.

"What the hell man. This isn't right. You should let them out."

"What the hell do you know anyway."

"I know that eating toxins and keeping poor defenseless animals locked in a trunk is not normal."

"You don't know shit dude. You're probably an enemy of the state. Why else would you be in the camp back there?"

"I just want to get home and will walk from here on."

"Suit yourself. You won't last long in the woods."

"I'll take my chances."

Ray waits for the car to pull out before continuing his journey- home through the woods this time.

CHAPTER 35
REDS

Donna drove while Lisa sat shotgun, holding Angela in her arms. The family made their way through the sprawling zigzags of the neighborhood a few short miles from the turnpike entrance. Abandoned cars were everywhere: on the side of the road, on the road and out in the fields.

The boys sat in the back. For a moment, it was almost normal, almost like when they were kids going for a ride with their cousin to the park but of course, things were not normal anymore.

A flapping noise interrupts the family bonding time. "Damn it," said Donna, "I think we got a flat." She pulled the car to the side of the road. "Great, I never changed a flat tire."

"In your whole life mom, you never changed a flat?" asked Lisa.

"I always had your father to change mine or would call AAA, which neither is an option at this moment."

"I know how to do it Aunt Donna. Dad showed me a couple of times and the last time I did it by myself, while he watched."

Lou scurried around the back of the jeep to get the tire and jack. Before he could open the trunk, Lisa screamed out, "What the hell is that!"

Three men and a woman whose faces were pale with eyes red as blood came lumbering over to them. They tried to speak but only mumbled. They kept coming closer as if they were in some sort of hypnotic state of mind.

"They look like zombies," said Louis.

The pale-faced blood-eyed strangers kept coming forward without saying a word. They were grasping with their hands as if they wanted to claw something. Donna screamed, "Lisa grab Angela and get out of there."

Edward, realizing he never loaded his weapon and had no time to retrieve it, reached for a crowbar in the trunk. The stranger and Edward are face to face. Ed winds his arm up and clocks the larger man on the jaw. Ed lands a direct hit but in doing so loses his footing. The stranger's head almost splits open as he falls to the ground, moaning.

Edward's momentum carried him forward and onto the ground as well. The woman threw herself on top of him before he had a chance to move. She scratched at his eyes with her dirty blood stained hands, while the other two parasites came over to feast.

"Do something Lou," cried Lisa, as Donna and Oliver made noises to distract the intruders. Angela covers her eyes and hides in the back seat.

Lou pulled out his Beretta, cocked the chamber and shot six shots at all three strangers finally putting them down and off Edward.

"My eyes, I can't see anything and they're burning!" Edward screamed. He rubs his hands over his eyes and then starts to reach for his stomach.

"Get a towel from the car Lisa before this gets worse," said Donna.

Donna put a towel over Edward's eyes as he lay on the ground coughing uncontrollably. His skin started to get blotchy and he wouldn't stop twitching.

"I think he got the same thing as Aunt Laura," said Oliver.

"Well, we need to get him in the jeep right now."

"Mom if he's contagious, we should put him in the trailer so we don't get infected."

"Are you serious Oliver. He's your cousin. Where's your decency."

"I'm trying for all of us not to get sick mom. Look at his eyes. We might all die because of his coughing or if he scratches one of us. He's starting to look like those things that Louis just shot."

"He's right mom," said Lou.

"Fine, unload something from the back and help your cousin into the trailer."

Oliver and Lou moved at a frantic pace changing the tire hoping no more blood-eyed wanderers would pay them a visit. Lisa joins Angela in the back seat. The boys finish off changing the tire and jump back into the jeep with Oliver riding shotgun.

"We need to get Ed and Angela to the nearest hospital. We can't make it up to the mountains without medical care. Who knows if there are any clinics left up there," said Donna.

"Granview Hospital is only a few more miles up the turnpike," said Lou," I remember going there to see a friend who fractured his arm a few years back when he was wrestling."

"Fine. Sit tight till we get there."

A few more twists and turns and the family caravan makes it to the turnpike, but now Donna regrets her decision.

CHAPTER 36
ROAD LESS TRAVELED

As if everyone who owned a trailer finally decided to bug out, they form a trail - miles long on the turnpike. More trailers and RV's than she's ever seen in her life cause a bottleneck. On the other side of the highway going south, into the city, only a trickle of cars flow.

Donna manages a smile: "Your father wanted to buy one a couple of years ago kids."

"An RV?" asked Lisa, "There for dorks."

"Well, sleeping in a car or an RV. I know which one I would chose young lady."

"I'd rather have my own bed. How we all gonna fit in that cabin in the mountains, anyway."

"We'll manage Lisa."

"Good job mom. Now we'll be stuck on this road all day. I hope we don't run out of gas."

"You're not helping at all Lisa. Try not be make things worse: keep Angela amused back there by playing Patty Cakes or something, okay."

"Thank God the next exit is for the hospital," said Donna, "although it'll probably take us a half hour to go three miles."

She senses that Oliver wanted to tell her something and asked, "What's on your mind dear?"

"Do you think it's a good idea to make it to the hospital? I mean they might think we're all infected when they see us."

"Ed's the only one whose infected and he needs help. And Angela might have internal bleeding. That poor girl should've been taken right away: going to that farm was a mistake. We have to go and get her checked out. End of story."

"I know mom but it'll probably be guarded by troops protecting the staff."

"Yeh, so what. It's a hospital Oliver. They're supposed to help the infected."

"Mom, in the city, people wouldn't dare go near them."

"That's crazy dear. Besides, we're not in the city, are we?"

The family can see the hospital from the highway. They decide to hug the shoulder of the road and get off on the exit ramp. Trailers and cars honk at them as they zip along.

As the family pulls up to the large concrete and glass behemoth, a large sign reads, INFECTED ARE TERMINATED.

Black smoke is billowing from the rear of the building as white ash falls to the ground and lands like dirty snowflakes on the jeep.

Donna continues going forward and then sees armed soldiers from the CDF, Homeland and National Guard lining the entrance.

"They're not gonna help Edward here mom…we should turn around," said Oliver.

"I just can't turn around. They'll know something's wrong. I'll ask about parking."

It's a one way leading to the front entrance as a CDF soldier stops the jeep. The soldier moves to the driver's side while two others are on Oliver's right. The soldier gestures for Donna to roll her window down. Before Donna can ask about parking, he asked, "What's the emergency or problem lady?"

"We came off the highway to see if we could get a friend treated for some wounds."

"What kinda wounds?"

Angela realized that Donna is talking about her said, "I'm ok. I feel good."

"We picked her up a while back. She lost her parents today."

The soldier peers through the window and although Lisa is trying to cover the bloodied skirt, he notices.

"What happened to her? Is she bitten?"

"No, not at all. Someone close to her did it. Can we please just go in?"

"No, I don't wanna go!" shrieked Angela.

"Please mom. Let's go," said Lisa.

"Not so fast young lady. We'll decide when you can go. You sure nobody's been bitten?"

Donna hesitates and is confronted with a difficult decision: risk getting caught in a lie or exposing Edward to the goon squad.

She is spared the choice.

A large knock is heard from the rear of the trailer.

"Whaddaya got back there, lady?"

The other guards are pointing their guns at the family.

"Step out of the car, now."

Donna obliges and as she unhooks her strap, said to the kids, "It'll be all right. Don't say a thing."

More knocks come from the trailer.

"Better not lie to me or it'll be your last... What's in the back?"

"He's my nephew. He's sick."

"You mean bitten?"

Donna nods her head in agreement.

"Live one here Corporal. Bring the stretcher."

The other guards whistle to some aides who bring a stretcher to the rear of the trailer.

"Please sir, he needs help."

"Oh, we'll help him all right. And don't say sir to me. I work for a living."

Donna is grateful for not lying as she knows this soldier has had his share of grief and death, and would be in no mood to forgive.

One of the subordinates rolls the trailer door open. Ed lunges forward but is knocked down with welcoming bullets from the other soldiers.

Donna sheds a tear but controls the urge to utter a sound. The only screams come from Angela and Lisa as the bullets zipped through her cousin.

The aides remove Edward from the trailer and throw him on the stretcher.

"Where you taking him?"

"Where all the infected go. Can't you read the sign?"

CHAPTER 37
NETWORK

The contagion once prevalent in the Northeast had spread across the country. No city or suburb was immune any longer. The denser the population the higher the probability of infection. The Stingers were still around and their favorite targets were multiple: other bugs, crops and humans, especially the ones with the vaccinations given by the CDF last year.

"Momma, what's wrong? Do you need something to eat?" asked Marcus.

"I'm not hungry baby, just thirsty," said Marcus's mother, Tianna.

"I think I got the flu of some kind and it's really bad, baby."

"The guards have mostly left momma; I could get you to the hospital."

"The hospital's no good for me son. They'd just put me out of my misery soon as they'd see me. You know that."

"Well, I could take you to one of our clinics down by the pier. They got all kinds of medicine for people. They don't work for anyone in the government."

"There's no point in taking a chance out there, baby. Who knows if what they got could help me anyways. Besides, I'm no good to you without my eyes. I'd just hold you back and I need you here for your sister. Promise me you'll take care of her."

She then put out her hand for Marcus to grab it.

Marcus held it for a moment as his sister looked on crying. His mother coughed for a few moments, closed her eyes and was gone.

If the bugs, virus and roaming mobs weren't bad enough, now the Bottom Dwellers and Untouchables had a common enemy- the Reds. It appeared that the reaction of the P2040 toxin dropped by the Stingers reacted in people, primarily the Bottom Dwellers who had the original vaccination and caused them to turn into some sort of a walking parasite. The Reds had eyes that bulged and that were the color of blood. They walked in a trance with blotchy skin, almost peeling off.

If you were lucky, the virus would kill you after a few moments of unbearable pain, if you weren't, you wandered the streets with a rage and thirst for liquids: any liquids. Others, went crazy with the reaction but a few were immune to the poison.

Since most of the infected were contagious, nobody tried to help them. It was the law of the jungle now. It had been for a while and everyone was on their own.

It was night in the city and the residents adapted to living with their newest enemy. This enemy wasn't equipped with sniper rifles only their grasping hands. They wandered around in what appeared to be a state of dementia. At first, some would appear harmless but after a day or so, they began to lunge and grasp at anyone in their surroundings.

Everyone has an Achilles heel and people quickly learned that ultraviolet light would keep the Reds away to some extent. Long rows of UV light were hung in doorways and alongside major streets. With the stench of bodies for a background, the inner cities became a glowing laboratory of garbage, rats and bugs.

The resistance is named the Network. It was initially comprised of rival gangs in the cities. When enough of their members were killed by each other, an alliance was formed. The common enemy was of course the CDF guards who had orders to shoot at anyone who was deemed to be disturbing the social order.

Gabriel was now a well-guarded resistance leader in the city. He commanded not just an army of followers but also the respect from the people rich and poor. He approaches the congregation to give a speech.

"New demons roam the streets my brothers and sisters, sent to us from our friends in Washington."

"Whether by design or negligence, it makes no difference to me and I'm sure to you who or what brought them here. We all pay the price for greed, power and misplaced control."

The crowd at the church is packed. Men, some as young as twelve, guard the hall with automatic machine guns. There is a picture of Jesus and next to him is a big N enclosed in a red circle and underneath it are smaller words that read, "The Network is you."

"An alliance is called for my brothers and sisters. The Untouchables as they like to call themselves high up on the hill, need our assistance in defeating these red-eyed demons."

A man called out, "Where the hell were they when we needed them?" The people in attendance cheer and stomp their feet.

"It's true. We were alone in the darkness my brothers and sisters, but the night is even darker now. The Untouchables have resources and supplies we need. And in exchange we have guns and people."

Another man yelled out, "People to die for them, that's what they propose, sacrifice for bread, just like every other war." The crowd again erupts. The hall is alive with energy.

Gabriel waits a minute until they settle down and then clears his throat.

"Yes, this is a war my brothers and sisters and I honestly say to y'all, it has many fronts. We have the CDF, bugs, famine, martial law and now these red-eyed demons roaming our streets. They don't discriminate. They are equal opportunity killers. I chose to fight and settle the score at a later point. The choice is yours. What say you?"

The crowd initially upset with the choice of an alliance with the Untouchables rallies behind their leader and supports the decision.

CHAPTER 38
THINK QUICK

A few miles from Vatican City, Italy, the Central Authority of the Order holds an emergency meeting. The well-heeled dignitaries including Burkman are sporting two thousand dollar suits as they come off their private jets. They are escorted by their bodyguards and a few of them are carrying flamethrowers in case any Stingers attack.

The gathering takes place under an old stone building built hundreds of years ago. The invitations were sent to all three hundred members of the committee but less than one hundred arrive. The grandeur of their former gatherings is long over as the remaining members of the Order huddle like rats, plotting their next move.

Salvatore Bertolli, head of the Order in Europe welcomes the arrivals.

"Brothers of the Order, thank you for arriving under an extremely difficult and hazardous situation. We have much to discuss and little time. Plans have a way of taking a life of their own. It seems as if the vaccinations were proven not to be as stable as we had hoped." Burkman puts his head down in shame and disgust.

"Nevertheless, the ends will justify the means. We will have a drastic population reduction per our original and long-standing plan but some of us may not live to see it. We have no control over the virus that has spread nor these flying bugs from various countries. The genie is out and we don't know what effect there will be on the future of the continents."

Bertolli sips a glass of wine and continues speaking: "The options we have at this moment are to relocate to a welcoming country or accept the fate of the Western Hemisphere. I'm afraid after losing Masters and other top government officials it won't be long before the tentacles of the American administration come knocking on our doors in the middle of the night."

Burkman raised his left hand and said, "Brother Bertolli, my contact in Beijing has agreed to have a sit-down and discuss our proposal with them. They are asking for ten billion Euros to have the meeting."

Another member from Brazil raised his left hand and said, "It is the end of the Order if we accept relocation to the East. They will never adhere to our tenants. This is blackmail and theft of our hard-earned money. We should stay in Europe."

"We need to regroup and find a suitable host country," said Burkman, "I am open for suggestions but inactivity will surely mean exposure and death of the Order."

"Is Jerusalem still an option for us?" asked Bertolli.

"It may be but they have their own conditions as well. I propose we send a delegation to both locations and see what is best for the Order and then convene a final vote on the ultimate location."

"All in favor?"

They all raise their left hands and quickly make their way to the exit.

CHAPTER 39
CLEAN UP

Marcus has moved from an informant and disseminator of resistance ideas to the leader of the Westside chapter of the Network. His kills were in the hundreds now, including CDF, Reds and Untouchables alongside their private bodyguards. When he got his original scholarship all those years ago, he aspired to become a journalist. Now, he intended to run the city under a new government giving autonomous control to each community with only the armed Network being centralized.

Reds moved up and down the narrow stone streets. Many of the walking parasites lay alongside the gutters with rats gnawing at their eyes. Guns and ammo were long ago outlawed but you would never have believed that, for the locals were armed to the teeth and shot at anything that came towards them. Network members were forced to wear caps denoting a pledged member and a tattoo with the letter N on their right hand and on the right side of their neck.

Stingers once prevalent in the city, chose to attack only at random. It appeared that another effect of the Reds' infusion into society or rather a transformation had been to limit the Stingers from attacking.

"Do you think those bugs know some of us are infected?" asked Marcus to his newest recruit Jamil.

"I don't know boss. I haven't seen any in weeks. I hope they stay in the country and let us be. We have enough shit to deal with."

"Let's hope they stay away. It's good they aren't here while we take care of business but we need to find a cure for this virus or we'll all get it."

"Do you think the government has a cure and is saving it?"

"Nobody's stupid enough to trust them for a cure. I'm afraid we got to solve this situation ourselves. I know we have a unit at the university doing research and have plenty of those things to test on. We just need to figure this out first then deal with the bugs or there won't be any of us to resist anything."

"Take aim, there's a horde coming down Market," blasted a voice over Marcus's radio.

"First things first, before we save the world," said Marcus, "We save ourselves."

They both locked their M-16's and tapped the bottom of the magazines, just like they used to do it in the movies. The armory for the M16's was attacked by the Network a few months earlier. It was guarded by the loyalists of the CDF who put up a valiant fight but were killed in the end. Marcus led the charge on that day.

"You take the first shot and remember what I taught you, breathe slowly and focus. You don't have to rush unless they're right up your ass," said Marcus.

Jamil misses his first target but then looks to Marcus for encouragement. "You can do this bro, just take your time and focus."

Jamil lands a direct hit – right between two red blood stained eyes.

Both young men start to pepper the Reds as they made their way down to the river. Their slow pace and bulging eyes make for easy targets for the two young marksmen. They cleaned up the block and then head back to headquarters.

The sun was setting on the city and the Reds were more aggressive and prevalent at night. The newly infected, if not brought down immediately with death, roamed the daylight for a day or two but after that they mostly made their appearance under cover of darkness and always thirsty.

Marcus, Jamil and two other foot soldiers made their way back home. When they reached their destination, a slew of Reds was waiting for them. They clawed and grasped at the front door to the building. Moments earlier, a child was taken down by one of the walking parasites and he lay curled up under the overhang in the back of the building.

Marcus waved to Jamil with a raised fist. Jamil instantly understood the gesture and ran to another building. He came out a few minutes later with a long metal tube attached to his shoulders.

The little boy was seen playing around the neighborhood in good times and in the darkest of times. He would play with just about anyone who would walk by.

Jamil yelled out, "Die you mother fuckers" and squeezed the trigger on the metal tube he produced. A long bright flame protruded from the tube and covered the faces and clothing of the Reds hanging outside the building. The stink of the burning infected flesh was so putrid that Marcus had to put a scarf over his face. Residents, locked in their houses, peered out of their windows to cheer the carnage.

The clan of soldiers allowed the Reds to slowly burn without wasting any ammunition. Their charred flesh melted and fell to the ground with a faint purple and yellow tint in the smoke rising to the sky, only their eyes showed but they posed no threat any longer.

More recruits were inside waiting to hear from the legend, Marcus, who had become something of a folk hero in the city and was nicknamed the Blood Warrior. The new mission was to go up to the hill and ensure the shipments had a safe passage back to the west and north side of the city.

Marcus and his team met up with King George, a young entrepreneur who made his fortune in technology and decided to stay in the city. He was the leader of the Untouchables in up on the hill.

As with the Network, the Untouchables had chapters throughout the city and in various cities across the country. Their common bond was the "special" vaccinations they received years ago but also their affluence. What they lacked in bravery they made up with warehouses of ammunition, dried goods, oil and other commodities. They had plenty of private mercenaries to protect them years ago but they too fell victim to the contagion floating around, and now needed to form a new alliance.

King George held out his hand and said, "Good to see you my brother."

"You ain't my brother," said Marcus. "Rich bastards like you caused this shit and now we gotta clean it up."

"Look, we didn't cause anything. We only did what the government told us to do just like everyone else. We didn't hurt anyone."

"What about the vaccines y'all got?"

"We did what we were told, just like you."

"Whatever, let's get on with it. What do you need?"

"Your guys did a hell of a job clearing up the entrance to the hill. That shipment of trucks behind me marked with X's are for you. The others need to get out to the pier. That whole area needs to be cleared."

"For that, what do we get?"

"You get the trucks marked X tomorrow filled with medicines that we agreed upon yesterday. Doesn't Gabriel fill you in on the details?" said the King, sarcastically.

Marcus and his men escort the trucks to their neighborhoods and rendezvous at night to "clean up" the pier.

"This ain't right Marcus," said Jamil.

"What's wrong my brother."

"We're gonna lose good men tonight to bring supplies to those rich assholes."

"I don't like it either but Gabriel thinks it's the right thing to do."

"Well, it ain't him risking his ass down here, is it?"

"Jamil, that kinda talk is dangerous. You're free to tell me what's on your mind but without Gabriel we would all be gone by now."

The pier is crawling with Reds- hundreds maybe thousands of them. The docks have warehouses of supplies and ammunition but the Reds linger because of the water. No one would think of drinking from the river water in normal times but this was a long way from normal.

Most of the Reds lay next to the river line sticking their heads in the water for relief. Some slide into the river and can't get back out, which causes the water to become even more contaminated. Hundreds float along the banks of the river's edge, next to boats, long abandoned by their well to do owners.

Marcus and his team begin the task. They start unloading their ammo into every one of the diseased, formerly normal humans. Unless a direct head shot was made, it took dozens of rounds to take a Red down. This, of course wasted a large amount of ammunition. Jamil uses his flamethrower to light up dozens of Reds lying along the river and along the warehouses.

The stench and tarred rotten flesh mix with the charred clothes to form plumes of black and yellow smoke rising up to the sky. The smoke makes it hard to see any Reds approaching the team but Jamil keeps burning.

The rapid-fire succession of flames and bullets flying lasted twenty minutes. The dock was clear and Marcus surveys the damage done but also the toll taken on his men. Five dead including his best friend Jamil.

The Blood Warrior and the remaining troops made the dock safe for the Untouchables and in return were awarded two truckloads of canned meats and toiletries.

CHAPTER 40
FALLOUT

On foot and without a weapon, Ray enters the forest and away from any police or worse: people without anything to lose or an affection for purple toxin.

Brief flashbacks of grading papers seem to be ancient history as he treks his way through the thick bush. It's eerily peaceful but the environment is a little askew. The sun shines bright and gives visibility to the foliage that has a strange ominous tint of color to it.

A rabbit scurries by slamming itself into a tree. Its head is bleeding profusely while the legs flounder about. All Ray can do is watch as the creature lay on its side kicking its feet, glazing at him with hollow eyes. If its mission was to die a slow death, then it was a success.

What possessed it to do that, Ray thinks to himself. *The toxin sprayed must be having side effects to the whole ecosystem now.*

A snap of a branch alerts Ray to look up. Before he can move out of the way, a sparrow falls on his shoulder then bounces to the ground.

Exhausted and thirsty, he moves quickly to get out the inner forest.

Dead animals are all around him now: fox, deer, squirrel, etc., lay still on the ground. Their eyes are expressionless. No traces of a hunter's bow or bullets are evident, which is fine with Ray, since he has no intention of giving a proper inspection. His thoughts are to get home but realizes now that he escaped one prison for another.

His thirst is insatiable at this point and for a millisecond considers licking some of the droplets on the low hanging leaves. Logic prevails and he keeps moving.

A welcome breeze comes from the clearing causing the leaves to rustle and smack one another. Then, hundreds of gnats and flies fall from the trees like black confetti all around him. Ray wriggles his body and brushes the ones landing in his hair. Furry animals were one thing but millions of dead insects falling from above evoked a visceral response within him. He runs without any direction. If only to escape this dreary environment of death, he briefly ponders thumbing on the interstate again.

Thoroughly creeped out by this latest brush with mother nature, he scurries to the clearing where the bush is thinner. He stands on top of a cliff overlooking a river, perhaps a quarter of a mile wide. Down on the water, dozens of boats line the banks of the waterway. On each boat, several armed men stand vigilant. Large nets cover the main part of each vessel.

Ray waves his arms, thinking that if any of the men shoot at him, he would be far enough away to avoid being hit. The men don't seem to be phased by the sight of a middle-aged man jumping up and down on top of a hill, waving his arms. One of them holds up a battery held radio and says a few words. From another boat, a man comes out from underneath the bay doors.

The two men chat once more with their radios and then one of them gets on the bullhorn.

"Who you with?"

"No one. Just thirsty and trying to get home. Do you have any water to spare?"

"Take a look around. Plenty of water down here. Can't you see?" Men on other boats and some women are now out in the open, laughing at the suggestion that Ray come drink from the river.

"It's fresh water man. Or at least used to be." Again, more laughter from the peanut gallery.

Ray, defeated, turns away and starts walking back into the woods.

"Hey man…just kidding. As long as you're unarmed and alone, come on down."

Stuck between some medieval forest built for Hades and psychopaths driving fast purple cars, Ray chooses to descend down the bank of the river to another misguided adventure.

A 24 ft. cabin cruiser glides to the edge of the river. A large bearded man and a young girl meet Ray with a jug of water.

"Whatcha doing in the woods man?"

"Trying to get home. I live about ten miles north... I think."

"Can I please have some water?"

Ray drinks as the girl said, "See any stingies out there?"

"Stingies?"

"Bugs man," said the apparent father.

"Only dead ones. Lots of dead things up there."

"The ones that do the spraying. That's the only ones we care bout."

Ray drinks nearly half the jug of water.

"Name's CJ. This is Caroline."

"Ray. And very thankful to meet you. I thought I was gonna die of thirst up there. What are all these boats doing here?"

"Last time those things sprayed, killed hundreds, maybe thousands in our town. The way we see it, they focus on the cities. Most of us own these boats, some needed to be taken."

"You think you'll be safe on the water?"

"For now. We get by. Haven't seen them damn Stingers for a while now. It's like they were sent here to kill and now they're gone."

"Do you think it's possible to take me upriver about ten miles? I don't have any money, though."

"Money's useless anyway. Where you been? I'll offer you a trade."

"I don't have anything to offer."

"Everyone's got something to offer."

"Name it."

"We still need things from the cities to get by. We purify our own water but necessities like fuel are always needed. Aint no charging stations on the river Ray."

"And toilet paper too dad," said Caroline.

"Yeh, that too. We'll take you to the next town up and give you two jugs. Fill em up with gas and grab a pack of toilet paper and we'll take you up the rest of the way."

"How my supposed to get the gas without money. All my accounts have been locked out."

"We're sending Big Tony with you. He's a good shot. You get in. He covers you and you get out. Do it all the time. Just do as he says."

"I don't think I could kill anyone for fuel."

"Well, you got no choice now. Do yah?"

Another man, Big Tony, presumably, comes out from the cabin door with two large jugs.

"Let's roll."

CHAPTER 41
DESPERATION

Ray can see the Texaco sign on the far side of the river. CJ steers the boat to a half burnt out dock on the bank of the river. There are no boats on the dock only cars lining the pathway.

"You won't have much time. Fill up and split. Tony's got your back."

Tony and Ray slog their way through the mud up to the edge of the station. There are several cars parked in the lot but nobody is filling nor charging any of their vehicles.

"It looks like it's closed," said Ray.

"Look man. We need that juice. It's not closed. Fill up on the pump closest to you and head back down. You get into any trouble; I'll take them out."

Ray has a revelation in the second after big Tony makes his tough guy speech: these water dwellers, who stole the boats and gas aren't going to waste any of it taking him upstream.

Ray doesn't want to think about it too much but the thought can't escape him: *Would they kill me on the river or leave me in the woods?*

"Hurry up man. If we wait too long, others will see us."

Ray grabs both the jugs and heads to the nearest pump. Both canisters are placed on the ground. As he looks around, three cars in the bay are abandoned, two have their windows broken.

His heart races as he fills the first jug, seemingly taking forever.

"Come on. Come on," he muttered aloud.

In the shop, he sees several people milling about and one of them turns back staring straight at Ray. The faces of the men are blotchy and from a distance, Ray can see their eyes are red as blood. He remembered that look, for they were on the faces of the strangers at DC 10.

As Ray finishes the first jug, they rush to the door to get out.

"Fill the other jug before they come," yelled Big Tony.

"I don't have time. We gotta go now."

Three red-eyed walkers are only a few feet from Ray who decides to leave the jugs and runs to the end of the station, at first hiding behind a large SUV and then making a dash up the street.

"What the hell man," screamed Big Tony.

Ray pays him no mind and continues sprinting away.

Tony grabs one of the jugs and with the other hand starts to pop the red eyes with his Ar-15.

"Take that bitches," he said.

Tony then vents his anger at Ray by taking a couple of shots at him, who is a hundred feet up the road by now with not one hitting his target.

Big Tony then grabs the other jug and swings his rifle to his back. From inside one of the parked cars, two more Reds come creeping at him. He barely has time to get his rifle in position before the jug filled with gas drops and spills onto the ground.

"God damn it!" he shouted, as he kneels to the ground to close the canister. His rifle lays next to him as a swarm of Reds approach from the rear. The first lunges at Big Tony while others go for his feet. Tony unloads of few rounds but only one of the Reds is affected. He lay on the ground, with his throat hemorrhaging, covered in gas and blood.

A few drops of rain start to fall and then a heavy downpour. Ray decides to hunker down under a tree for partial relief and watch the show at the gas station. He watches as the mutated humans rip into Tony. Heading back down to the river people will not be an option for him and following the main road up the line, will not be an easy venture, as well. Some guilt fills him; but he calculates this would have been the person to kill him anyway, so the feeling doesn't last long.

As if their thirst has not been quenched, the Reds look up to the sky with their mouths open. Blood must not have been their only desire, water also appears to be a necessity for these demons.

Then, one of the Reds makes a sound that sends a chill up Ray's spine. A long high pitched wail comes from one at first, and then all of them join in. The screech is deafening and causes Ray to cover his ears. They rub their eyes and fall to their knees, clearly something about the rain had triggered a negative reaction in them when the droplets had hit their eyes.

The rain offers Ray a clear choice. As long as it came down, his only threat would be from humans. He begins the journey home, alongside the main road, thumbs in his pockets.

Ray traveled this section of the interstate thousands of times and knew the exits by heart. A few cars zip by, although many are slowed by the parked cars on the road. More of them are off to the side of the road.

Were they abandoned or attacked, he thinks to himself. He then notices something that answers his question: the majority of the cars had a purple residue on them.

He can't explain why there were no people in the cars but conjectures that the gas from the spraying had made them sick, which made them pull over and leave their vehicles.

If that were the case, his hypothesis would be correct with keys still in the ignition. Indeed, as Ray checks the empty cars, most have their keys still in them. As he methodically races from one vehicle to another, he hopes that one infected person had the inclination to turn off the engine before wandering off into the woods in their new state of mind.

A red jeep with sporty wheels, probably a teenager's, is turned sideways as if the driver had to make a quick stop. Ray peers inside and sees the keys lying on the floor. He doesn't want to get disappointed any more than he already is by getting in, so he leans over to turn the key into the ignition. The rumble of 4 cylinders never sounded so sweet. He hopped in and began the commute home.

The masses now had a new enemy: one that struck without being seen but its effect was greater than any bullet or malnutrition. At least with those, you knew the cause. Now, your neighbor's cough could result in the same slow death as a torture victim in a prisoner of war camp.

The virus spread slower than it had in other countries but resulted in the same outcome of a panicked and abused populace fighting for survival from enemies all around.

CHAPTER 42
PIT STOP

Angela reassures Donna that she is fine and pleads to leave but the soldier orders the family to park at the end of the lot and have a doctor tend to Angela's wounds.

"We won't be long guys. I promise. Angela, we're just going to see if you're hurt inside ok honey?"

"I'm ok."

"I know you are dear but you might have a boo boo inside and you won't know right away. It can cause you to get sick later."

"Will I get like daddy did?"

"No sweetheart. We just have to see if a doctor can check you out and then we'll be on our way, Okay?"

"Okay."

The minute Donna walked into the hospital she realized it was a mistake, but she had no choice except to proceed forward. Nurses and doctors strolled through the lobby and hallways, however, there were more armed service personnel than staff. And they were everywhere.

No retiree earning part-time pay welcomed them at the reception desk, only more green fatigues. "How can I help you?"

"Can I have this young girl looked at by a doctor for internal bruises?"

"Is she your daughter?"

"She has no one left to care for her."

"That's not what I asked you."

"We found her on the side of the road and it looks like she was hurt in some way. I'm taking care of her now."

"A good Samaritan in this world. That's refreshing."

"I couldn't just leave her alone, could I?"

"I'll take that as a no."

"Have a seat and we'll call you if we have someone."

"What do you mean if you have someone?"

"Mam, I won't tell you again. Have a seat."

As the family sat in the waiting area, they hear screaming coming from a distant part of the hospital. It's drowned out by the sweet sounds of an old country and western song.

"Mom we should go."

"Lisa, we can't attract any more attention to us. Please…"

"But what they did to Edward –"

"You're gonna scare Angela. Please, just stop and help for a change, will you?"

The dirty flakes that welcomed the family earlier upon arrival again start to fall outside.

Lou and Oliver go over to the window to watch the flakes fall just like to use to watch snow falling when they were younger, and school was called off for the day.

Lisa sees two trucks with trailers attached, pulling up to the side of the hospital with a large warehouse door painted black. The first truck is much larger than the second one and pulls up to the door first. Armed men and women come out of the hospital and move to the back of the truck. Other staff, most likely subordinates, lower the back door to the trailer.

Donna covers her mouth as Angela moves over to the window to get a better view.

"Boys come over here please."

The boys ignore their mother and stare in horror as the trailer door opens. Body parts intermingling with other bodies are lined up in the trailer. Animals, as well, make a heterogeneous mixture of carcasses and humans. Young and old, dead piling on top of one another -rows of smaller animals, cats, squirrels, rabbits rest on top of larger canines.

Forklifts arrive unloading the dead and take them inside the door that was painted black.

"What happened to the dogs," asked Angela.

Donna without hesitating, said "I think they ate the apples dear."

"Mommy said not to eat them."

Donna didn't wait to see what the other trailer had behind its door and went back over to the sofa, holding Angela's hand.

"Mom, they won't know we left. Let's just go," pleaded Lisa.

"They must be infected and are going to be burned," said Oliver.

"Why'd they have to burn them? Can't they just shoot them?" asked Lou.

"If they leave them die in the open, probably other animals or insects will feed on them, which will spread the virus to more people."

"You're such a smarty pants," said Lisa, "I guess you did learn something at college."

"Yeh, for the couple of months that I was there."

After all the dead had been removed from the first trailer, it slowly pulls away. The other truck and trailer move to the warehouse door painted black. This time many more armed servicemen come over.

The soldiers aim their weapons at the trailer. As the rear door opens, humans, alive this time, are packed inside. None try to run as the soldiers stare them down, sealing their fate.

"They don't look they're even infected or hurt," said Lou, "Why'd they bring em here?"

Soldiers order the people to step off the trailer and into the hospital. They are given shots on their left shoulders as they enter the door that was painted black. Some cry and are hesitant to enter but none attempt to escape.

"Do you think they're gonna kill or burn em too, Ollie?"

"I don't think they'd waste time and money giving them shots if that was the plan. Something worse is in store for them."

"What could be worse than killing them?"

An aide comes over to Donna and Angela. "Follow me please."

"Boys sit here with your sister while I go with Angela."

Angela sits with Donna in the little room; first being probed by a nurse, and then told to wait for the doctor.

Doctor Patel comes in the room and shakes Donna's hand. A loud scream is heard again coming from down the hall.

"What was that doctor? Are they operating?"

"No worries. Let's see what's going on with this young lady, shall we?"

The doctor feels around Angela's stomach and checks her wounds. He has the nurse reapply a proper gauze to some of her wounds.

More screams are heard, which causes Angela to tense up.

"Can't they give him something?"

"Mam, no need to worry about them. They are helping with the cause and are vital."

"What cause?"

"Finding a cure to the contagion, of course. Testing on the dead is futile. We need live specimens."

"My God. That's inhumane. What gives you the right to do such a thing?"

"The piece of paper hanging in my office, that's what."

Donna brings Angela closer to her.

"No worries mam. We have more than an ample supply. Your services will not be needed. At least not today."

CHAPTER 43
SPINNING IN CIRCLES

After getting checked out by Dr. Patel, and describing the grotesque duties at the hospital, he informs Donna that Angela doesn't have internal bleeding and will be fine. Donna and the kids pull out of the hospital but don't head for the highway. Dodging abandoned cars at a predictable and cautious speed, they head north on a two-lane road.

Oliver looks in the rearview mirror and sees Angela sleeping in Lisa's arms while Lou is loading another magazine for his Beretta. "I guess we're stuck with her now."

"She's got nowhere else to go…losing her whole family today, poor thing. No one should have to see what she saw and everything else she had to go through today."

Oliver nods in agreement. "Do you think we'll make it to the cabin today mom?"

"We used to do it in a few hours. It shouldn't take that long. I hope"

"That was before. It's different now."

"Tell me something I don't know. In either case, we got no choice dear."

Leaves and debris clutter the road ahead. As they progress further up the road, more junk and broken trees litter the road, almost as if they were purposely put there. Abandoned cars were one thing but getting around a tree was an entirely different type of ordeal.

"Should we go back and get on the highway again?" asked Oliver.

"We already know what that'll get us. We have to make it around?"

"I don't think it's a good idea."

"Well, we have to try."

Donna slows down and goes off the shoulder looking for an entryway to get the car and trailer through. She manages to squeeze her way into one passageway mildly scraping the trailer. She cautiously breathes a sigh of relief.

"Oh no."

The clearing through the first blocked set of trees revealed other ones bigger in size laying on the road in front of her. She's now sandwiched between more fallen trees and debris ahead and the barely passed through the opening they just came through.

"Go around mom," said Louis.

"If I could Lou, don't you think I would."

The car stopped on the side of the road.

"There's no way to get around those trees with the trailer attached," said Oliver, "and maybe not even without the trailer."

Donna and the boys go out to inspect the surroundings.

"We need to ditch the trailer," said Lou.

"We can't do that. It's got most of our food and clothing in it," said Donna.

"It's either that or we move those big trees. I'm pretty strong mom but not that strong."

The boys unhitch the trailer, taking some water and other valuable belongings that could fit into the back of the jeep.

The trailer slowly drifts back into the opening just passed. Around the abandoned trailer, come two blood-eyed walking corpses for the family to confront.

"Lou get your gun! Bug eyes coming from the opening," said Oliver.

Oliver then realizes the other guns taken from his uncle's house are stashed away in the trailer.

Lou takes aim and shoots at the first one closest to the jeep. It knocks it back a bit but the Bug-eyed demon continues to drift towards him and the family.

"Shoot again," said Donna, "and aim for their eyes."

Lou fires again. Three shots echo in the distance but they don't come from Lou's gun. The Reds are knocked down but the last bullet finds its way to Lou's head. He falls to the ground, gun at his side.

Donna lets out a loud shriek, "No!"

She kneels on the ground to see if Louis can be saved. He isn't. The bullet split the side of his head wide open. She covers the wound as if the gesture could prevent the damage already done to her son, but blood painted on her hands is the only reward.

Three burly men with beards wearing hunting gear approach.

"Are you guys ok?" asked one of the men.

Donna springs to her feet. "You murdering son of a bitch! Why did you do that? You killed my son!"

"Sorry mam. We were trying to protect y'all. We were shooting at the Reds. He caught a stray is all."

Oliver stands in front of his charging mother in an effort to prevent more loss to their clan.

"Sorry, you piece of shit, I'll kill you," screamed Donna, as she pulls out her revolver to shoot the men but they were too quick. One of them kicks her face in with his rifle butt while another puts a gun to the back of Oliver's.

On all fours, Oliver contemplates picking up Lou's pistol, which is only a few feet from him. Before he has a chance to demonstrate his bravery, a vicious blow strikes him down.

The shots and screaming bring Angela and Lisa to come out from behind the seat. Lisa, stunned at this point, falls to the ground crying, still holding Angela's hand.

"Get up boy," said the third bearded man, as he pushes Oliver to the back of the trailer.

"Stay in there, boy, so you don't cause us to do something we just might regret."

All three men look at Lisa as if she is a wounded deer ready to take the final shot to put her out of her misery.

Lisa's been around the block and knows a menacing look when she sees one.

Her intuition is confirmed as one of the bearded men unbuttons his pants.

"Please don't," sobbed Lisa, "I'm infected too." She clasps her hands together as if begging might calm their bloodlust.

"Nice try bitch. If you was bit, your eyes be red as your last period." All three chuckle like hyenas and move a little closer to both of them.

"Angela run and hide."

Angela sprints up the road and hides under the bushes blocking the entrance to the road. The men don't bother with the chase.

"We'll get that one later. Got years to train her right," said the largest of the bearded ones.

They move closer to Lisa and now are only a few feet from her when suddenly a humming is heard from above and the skies darken, just a tad.

"Oh shit, it's those fucking bugs again. Maybe they'll spray."

The Stingers weren't spraying this time but found their targets: three rather large ones. Hundreds of the Stingers descended in a matter of seconds decimating each man. Lisa darted to the trailer and locked herself inside with Oliver, who had his hands open pulling her inside.

Angela started to make her way towards the jeep but Lisa yelled, "No Angela stay hiding. We'll get you later."

Angela didn't listen to that command. She ran towards the jeep as quickly as her little legs could manage.

Lisa halfhearted opened the door to get out but Oliver pulls her back inside.

Every second of the next minute tortured Lisa as she had to hear the little girl wry in pain and muster a faint cry for help.

"What have we done Ollie? We killed that poor girl."

"No we didn't Lisa. Those bastards did…We just saved ourselves."

"What about mom? She's still out there."

"We can't go yet."

The two of them huddle and cover their ears until they're confident no more Stingers are outside.

As quickly as the Stingers came, they left.

Lisa and Oliver peek ever so slightly through the opening. They saw the three men bloated and bitten, stomachs even bigger than before. Donna was also lying there but she didn't appear to be bitten. On the side of the road, only several feet from the jeep, lay little Angela, with welts and blood all over her petite skirt.

Lisa runs over to her while Oliver inspects their mother.

"Mom, get up. Please…" She only lay there motionless.

Oliver finds a bottle of water and pours it over his mother's face. Donna slowly comes out of her slumber and glances at the carnage left by the Stingers.

The three of them sit together looking at their brother and Angela for quite a while before Donna said, "We need to bury them quickly before any more people see us."

They quickly realize there is nothing to dig in the ground and make a troublesome decision: the battered threesome pull Louis and Angela to the edge of the road overlooking the cavern below and slide them off into the river.

The three of them get back in the car. Donna is the first to speak, "We're going back home. If this is the end, I want it to happen where I raised my children."

They turned the car around and headed back to their fine suburban home.

CHAPTER 44
REUNITED

Donna makes her way back to their old neighborhood just before dusk. The family takes several turns and then approaches their cul-de-sac. Not a soul is out except for the occasional dog running wildly through the street.

"Whose truck is in the driveway?" asked Oliver.

"I don't know. We need to be careful, most likely someone seen us pack and leave and then took over the house."

"Oliver, do you have your gun loaded or the one Louis had?" asked Donna.

"Yeh mom but only a few rounds left in Lou's. I need to load the one I got from Aunt Laura's. I have to check Lou's bag for the rest of the ammo."

Donna parks on the side of the house leaving the car run.

"Should we go inside?" asked Oliver.

"Let's just sit here for a while and see if anyone comes out."

They sit for a few minutes and then notice someone moving around behind the curtains. They get a little nervous.

Lisa then said, "Let's get out of here mom."

"We can't just keep driving around with nowhere to go. Sit tight for a minute."

A few dogs are heard barking from a distance. "Mom we should go."

Donna puts the car in drive but stops suddenly. They all notice it is their father peering out from behind the curtains.

"Oh my God, I can't believe it," said Donna, as she turns the ignition off and flees from the jeep.

Ray sees that it's Donna and comes out of the house. They all embrace each other quickly at the porch and then retreat to the living room. They both explain what has happened over the past year. It is a bittersweet homecoming for all of them.

"Where's Louis?" asked Raymond.

Donna begins to cry and moves to hug Raymond once more.

"What happened? Where is he?"

"Some piece of garbage shot him while on the road," said Oliver.

Raymond bangs his hands on the table. "Well, where is he?"

"We couldn't bring him back dear."

"Whaddaya mean. You couldn't bring him back. You left our dead son to rot on the road."

"We had no choice honey."

"Don't honey me. Where's Lou? I'm going to get him."

Oliver realized he needs to interrupt for any more words coming from his mother will only anger his father more. "Dad, we wanted to give Lou a proper burial but we had nothing to dig with, so we placed him in the river."

"The river?"

Ray reluctantly accepts this excuse and goes into the living room.

As the family had done so many times in the past, they sat down to watch the news. There was no sugar coating the dramatic changes happening in the world, especially in the Western hemisphere. On that night, the family watched in horror as the statistics were read on the air of millions across the globe infected or killed with the various strains of viruses floating around.

The president gives a briefing from inside the bunker: "We have credible knowledge of a secretive force that infiltrated the highest forms of government, media, business and military, with nefarious and evil plans. We have uncovered many of the saboteurs and traitors to not only this nation but also the global community. Justice will be swift and not merciful."

A commentary from the news anchor has to put on the best face possible:

"The situation may have reached a tipping point, as there are reports that the contagion has reached a leveling off. There's still is no word on the status of the Stingers and crop failures, and it's still much too dangerous to harvest. A spokesperson for the President confirms to us that there indeed is a secret cabal of organizers plotting to bring down the western world by unleashing deadly pathogens onto the public. The cabal is not believed to have been linked to any country."

"That's the government at its best for you: finding out when the shit has already hit the fan," said Raymond.

"Honey, do you think you should talk that way dear, after what we all just went through. Maybe the government is still watching us."

"If they still think that I pose a risk to the state, then we really don't have a future. I met Allen's old professor at school when I was in the camp. We escaped together but he was killed by one of those walking parasites. My mind is at peace with Allen's life and his deeds. It was something that just got out of hand."

They finished watching the news and huddled around the coffee table drinking leftover packets of tea boiled over the fireplace in a small pot.

"Ray, do you think it's safe to stay here?" asked Donna.

"Why, where do you want to go? Everywhere has the same problems."

"I know but your brother is up in the mountains. We tried to get up there but had troubles."

"Is that where Lou got killed?" asked Ray.

"Well, it was a long journey. We took Edward along with us. Laura died of the virus a day before and were moving up north when we ran into those bastards who shot Lou."

"What about Edward?" Was he shot too?"

"No. Some sort of diseased person came at him and he got sick. He was shot at a hospital by guards because he was infected."

"I know. They're not taking a chance on anyone infected."

"I don't think it's smart to stay here too much longer. I know we all had a hard time out there but I believe our only shot would be to keep moving. We should be with your brother."

"I tell you what: let's sleep on it and make a decision in the morning."

CHAPTER 45
RUN TO THE HILLS

The long wail of the fire siren wakes up the family. Each one of them looks out of their windows and sees thick black smoke coming from down the street a block or two away. Donna wonders if it was set by the owners or if it was caused by something else. Whatever the reason, the fire burned for hours before a response came from the fire department.

"What's the point coming now? The house is already burnt down," asked Lisa.

"They don't want any other houses getting burnt because of it Lisa," said Donna.

They took very quick cold showers and sat down for breakfast consisting of rice cakes and leftover tea.

After breakfast, they hold a short memorial service for Louis and Edward in the backyard.

"Ray, it's not safe here anymore. I don't think we should take a chance staying here any longer. We should get out."

"What makes you think that getting up to the country is going to make us safer?"

"Everyone is out to get over on his or her neighbor here. After Lou died, I thought coming back home was the best option. Thank God that we did if only to find you here but I think my thoughts were to die in a familiar place. The hell with that. I lost my whole sister's family and my son here. There's no future staying here."

"We need to be careful of others on the road dad. Can we just keep driving and not take the major highways?" asked Lisa.

"Sure, what the hell. I doubt there's going to be any teacher jobs opening any time soon anyway. I'm up for an adventure. Since everything is packed, let's just go."

Ray made the journey many times as a youth with his parents. It usually took three hours back then. This time it took nine. Ray and his family took the back roads but had to stop many times to clear the road from debris and cars that ran out of battery charge or gas. Remarkably, a few stores were open along the route. They saw Reds, maybe hundreds of them along the road and on large farms. The enclosed chicken and cow enclosures most likely presented them with resting spots during the day.

The winding road that led up to the mountain is littered with garbage and trailers. Corpses lined the ground, some fresh but most bloated from either bug bites or worse. A few children played out in the open seemingly oblivious to the macabre landscape surrounding them.

"It's been a long time since coming up here Ray. Are you sure this is the right way?" asked Donna.

"I'm sure but something tells me that the next three miles are going to be harder than the last two hundred getting up here."

He was right and only had to wait a few minutes for clarification. As they slowed down to the entrance that leads up to the mountain, they noticed on either side of the car were shotguns pointing at the family. "Get out of the car and keep your hands up," barked a man in his late fifties wearing a Pittsburgh Steelers jersey and spitting tobacco.

"What should we do?" asked Donna.

"Stay calm, we have to do what they say," said Ray.

"No we don't. Dad, they'll kill us," said Lisa, frightfully.

"We don't have a choice. Let's just get out slowly and do as they ask."

"What be your plans on our mountain?" asked the man with a full beard and trembling hands.

"My father has a small place just a few miles up the road. I believe my brother is up there now. He sent for us a while ago. We mean no harm to anyone," said Raymond, with his hands raised in a show of submission to the militia holding his family hostage.

"What's your brother's name?"

"Steven Brown."

"Don't mean shit to me. I ain't never heard of em."

The three men holding shotguns at the Brown family told them to get out of the vehicle.

After standing for a minute, the men order the family to get down on their knees. Raymond offers to give them the car and trailer full of food but his answer is a punch in the face.

"We don't need your shit from the diseased city," said the youngest member of the trio.

"Take it easy young buck," said Sam, the apparent leader of the pack.

After taunting the family with a mock execution and slaps to their faces, they are taken to a trailer with two large cages. One cage is full of dogs and the other empty. The family is pushed into the empty cage and told "not to go anywhere." This gives the trio a big laugh as they chew on their tobacco, openly displaying their rotten teeth as they chomp and spit.

The trailer park kidnappers radio into someone at the top of the mountain to try and make a trade. Initially, no deal is made.

"You can't trust those animals, they're just as bad as the Reds and would turn on you in a heartbeat," said the mayor of the mountaintop, turning to his private council the kitchen table, "We don't need anything they got."

"What are their names?" asked Steve, who by this time is one of the mayor's most trusted associates.

"Brown, I believe," said the mayor.

"No way, maybe it's my brother coming to the cabin. I told his wife to come up last year."

"Your name is Sterling not Brown?"

"I changed it to Sterling in the city before I left because I didn't want the vaccinations and chip implanted."

Noticing the possibility that Steve's family was being held hostage, the mayor had his minion's radio to the mountain outliers to see what they wanted for trade. Remarkably, all they wanted was to move up the mountain to a location where the rains wouldn't flood out their trailers.

The mayor thought it too risky but Steve convinced him to allow one trailer. The Brown's met at a rendezvous point up the mountain with dozens of

Blackstone's men including Steve. They briefly hugged each other and went back to the family ranch.

The two families ate and talked about the experiences of the past year. Steve told Ray they could build a small place for them if needed and that they were welcome to stay as long as they wanted.

CHAPTER 46
PLAN

The geniuses who weren't able to control events underground in their bunkers at D.C., decide to earn their bloated salaries by concocting a plan to eradicate or "neutralize" the infected humans. Enough of the toxin was introduced into the ecosystem by the spraying that it was now in the water cycle. The effect had been minimal to the general population, but the infected reacted strongly to the decreased pH in the rain: their exposed retina, not only caused an abnormality in their sight, but it reacted vigorously with the acidity in the rain.

The plan was to keep it raining long enough for whoever was left in the National Guard to easily track and kill the infected. No such plan existed for the Stingers and crop failures.

Theories regarding weather modification had always been lurking in the underground conspiracy world throughout America, but no government or military official ever admitted to it. Turns out, the kooks were right all along.

The President asks for a briefing regarding "Operation Noah's Ark" from his newly appointed chairman of the Joint Chiefs of Staff, General Walter Mudd.

"Will this work General?"

"Sure, Mr. President, we can target specific areas for weather anomalies, and yes can make it rain ninety percent of the time?"

"For how long?"

"Days... weeks, if needed."

"Now the downside. What's the effect?"

"Within a few days, we'll have massive flooding, more than two weeks- forget about it...the coastline will be effectively wiped out."

"But will we be able to kill enough of those Reds?"

"Sir, we'll have to be mobile and assuming they come out to drink, we'll blast the shit out of them."

"It's a risky venture but we gotta do something. Proceed with the operation."

The white streaks of puffy clouds line the sky up and down the coast, as every jet is utilized for the operation. Whether it works or not, Central Command doesn't share their plan with any other nation.

Indeed, the masters of the universe played God one last time. The rains came from all corners of the country, especially on the east coast. And so too, the Reds came out to drink and to get blinded. Evidently, their learning curve was well below the standard deviation. In an orgy of bullets and blood, the helicopter gunships and low flying jets decimate hordes of Reds attempting to quench their thirst.

The slaughter continues well into the second week after that the President asks for an update on the operation.

"Give me some good news General. We can't take any more shit sandwiches from you guys. Whatever is left of the country, we still need to go on."

"Yes, sir. Well… the operation is a success, maybe too much."

"What the hell does that mean. We don't have time for riddles. Are they all dead?"

"Just about everything that moved was targeted and neutralized sir but –"

"There's always a God damn but coming. Just say it. What went wrong?"

"Sir, we can't stop the rain."

The President bangs his hands on the desk. "We've condemned all of them to death."

Mother Nature has a way at laughing at us, especially when we try to trick her.

The rain eventually let up but only after three weeks. The General did get the estimation correct: there were no major cities left on the eastern shoreline, anymore. Nearly twenty-five percent of the population is washed out to sea or floating along some tributary.

Before all of D.C. goes under, the administration relocates to Colorado. Thousands of staff and logistical operators die in a watery grave alongside the proletariats in the suburbs. A few thousand manage to make it to the roofs of their apartment complexes, but in time they would wish they had been submerged along with the rest of their brethren.

The Stingers who lay dormant for the most part when the deluge of rain fell, came out with a fury in the aftermath. A target rich environment awaited them as tens of thousands of people languished on rooftops of houses and on high rise apartment buildings.

The flying demons attacked indiscriminately. They weren't spraying any toxin but their bite unleashed the virus that had infected millions prior to the rains. The infected soon outnumbered the non-infected on the rooftops and began to lunge at anyone in their vicinity. Faced with a choice of being targeted by a Stinger or a newly infected, thousands chose a one-way flight off the building. The water had receded, but not enough to cushion their fall. Most die on impact, a few managed to eke out an existence with their mangled bodies for a day or so.

Satellite footage is immune to any of the carnage left on the earth. Outside of Boulder, the administration views the new coastline of America, which doesn't include Florida, Rhode Island, Maryland and Delaware, anymore. The livable area for the majority of the other states along the coasts is reduced to less than one-third of their original capacity. There was, however, one correct decision in the latest fiasco concocted by the military: the operation was only enacted on one side of the country, not throughout the nation.

Deep within the Rocky Mountains, outside of Boulder, Colorado, General Mudd and a few of his subordinates offer their resignation to the President.

"What's the point General. You didn't misrepresent the plan. There's no way that you could have predicted the rains wouldn't stop. I own this calamity and if we survive will be known as the President who took down America."

CHAPTER 47

BLACKSTONE

Deep within the mountains, several miles where any hikers ever wonder, sits an armed camp enclosing a two-story modestly sized colonial house. It was built before the breakdown in the world by Dr. Stuart Blackstone. Barbed wire surrounds the exterior perimeter with another inner perimeter circled by a six-foot trench of water. The house is off the grid using geothermal, wind and wood as energy sources.

Blackstone was a Naval officer who went the traditional route at the academy and then finished up a twenty-year stint with Uncle Sam. Instead of consulting for a military contractor after his service, he pursued academia and received his doctorate in Environmental Science. When his brother, who was less ambitious as he, died of cancer at IS&G Industries, Stuart started writing and opening up his eyes. He soon discovered more than he bargained for and tried diplomatic channels to shut down IS&G. He was offered two choices: death or banishment.

The last stop on his Blackstone's journey was miles away from the beehive of the cities and slumber of suburbia. Nearly off the electronic grid, except for the occasional article criticizing big government, pharma and the military, Stuart sustained himself off the resources of the mountainside. Most thought he was a lunatic but a few regarded him as a prophet. To the mountain men and newly acquired Bottom Dwellers, he was the Mayor and he ran the mountainside.

The Mayor would put out weekly sermons on the status of the world and who was responsible for the reality they all faced. The real reasons were never quite clear nor true but the one fact he did know was that a hidden hand was behind all the mischief that started the calamity.

Steve and his family had made the best of their lives since coming up to the cabin over a year ago. It was not your typical cabin but rather a three-bedroom ranch that sat atop a hill alongside the Appalachian Trail. It had well water and a wood burning stove.

Steve was well equipped with enough guns to hold off a small army. He taught Tina, Thomas and Susan how to shoot small game: fox, squirrels and even rabbits were the usual nighttime entrees. It was a rule of Steve's that each family member walk around with at least a pistol, but the preferred method for patrolling the mountain would be a rifle, knife and a pistol.

Steve met Blackstone before the collapse when he was hunting in the woods. Several armed guards were escorting Stuart one day as they prowled the countryside in search of meat. Steve's marksmanship impressed Blackstone upon their first encounter and they quickly developed a friendship. Steve thought that the Mayor was the first intellectual he met that wasn't an asshole and they both shared a distrust of the government.

As in the city, a network of like-minded souls formed within the mountains. Their bond was to keep outside intruders from nesting in the mountains and that meant Reds, Stingers and people. Posts were set up with lookouts and Blackstone's compound became the central command for the Bottom Dwellers.

As the world slowly slipped into the shitter, the virtues of being disconnected to urban and suburban life drew thousands to the mountains. Daily, cars and trailers would make their way up to the hilltops. At first, people got along because of shared persecution, but the ones who could not fend for themselves became a liability and fell into despair.

It seems like you can call it civilization to some degree anywhere you go but after the natural comforts and food run out, the primitive animal is unleashed in all of us. The decadence that resulted in the cities and suburbs came to the mountains and hills.

Steve stopped counting the number of kills he had over the past year. It was good that he brought up thousands of rounds of ammunition because he needed it. No doubt, he racked up more kills in people than squirrels.

Steve became a trusted lieutenant in Blackstone's private army of the mountain. At first, they met weekly, but as the numbers increased and the natives became more ambitious, they needed to meet daily.

Blackstone called the new arrivals T-people, because they lived in trailers in the valleys and nested along the network of roads leading up to the hilltop. The

T-people were weekend warriors who bought trailers and made their way to the mountains seeking to sustain their family's future. They quickly realized that having guns without any training became a recipe for disaster. They shot wildly at anything that moved through the woods, with modest results. However, as the winter season arrived, the T-people fell apart.

Without adequate heat and a method for generating food, it became mayhem leading up to the mountainside. The T-people were never truly organized but as the first winter dragged on, the only viable way of sustaining themselves was to take, at gunpoint, anything from the newer visitors to the mountains.

"Steve, we got word that the T-people are going to make a run for the hilltop," said Blackstone.

"All of them?"

"No, not all but enough."

"What do they want?"

"What they always wanted. This hilltop, yours, mine and everything else. They're takers."

"They ain't never been organized. What's changed this time?"

"A little birdy informed me they formed an alliance for this one time and are coming tomorrow night."

"Well, what's the plan? Whaddaya have in mind boss?"

"We've never taking the fight to them and it's not my style but these are indeed desperate times. My goal has always been to live up here peacefully but I don't think that's an option any longer. We hit em tonight with everything we got and hopefully that will deter any further thoughts of coming up here."

"I agree Stuart but that means killing their families too."

"I think we could start with the armed men and then move to whoever is anxious enough to take us on. After that, we'll play it by ear, okay?"

"OK."

Susan and the kids stayed at the ranch while a two dozen men and women including Steve, arm themselves for their nighttime mission.

Steve and the other expert sharpshooters take sniper positions either in the trees or in the bushes along the route, one mile from the T-people hideout. Two scouts lead the way and immediately take a couple of shots at one of the campers.

This draws around twenty people out of the trailers tracking the scouts. The apparent leader of the T-people radios to another set of comrades alerting them to this preemptive strike by Blackstone. Another dozen or so T-people brethren take chase up the hillside. As they get closer to the scouts, Steve and the other snipers pin them down with high caliber shots. Several minutes of getting picked off one by one is enough for the leader to call for a retreat, but Blackstone and the rest of his troop set an ambush for them.

As the armed T-people make their way back down, they are sandwiched between hundreds of rounds of choreographed bullets flying at them and precision rounds from snipers on the other end. Outgunned and undisciplined, the T-people scatter and are picked off like fleeing birds at a pigeon shoot. Blackstone loses one man while all but two of the T-people survive- apparently fleeing for their lives.

Blackstone and the others decide not to proceed any further to the trailers.

"We aren't mercenaries," he said, "I hope they get the message and will not seek revenge for this action."

"I'm not so sure of that boss. I think we should finish the job down there."

"Steve, do you hear yourself. You came up here wanting to live off the land and now you want to hunt the rest of their families down. You know that'll mean killing kids, possibly all of them unarmed. That's not how I do things. Are you prepared for that on your conscious?"

"What's the difference? Without their arms to defend themselves, and alone down there, they'll be ripped apart by others as they come to the mountain. Is a slow death better than what we just did?"

The other men seem to nod their heads in agreement to what Steve has said.

"What separates us from who we just killed Steve is a code of conduct. You remember that don't you?"

"That was a world away boss."

"I won't live in a world without any rules. That's how we got in this mess. The fat cats took everything without any checks and balances- polluted the world with technology, pills, and robotics. No different from what the T-people did- just on a lower level is all."

"I'm not an educated person Stuart but I do know a few things and one of them is revenge. If someone just killed my dad, you better believe I'd be gunning for them. Mark my words, none of us are gonna sleep good knowing those kids down there will be coming for us some time down the line, seeking revenge for their parents."

"If we pull through this nightmare Steve, we need our humanity. Going down there and 'finishing the job' is not what humanity is about. It might as well be every man for himself. Is that what you want?"

Steve clearly not in agreement with Blackstone, and wants to continue with his line of persuasion but realizes the Mayor has made up his mind and said, "Fine, you're the boss. Let's go back."

Blackstone and the rest of the crew make their way back up the mountain. Steve and another sniper carry the lone dead person of the attack along with them.

A long recognizable scream is heard as they approach their cabin.

"That's Tina," said Steve, as he drops the person he is carrying and hurries to get closer to the cabin. The screams get louder.

The others join Steve and race to the cabin.

"Steve, slow down. You'll get picked off before getting in," said Blackstone.

Steve reluctantly listened and takes up a position outside the window of his cabin. The others flank the rear and side of the house.

As Steve peers through the window, his eyes widen and his face boils with rage. He races to the front door pulling the lever on his rifle hoping to get off one shot as he enters.

Blackstone can see Susan lying on the floor, face first with fresh blood pouring from her covered body. Thomas is sitting on the bed with a rifle to his head, petrified and with tears coming down his eyes.

Another man in his later years has Tina bent over and is having his way with her. He slams her head on the table, which knocks the scream out of her. She glances up barely conscious to see the door come flying open.

"Daddy!" she said, looking up at him.

Two shots, milliseconds apart, tear into the rapist. Instinctively, without thinking of Thomas on the bed, he covers his daughter in his arms as the other man holding the rifle is startled and moves back. Thomas jumps off the bed as the man regains his composure and fires a shot at him. It misses and before another one comes his way, Blackstone, who had the man in his sights, discharges a well-placed .308 Winchester round into the man's eye. His head lunges back as the rifle falls from his hands.

Blackstone and his men race into the cabin and finish off the man without using any more ammunition.

After he gets his daughter cleaned up, Steve, Blackstone and the others head back down to visit the rest of the T-people and to finish off the job.

CHAPTER 48
HEARTACHE

The ensuing weeks had all family members training with Uncle Steve on survival techniques. They were all taught how to hunt, fish and defend themselves. It was an arduous and stressful time with each other but for the first time in a long while things settled down to a comfortable albeit strange type of normal.

Steve explained defense tactics to Donna and Raymond and told them that Dr. Blackstone had developed some new methods to fight not only the bugs but also the crop failures. He told them that at least once a week a horde of Reds would try and come up the side of the mountain looking for water.

Blackstone believed and proved the theory that the Reds and to some extent the Stingers were submissive to salt water. Every house on the mountaintop was equipped with tanks for saltwater and hoses to spray at the Reds should they breach the interior wall. When sprayed directly at the eyes of the Reds, they would fall in excruciating pain allowing others to put them out of their misery with a knife to the head to save ammunition.

As the weather turned nicer, Tina and Lisa decided to venture off to test their archery skills. Oliver stayed at the cabin but Steve insisted that someone accompany the girls. Thomas volunteered to go with them.

"I don't want them going down to the valley, understand young man?"

"Dad, I'm old enough to handle myself," said Tom, "I can protect them."

"I know son but any sign of trouble, call on the radio, ok?"

"Okay."

Thomas and the girls trekked over newly melted snow slogging their way down a path. The girls move quicker as if they purposely want to leave Tom behind.

"Girls, what's your rush, hold up."

"Hurry up, slow poke. Try and keep up."

The girls move ahead of Tom and see a creek running down the trail through a cavern. Stains of purple flowed on the top and the sides as multicolored specks of light protruded from the pebbles and rocks below.

"Why's it purple?" asked Lisa.

"It's been like that for a long time now," said Tina. "I think it's because of those flying bugs that sprayed."

"You don't see them anymore, do yah?"

"No, not really, but we hear them sometimes."

"I saw them up close on the way up here. They came down and stung just about everyone."

Thomas was the first to see them before the humming got closer. He ran to the girls to get them under some sort of cover but they were too far away. He yelled up to them but they laughed and ignored him.

"Girls, turn back. Get out of there."

The humming got closer. The cold air didn't faze the Stingers who were known to come out at night but apparently evolved in the high elevation. They descended in a V pattern on the girls. Tina and Lisa ran as fast as they could back to the cabin. Lisa stumbled and fell over a log in the path. The Stingers were only a few feet away as the humming was at a fever pitch now.

Lisa pushed Tina away who jumped into the creek nearby.

"Stay in the water as long as you can Tina!" yelled Tom.

"Tom, what are we gonna do? They're all around," cried Lisa, as she makes a feeble attempt to swat at the tiny creatures swarming around her world, growing smaller by the second.

Tom covered Lisa with his body but the Stingers were relentless. They moved their way around the heavy winter coats and into the necks and faces of both Tom and Lisa leaving them neutralized and screaming in pain.

They were too far away to be heard but it wouldn't have made a difference.

Tina lay in the water periodically covering her face with ice-cold droplets and small rocks. Perhaps in a different scenario, laying in the cold water in the summer heat mesmerized by the purpled colored lights, it would have dazzled her; but today, it was a frozen horror show. She was petrified, cold and invisible. The only sound she made was the chattering of her teeth.

Shivering, crying and scared that she would soon be stung, she stayed in the water for what seemed to be hours but was only minutes. When she got out and inspected her brother and cousin, she fell to her knees and cried.

How in the world do I tell dad about this? She thought to herself.

She contemplated waiting for the others to arrive and wanted to scream at the top of her lungs, however, she couldn't scream even if she tried. Her clothes started to harden and freeze up after only a few minutes being out of the water.

She made the slow walk back to the cabin to deliver the horrific news to the family.

CHAPTER 49
WAR

The Chinese delegation met earlier in the week with the leaders of the Order who expressed a desire to seek refuge and to give a thorough briefing on what led to the present situation.

Burkman and two dozen of the highest-ranking members of the Order arrive in his private jet and land in Beijing under cover of darkness. They have a midnight meeting with the Prime Minister. There are no members of Chinese ancestry in the Order and most of the Chinese are skeptical of their designs. Even with billions to offer, they are rebuffed and sent packing.

Three nuclear-armed nations unaffected to this point meet in in Karachi, Pakistan. The cover for the meeting is traded but the real intention is to take advantage of the deteriorating situation in the Western world, especially in America. They call their pact the Eastern Alliance with an agreement to defend each other in the event of an armed attack by another country or countries.

"Mr. Prime Minister, do you think the situation will require us to take up arms?" asked the Ali Khan, the Pakistani ambassador.

"We met with the originators of this crisis. It seems that they cannot control the events any longer and the Americans are going to eliminate their movement. They wanted protection and disclosed their true intentions for the world to us. We are not in agreement with the reduction in population. We have adhered to the Western demands for too long, slaughtering millions of our daughters and it's time we take our rightful place as rulers of the world and restore our dynasty. We will increase our population going forward – not reduce it. We sent those demons back," said Yuan Mei, the Chinese Prime Minister.

"Would it not be wise to just wait until the virus has spread to such an extent that their countries are no longer viable?" asked Mr. Khan.

The Chinese Prime Minister agrees with the question and then said, "Waiting is a good option but we are not sure that the contagion will be limited to the Western hemisphere. In fact, Russia is infected and they are our neighbors, as you are aware. Let us not forget if this contagion continues and spreads throughout the world, the priority will be a cure and we may need the West."

"I don't agree. We should strike now and at least get our peninsula back from those devils. It would favor Pakistan as well. You could get Kashmir back in one strategic blow," said the North Korean ambassador.

"The Americans as with any empire do not go down so easily. I don't think they would come to the aid of India but letting the peninsula go after all these years will not be an option for them, in my opinion," said Mr. Khan.

"We have received a message from the American Ambassador before arriving to our summit. They are requesting that we provide fresh water and grain shipments to them in exchange for concessions," said Mr. Mei.

"What are those concessions?" asked the North Korean ambassador.

"They are turning a blind eye to an aggression from the north, provided there are only conventional weapons in the theatre. It appears that patience was the preferred strategy to use against the west."

Thousands of rockets and missiles rain down on Seoul, South Korea one week following the summit in Karachi. Millions of civilians evacuate the city as six hundred thousand South Korean Army units' march north closely followed by twenty-eight thousand American forces. They cross the 38th parallel after four days of around the clock bombing from the South Koreans and American warships off the coast.

If ever there was a meat grinder, this was it. Thousands were killed or maimed daily on both sides. Without the American Air Force, South Korea would have been doomed quickly but every type of conventional bomb was dropped on the north stopping their advance. Then, early on the thirteenth day, the North Korean leader forgot about the virtues of patience and unleashed two of his prized possessions on Seoul. Residents of the metropolis awoke for the last time for in an instant, two thermonuclear bombs hit the center and outskirts of the city. Seoul was reduced to ashes and smoke in seconds. The fallout killed many more thousands in the ensuing days and months.

The armada off the coast of Korea braced to launch its arsenal of special weapons to the north while the admirals stood by waiting for the order from

Washington. It never came. There was no point. The immediate blast and following radioactive dispersal left nearly fifteen million dead in Seoul. For all practical purposes, South Korea was lost forever.

"Mr. President, Korea is lost. We must strike back on Pyongyang now!" ordered General Stack, Supreme Commander of the Pacific fleet.

"I think you're forgetting who's in charge here General. If it's a lost cause, then why strike the north and risk further retaliation and nuclear response?" asked the President, rhetorically.

"Inaction will only invite further belligerence, Mr. President. We can't let them get away with this, you must order the strike."

"I have listened to Generals enough during my term and all that it's brought to me and the country is more misery. No, I will not order a strike. We're not at recess, you simpleton. If you could think rationally, then you would realize that would mean China will retaliate on us. Moreover, I know you are perfectly fine with that but I believe we have enough problems."

"But sir –," He tried to continue but could not. "You're relieved of your duty. Get him out of here right now."

Two large marines grabbed the General by his sleeves and escorted him out of the bunker while a call came in from the Indian Prime Minister.

"Mr. President, Pakistan has unleashed its military into the demilitarized Kashmir region. This is a courtesy call to let you know this will not stand and we will retaliate."

"Mr. Prime Minister, our administration strongly encourages you not to retaliate and allow Pakistan to take the region."

"This cannot stand Mr. President. My Generals are massing our legions as we speak and I will order an effective response as soon as this conversation is over."

"Mr. Prime Minister, I believe you should reconsider that decision. China has an aggression pact with Pakistan and a strike on them will invoke a response from China."

"Well then, we will expect your support to prevent that from happening, Mr. President."

"No sir, you cannot count on that. You are on your own."

China did not have to intervene militarily on the Korean Peninsula nor in Pakistan. They remained on the sidelines and watched as Pakistan and Korea were weakened.

Deals are made in public and some are made in private. India had a backdoor deal with the Chinese not to interfere with the Pakistani advance if nuclear arms were not introduced into the theatre. Although of different sects, Pakistan and Iran were the only two Muslim nations that were equipped with nuclear weapons and the Iranians were not going to allow Pakistan to be swallowed up by India. A million-man army flowed across the Afghanistan border into India's western front. This allowed the Pakistanis to save face and regain any lost territory.

The fighting continued into its second month with hundreds of thousands of casualties on the Indian subcontinent. When it looked like the advantage was in Pakistan's favor, an unexpected ally came down from the north.

Russia, initially infected with the virus, suddenly exploded with the contagion across their southern border and into the Afghanistan/ Pakistan region. Pakistan offered a truce but the Indian's realized it was their chance to finally put an end to the conflict and resisted any peace offerings. They continued to crush the Muslim hordes to the north and west until most of their troops started to come down with the contagion.

Indeed, the plague had reached the subcontinent and spread to millions of Indian troops who threatened to bring the virus back home.

Five nuclear-tipped rockets were launched at India's own men to prevent the virus from coming back to their cities. This wild gross miscalculation and tactical use of the nuclear option convince the Muslim alliance to stop any further aggression, but the impediment of the virus was only short lived. It continued to spread from Bangladesh and into the eastern regions of the Indian subcontinent.

China, who thought they could sit this one out soon realized that microbes do not discriminate. The plague continued across all of Asia and to the southern shores of Vietnam.

The effect on the world from this new wave of savagery and bloodshed between nations had its greatest impact on Japan, who vowed not to let a nuclear-armed Korea, especially the North be at their doorsteps.

The Japanese Prime Minister called a special meeting with his cabinet to discuss the crisis on the mainland.

"We have not initiated any militaristic moves in nearly one hundred years and do not wish to conquer any lands or peoples but we cannot stand by and watch as other neighbors in our hemisphere develop conventional, nuclear and other forms of warfare that jeopardize the future of the homeland. We will develop our own defenses against this new threat," said the Japanese Prime Minister to his cabinet.

All who are present agree with the necessity to prepare for war.

CHAPTER 50
RISING SUN

Masters at imitation and ingenuity for generations, the Japanese saw the world imploding and realized their island was not going to be a buffer to the assault any longer. Their scientists along with the Americans worked around the clock on a cure for the virus but also a strategy to weaken Korea and China as they struggled to put down their own Red menace.

Since there were different strains of the virus, it was difficult to formulate an antidote; however, at their joint research facility in Osaka, the government provided resources to try and fulfill that objective.

On the second and more militaristic front, some high-ranking officials in the Japanese military wanted to proceed in another direction and held a private meeting with the civilian leader.

"Mr. Prime Minister, the committee implores you and the government to consider the possibility of giving us the ability to make a weapon from these creatures and to give authorization for Operation Rising Sun," said General Hito.

The Prime Minister is surrounded by other generals and his chief of staff who smile and encourage him to pursue the venture.

"Mr. Prime Minister, we may never get a chance like this again."

"General, how quickly can this be accomplished and what are the chances of failure in this endeavor to the homeland?"

"Sir, there is nothing special in the development or the procedure for these weapons. The Americans have been doing this for quite some time with varying degrees of success. We worked with them on several occasions in Africa implementing the technique and could continue with their assistance in Osaka on that goal."

"If it was so effective, then why do we have such chaos in the world?" asked the Prime Minister.

"Sir, the Americans had many high-ranking rogue agents that swore allegiance to a foreign cult. Their motives were different from ours."

"I hope you are right. If the Chinese and Koreans survive this plague on their doorsteps only to find another attack linked to us, we may not live to see any more sunrises."

"Sir, there are millions of these things around the globe; there is no way that we can be blamed for more of them coming out of the east. We can always admit to the manufacture of these creatures for defenses purposes in the event they make their way to our shores."

"I hope you are correct in this analysis, General. I am not fully convinced but proceed with caution."

The government of Japan convinces themselves that the idea of bugs for warfare was ingenious and secretly worked with the Americans to produce their own crop of these deadly troops. Huge automobile conglomerates such as Toyota and Mitsubishi were converted to manufacturing facilities for raising millions of flying bugs for battle.

They weren't the only ones to have nefarious designs for the planet. Simultaneously, this strategy was being worked on in various capitals throughout the world, including Beijing, Islamabad, New Delhi, and even in the Middle East.

Instead of coming together as one race of people to come up with a global solution to the crisis, countries already reeling from the plague and Stingers focused their attention on taking advantage of their neighbors weakened state to annihilate them.

The madness was everywhere.

Is the idea and notion of peace between nations only in fairy tales? Was this the case throughout the early days of recorded history and basic animal instinct: continually looking for weakness in an opponent or in a tribe and then purposely planning their demise for control and dominance?

The obvious answer might be yes, and one only needs to watch a nightly sporting event to witness legions of fans cheering the destruction of their opponents, which has become a multibillion-dollar business or at least used to be.

Thus, it began. Japan who was isolated from the world and was not affected by the virus, Reds or Stingers used their knowledge and skills to work on two fronts with the assistance and military pressure from America.

The research facility on the mainland of Japan, located ten kilometers from Osaka's city center was named Sector 11. It was housed by leading scientists from

America and the homeland. The public mission mentioned to the world was a cure for the viruses.

America still had military strength even in its dismal state and their mission was a solution to the Reds menacing their country. The Japanese were focused closer to home. They wanted to launch Operation Rising Sun using the methods developed at Sector 9 years ago and worked in conjunction with the military to accomplish that goal.

It took weeks to develop the new race of Killer bugs from the east. But by using the DNA of captured Chinese prisoners, the Japanese developed a race of Stingers that could target only people of Chinese descent or so they thought. The bugs were programmed to go after the enemy and then explode after making the sting so their origin and chemical structure could not be analyzed to the source of their creation.

The Japanese over the course of several months finally perfected their own army of killer bugs. They launched their Stingers to the west of the island.

The Generals watched and eagerly awaited for the reports to come back.

The Stingers swarmed together and left for the Chinese mainland blackening the sky for miles. When they had reached their destination and city centers, they descended on residents as programmed, but instead of a planned one one-person bug attack, they primarily focused all their aggression on a few people.

For all their planning, the outcome was that hundreds of thousands of these killer bugs annihilated a few Chinese and then exploded in a mass of organic material hurling their collateral damage onto a few people. The result was a gross imagery and an uncomfortable inconvenience having people wipe the debris from their eyes.

The generals were brought to Tokyo for an update on Operation Rising Sun.

"Well, General Hito, what has been the result of billions of yen on this project that you and your comrades promised would give Japan a foothold on the Chinese mainland and forever regain our dominance in the world," asked the Prime Minister, incredulously.

"Sir, the early results proved that the flying insects as weapons have the potential but we must continue development. We have had a minor setback but it would be unwise to stop at this point. In my opinion, we should continue."

"I'll tell you what is unwise General, for me to listen to any more of this foolishness. You have brought shame and dishonor to our people and most likely a nuclear retaliation from the Chinese mainland. Have you thought of that?"

"The Chinese would not dare. They have too much to lose and besides we have America as an ally."

"You fool. The Americans are for the Americans as are the Chinese for the Chinese. This is natural and to be expected. You are supposed to give me good advice. The smart strategy would have been to wait for the other countries to get weaker and were on their knees, now we look like the devils for launching the attack."

"Sir, we have other options for these bugs and have developed toxins for their release. We need another opportunity to demonstrate how effective these weapons can be."

"Enough of this madness! History proves that one mistake leads to another without a correction. We will not pursue any more of this. I hope you do the honorable thing and relieve yourself of duty: the old fashion Japanese way."

In this regard, the General does not disappoint. He took a three-hundred-year-old Samurai sword and performed his duty well.

The Chinese, not wanting to be outdone by their neighbors across the sea had some quality artistry to show off as well. Their factories and facilities churned out their version of flying killing insects and spread their form of madness up and down the coastline, primarily on the Southeast region of Asia.

Up until a few years back, the countries of Southeast Asia nearly rivaled the much larger country of China to the north in industrial production. The importation of Chinese Stingers into the region reversed years of progress by decimating its young workforce.

Other capitals followed suit and across the Asian continent, flying bugs that were programmed to target other countries and people performed their dastardly deeds without any hesitation.

From the Indian Ocean to the South China Sea, millions of these flying troops attacked other bugs, troops and civilians that got in their way. The smaller yet quickest Stingers came from India who had programmed their bugs to return to the factories after launch and didn't implode.

Chinese and Indian bugs gave the most ferocious battles known to date in the Bug Wars of 2043. They would sting and fight each other until one group held the upper hand and drive the others away. They would then feast on the spoils of victory: the residents, crops and people down below. One country would gain territory over the other for a short while but not one country capitulated and lost anything other than their minds in this new form of butchery.

CHAPTER 51
SEMITICA

The final war of the Levant- states of Syria, Israel, Lebanon, Palestine and Jordan- ended almost eighty years of aggression and armed futility in the year 2025. Aided with Russian firepower, the Syrians advanced first capturing the Golan Heights back from Israel. Soon after that, Jordanian troops crossed over into the West Bank and onto the edges of Jerusalem. Israel, who had been demoralized because of the 8.5 earthquake in Tel Aviv and along the coastline, did not have the resources to effectively fight back. Their other cities struggled with the existing population fighting the insurgency of the Palestinians. Many local religious leaders thought the calamity was brought on by God and urged the citizens not to take up any arms.

Finally, with their backs against the wall and on the brink of annihilation, Israel let loose on two of its coveted resources: two miniature nuclear-tipped missiles, one in the northeast deserts of Jordan and one in the western edge of the Iraqi Desert. Although the human casualties were in the tens of thousands, the psychological effect was immense.

Out of the ashes and radioactive decay arose Suleiman Hamshuk and Shimon Barak, the Syrian and Israeli presidents, respectively. Both men having lost close relatives in the carnage realized that enough was finally enough.

The long-awaited peace treaty was not signed between warring parties but between cousins. The visionary leaders agreed to form a united country for all Jews, Arabs and Semites who wished to live together. They called the country SEMITICA.

Semitica, comprised of the previously autonomous regions of the Levant, held their capital in Jerusalem with the old Arab capitals remaining as state capitals of their respective regions. The newly discovered oil and gas fields of the Syrian

Desert combined with the technical expertise in Israel and surrounding entrepreneurial spirit in states such as Palestine made Semitica a global powerhouse not just in the region but the world.

The unique power-sharing agreement, kept the President a Jew with veto power and a Sunni as Prime Minister, effectively running the day-to-day operation of the country. Finally, a Christian and a Shiite formed the Supreme Council with each having veto power to overrule critical decisions. A true one hundred percent consensus was needed for any legislative action.

At first, radicals and hardcore zealots on all sides tried to sabotage and destroy the new nation targeting of all places holy sites in Jerusalem. If not for the visionary leaders Barak and Hamshuk, the newly constructed republic would not have lasted, but in the ensuing years, Semitica flourished.

This new alliance of Semites didn't please everyone in the region. Turkey and Iran, bitter rivals for many years formed an Islamic pact to return Damascus to the Arab and Islamic world. First, they tried diplomatic and economic sanctions against their one-time ally but that quickly failed. Next, they tried the military.

One million men poured across the eastern Syrian desert into Deir Ez Zor and got to the gates of Palmyra. The ruins that stood for thousands of years were smashed as a prelude to the savagery planned for the capital.

In the North, the other advance led by the Turks seized Aleppo and were marching towards the industrial city of Homs. During the last battle for the city of Hama, the Syrians put up a valiant effort but the Turkish troops in a frenzy of killing and bloodlust, slaughtered every military personnel and spared relatively few civilians. Outgunned and with a weakened Air Force, the Syrian state was desperate. The Turks who once ruled over the country nearly two hundred years ago were positioned only a few kilometers from the center of Damascus.

A frantic call is made to Jerusalem from Damascus whereupon the leader of the Syrian state requested assistance from their joint command located in Tel Aviv.

The capital of the newly formed nation of Semitica did not disappoint. Missile after missile rained down upon the troops occupying Syrian territory as well as landing in the capitals of Tehran and Istanbul.

As in a hand of chess, the Iranian and Turks believed that they could capture Damascus before enough of their citizens and troops would be killed. When the call came into each capital that the next round of missiles would be tipped with a special payload from the joint command, the message was received loud and clear. The armies moved back across the borders and no new escalation was attempted at a member state of Semitica. This destruction moved the Syrian people to form a true peace with the other states, especially, Israel in their union. A peace that meant sharing of cultures, language and bread – not just a piece of paper declaring peace between leaders.

Semitica bloomed after that for nearly a decade until the Western world descended into darkness with the bug, crop and contagion crossing into the eastern world.

Burkman and his comrades of the Order met with the Supreme Council to discuss sanctuary and to avoid any retaliation from America or Europe. They told the council they were bringing one trillion dollars to the table as tribute for their acceptance into Semitica. The looted funds were stored in the Bahamas and in Swiss bank accounts and they were willing to transfer it all over to Hamshuk and Barak.

The leaders of the Order explained their rationale for orchestrating the demise of America and much of the Western world.

Burkman explained the logic to the council, "We could rule the world with less people to manage and all the resources at our fingertips. And we only ask that you conform to the Order of the brotherhood."

Other members raised their left hands and professed their loyalty to the Order and allegiance to one another.

"You have the nerve to come to our chamber and profess allegiance to some sort of blood cult with goals to rule the world and believe we will support this. I don't know what else you are drinking besides the blood of animals or people but this will never stand."

The members of the Order look at each other in disbelief.

"In addition, it is my understanding you met with the Chinese first. Is that true?" asked Hamshuk.

"Yes, that's correct Mr. Prime Minister but those heathens are against any more population control and don't believe in the brotherhood. We feel you would understand."

"What makes you feel that we are for a reduction in the population. Who gave your group the authority to kill millions of people for some New World Order?"

"Mr. Prime Minister, if you will just allow us time to explain the benefits of the Order…"

"No, you have no other places to hide and like cockroaches, you scurry around the globe seeking refuge from retribution. The Chinese are not foolish and neither are we. You think that we are a backward people who will idolize false deities and humanity. We cannot be bought and you have made a great mistake. Your future is sealed."

The members of the Order realize they made a grave mistake coming to the Middle East and frantically mumble to themselves. They then offer payment to the leaders of Semitica for safe travel to New Zealand.

"You need to pay for your deeds. You have tried to remake the world in the vision only God can do. Your folly has brought calamity to the world. If the Americans and Europeans realize you were here and we let you escape, we will look complicit in your actions. You must atone for your evil deeds."

"We make no insult to your state and people, we thought you would accept our terms and allow refuge. Accept our gift as a deposit for perhaps consideration into the future and we will be on our way."

"No, you thought we could be bought with trinkets of gold because we love money. Isn't that so?"

"No, Mr. President, we meant no disrespect."

"Take them away," said Hamshuk. "We will show you what we think of your brotherhood of devils and false Gods."

Retribution was swift but not merciful for the representatives of the Order. Their hands depicting their deity were cut off and placed in front of them as they are buried up to their necks in the desert sand. They are left there for hours in agonizing pain, losing copious amounts of blood, contemplating their grizzly future and past deeds.

Finally, their faces and heads were smothered in honey. Scorpions and snakes were brought from miles away to feast on the apostates. Not one of them pledged allegiance to the brotherhood any longer but rather prayed to God for forgiveness.

Several miles further up the desert just outside Beersheba resides a facility the Semites have named the Damascus Gate. Like their counterparts in the USA, it is a military factory working on the latest technologies for warfare. Unlike in the USA, Damascus Gate has a sole mission: to manufacture a race of bugs not for warfare against humans but against the Stingers and Reds that have infected the world.

Benjamin Elizeir runs the facility at the Damascus Gate. He is a career military person who fought in many battles and earned the respect of all people throughout Semitica.

"We have been tasked by the Supreme Council with rollout of these creatures by weeks' end. Are they ready to deploy?" asked Elizeir of his General Manager, Ali Muktar.

"Sir, we have some final modifications to the troops. They will be ready and on schedule as planned."

"Good, the future of the world will depend on it. We cannot afford to have the mission fail. It is our time to show the world what the Semitic mind is truly capable of."

"Yes sir. They will be ready."

Each tiny brain of the insects is equipped with a microprocessor implant representing the most cutting edge technology in the world. These microprocessors are tied into the DNA of these new Stingers that have the capability to make high-level decisions: artificial intelligence for bugs.

The mission of the desert Stingers is to seek out every other Stinger from California to the Chinese plains and eradicate them. In addition, any Reds that are seen, the desert Stingers are to seek out their eyes and remove them, which allows the locals time to kill them more easily.

The workers perfect the technology and manufacture millions of the desert Stingers for a mass invasion of the world during the summer of 2043. The Damascus Gate facility not only produces the first generation of AI Stingers but has ample room for the insects to multiply. There is no need to implant the second generation because the genetic information is passed down to their offspring.

The 110-degree heat provides a good backdrop for the release of the Stingers as the military men and women unleash the hatches from the facility. The humming of the creature's echo like a dragon erupting from the underworld. The sky is darkened with a dark brown mass that moves in several different directions.

Reports come back almost instantly of the success of these warrior creatures. With a voracious appetite and relentless zeal, they attack and kill every Stinger from the East while simultaneously plucking the eyes out of every Red they encounter below them.

At first, people are afraid to come out when they see these larger and smarter hornets attacking over their heads, but then they quickly realize they are the saviors to their respective homelands. Streets are lined with children waving to them as adults clap and cheer their arrival.

Like wasps devouring honeybees, the desert Stingers rip the heads off the old Stingers in midair and continue in flight to the next bug. The programming that allows them to target the rotten diseased DNA of the infected masses makes it easy to cleanse the world. They would rest for a few minutes and then continue their aerial march from country to country and creature to creature.

CHAPTER 52
TURN ABOUT

The success of the desert Stingers compels the world to view Semitica with a degree of respect that was not known in that part of the world for a thousand years. Exposure of the Order and its Machiavellian designs satiated many in the world. President Barak went on air explaining their punishment and how their tentacles of influence had stretched across military, business and the multinational corporations, primarily IS&G. Many low-level Order subjects either killed themselves or were rounded up and executed. The few that escaped went underground like cockroaches avoiding the light of day.

Barak was invited to the United Nations to make a speech.

"Fellow citizens of the world, the time for pain and blaming other countries must come to an end. The effect of greed, power and misplaced authority is on display for all the world to see. Semitica offers the world a new approach to living where former enemies can live in peace. It is our right to seek retribution from the evildoers to this worldwide calamity but we ask no retaliation to any one country or continent."

As with everything in life, for every cause there is an effect. And so is the case with the dramatic warriors of the desert. The residual fallout of the P2040 and M2200 spraying left much of the countryside and waterways polluted. Only a few countries had drinkable pure water. Many died from cholera and other water-borne diseases.

The desert Stingers never returned to their base in the Negev but there were reports that they drifted north to Iceland to hibernate. Whatever the outcome, people were content that they killed every Red on the planet.

Much of the landscape was toxic from the pesticides and spraying did earlier. The only real plants that seemed to flourish were weeds, dandelions and other less edible vegetation. Native borne insects that fed on vegetation started to mutate and display unusual physical characteristics. Although there didn't appear to be predators for farmers to be concerned with, tilling the fields still became a dangerous occupation.

However, for the first time in years, a collective sigh of relief swept across all of humanity. The rebuilding and healing phase came next. The United Nations returned to New York City and the President of the USA addressed the world along with other world leaders pledging support and a new era of peace throughout the world.

It was short lived.

The AI Stingers that were thought to have hibernated north came back with a vengeance a few months later. Their intelligence must have increased, for they were known to have been busy building their own type of cities high in the trees. Millions of them worked in unison constructing large oval shaped dormitories where they congregated and planned their next move.

As unusual as it would sound, the AI Stingers had a central authority protected around the clock with the largest and most aggressive troops. They had scouts that would patrol their homeland for anyone unlucky enough to trespass. Had the military been aware of their maleficent designs, they could have used conventional bombs to eradicate them during the window of opportunity that was available.

The AI Stingers, no longer content with bugs and diseased humans, turned their attention on people. There was no apparent logical reason for the change: most likely the feeling, if there is such a thing for insects, or the passed down trait of dominating others similar in design to their programmers, was a plausible answer to this new treachery and madness.

It was panic and pandemonium all over again.

The nuclear-armed countries were at their wit's end and convened another emergency meeting at the UN, which was now functioning back in New York City. Permanent members of the Security Council that now included Semitica, questioned them about new AI Stingers and their whereabouts.

"We find it strange that the regions of Semitica and the Levant are not affected by this latest crisis. Why haven't the AI Stingers returned back to their bases in the Levant?" asked the Chinese ambassador. The Russia, Korean and even the American ambassador glazed at the ambassador from Semitica for answers.

"My fellow ambassadors, we offered the world a solution to the crisis and exposed the group behind the madness. Are you insinuating that we are behind this latest calamity onto mankind?" asked ambassador Harrir.

"There are no accusations at this time Mr. Ambassador. We wish to know if your country can return these things back to their bases in the desert so we can more easily destroy them," said the Korean ambassador.

"We have tried and will continue to present another solution to the world but rest assured that these Stingers are not under our control and we will do whatever is in our power or what is the consensus of this panel to assist. We wish to do what is in the best interest of the planet and are open for suggestions."

The citizens of the world could not tolerate another round of flying death from the air. Out of sheer frustration and backed up with no clear rationale other than vengeance, Russian, Chinese and Korean missiles tipped with hydrogen bombs decimated the bases of the AI Stingers in Iceland. A once serene and beautiful country was reduced to a barren radioactive wasteland. Of course, the Stingers were not home for the arrival of their foreign gifts but it made no difference to the leaders of the countries releasing the bombs. They had to show some sort of action, misplaced and foolish as it was.

In Jerusalem, a cabinet meeting was held to discuss the recent events and the mistrust displayed at the United Nations. Although Harrir told the truth at the security meeting in New York, he sensed that some of the countries didn't believe him, which was conveyed back to the cabinet.

"We have hundreds of our own missiles that can target the countries that accuse us of this situation. I know they are planning something evil for us. We saved the world and this is how we are to be repaid?" said Barak, rhetorically to his cabinet.

"Sir, we cannot fight all those countries that are nuclear armed. It would be sheer madness and suicide," said Daniel Kibbut, Finance Minister for Semitica.

"You are correct Daniel. We can't fight them all nor do we wish a fight, but they should know that the leaders of their capitals would not be safe if we become a target of their aggression. It is the same old story repeatedly; they say we lie and cheat and wish to take over the world. They are the ones who brought this destruction to the human race. Do we not have a right to be paranoid? General, inform the high command to be on alert."

The AI Stingers continued their rampage. They now have evolved a form of communicating with other members by using strange chirping sounds in the air on when and who to attack. They would use military techniques such as flanking and ambushes for their enemies. Locals who could not wait for the military to come and assist use primitive flamethrowers to defend their territory. It would be to no avail for the bugs would seek out the gas lines and attack from behind, disposing with the operator in short order.

This continued for weeks with no end in sight. The AI Stingers quickly learned that it took too long for a person to die with their stings and thus developed a new technique to put the population down. The previous generation of "dumb" Stingers had man-made toxins packed into them. These new AI Stingers went to the source for their toxin. Some of the waterways and canals were heavily polluted with the P2040. The AI Stingers recognized this and would swoop down to fill their bellies with the old toxin and then infect the awaiting masses on their return flight.

CHAPTER 53
RESOLUTION

One last shot at a military solution was in order and in one more laboratory. This time it came from Mexico, who hastily arranges a meeting between both the Mexican and American presidents.

"Mr. President, Mexico has been a good neighbor to us for hundreds of years. Your homeland has not been affected to the extent that ours has been. We have come to understand that one of your facilities may have a solution to this crisis. Is that true?" asked the American President.

"Sir, we have been working on a device that may help this worldwide disaster. You know some of us are intelligent down here and if given the opportunity will contribute positively to the world. You do know that we have more than tequila and tacos? Does that surprise you?" said the Mexican President, with disdain in his voice.

"Mr. President, we have always recognized the good nature and ingenuity of your culture and people. We have the highest regards for our neighbors."

"Yes, so much regard that you prevent us from coming across the border. We do feel welcome and appreciated. Now, it is our time to be the bully."

"Can we focus on business and take personalities and bias out of the equation?"

"You are correct Mr. President. Let us get down to business."

A large facility known as the Conquistar is housed outside Mexico City. It was owned by a private individual who subcontracted work for the military and government. When the government wanted a project to be accomplished, they turned here.

President Enrico Enbado informed his American counterparts that their researchers had come up with a solution that would annihilate the AI Stingers and any leftover Reds that were still drifting around. They had one stipulation: removal of the wall separating the two countries and the return of California, New Mexico and Arizona to their homeland.

"What you are asking for Mr. President is a removal of a quarter of our population and a transformation of our republic. We cannot allow this," said the American President.

"We are not negotiating some sort of a trade deal, Mr. President. The terms are non-negotiable and binding. I realize that you still have nuclear weapons and can threaten us with destruction but we also realize that without our help you will be destroyed as well. Our terms are generous and should be taken seriously. You have one day to respond to our demands."

"How do we know what you say is true and that it will work?"

"Of course, 'trust but verify' as one of your predecessors once said. I understand. We can try it on a small scale and then you will have your proof."

Desperate for help and on the brink of total hysteria once again, the Americans agreed to the demands.

The Mexicans would need the American satellites that were in orbit to accomplish the task. Their scientists had come up with an electronic algorithm that needed to be broadcast at high frequencies for the AI Stingers to receive. Once receiving the signal for several minutes, their brains would explode and they would fall to the ground.

The President of the USA wanted to do a trial run in one location before deploying it across the whole planet. The scientists and military from the Joint American command informed him that it would be unwise to proceed locally, for the AI Stingers would realize they were being targeted with a telecommunications signal and would quickly adapt.

"Mr. President, after consultation with our legislators and military people, we have agreed to the terms and have the papers to sign at your convenience."

"That is excellent news sir. We shall sign the terms and annexation of the states in Los Angeles tomorrow. If any of your citizens wish to stay and be citizens of Mexico, they are welcome. We have an open border."

They finalized plans for the weapon and coordinated the launch of the signal between all major governments on the planet. All systems were green for go. At 0600 hours on the first day of the New Year, 2044, the signal was broadcast across the world.

The result was a success!

When the signal was transmitted, the bugs reacted violently and were under no guidance and control of their own. Some attacked other Stingers. Some ran into the nearest mountainside, but the majority just popped in midair. All the AI Stingers died after only a few seconds and fell to the ground. Millions of the brown and toxic creatures littered the countryside, suburbia and cities throughout America and the world.

The Reds were stopped in their tracks as well. When the high-frequency signal hit their ears, their eyes went from blood red to glass and their bodies curled up into balls dropping as if a giant pesticide had been sprayed on them. Some made it to the rivers where they plunged themselves in, only to drown moments later.

The one adverse effect to this collective telecommunication broadcast was that the signal reacted with the millions of people who were given the original vaccinations in the early days of the outbreak, primarily the Untouchables, military and civilians who could afford the vaccinations. The electronic signal acted as a catalyst in the nervous system of people who were given the "special" shots in the early days, compliments of IS&G, and it left them reeling with pain for a few moments before collapsing with a brain hemorrhage.

The contagion that affected millions of the poor and commoners was now to be experienced by the one percent of the global population. Tens of millions of well to do people died instantly across the world. The ones not given a vaccine shot or who had one manufactured for the masses were unaffected.

The signal had a high-pitched sound that everyone could hear. It stopped people and animals in their tracks but was deadly to only the chosen few. The rest had no more than a splitting migraine headache that lasted for a few hours afterward.

Oliver came from outside to see if his parents had heard the siren and if they were all right. He called for them but got no reply in the house. He looked around frantically upstairs and downstairs but found nothing. He then went around the cabin to the swing his parents would sit on after dinner.

He found both of them holding each other on the ground next to the swing. They were motionless. Tina was just staring at them in disbelief, crying.

Raymond, who had to be inoculated because of his professional job died on the mountain along with Donna, side by side.

Oliver, who was absent that ill-fated day in school when the vaccination shots were being given to all his classmates, lived. Steve and Tina survived for they had run to the hills before being vaccinated years earlier. He and his daughter never returned to suburbia opting instead to stay in the mountaintop working in the fields living off the land and homeschooling.

"Son, we have much work to do cleaning up the environment and this world. We can't leave it up to others to fix the problems. You should mourn the loss of your parents who loved you but then I would like you to assist me on the other side of the mountain," said Blackstone, who of course was immune to the signal because of not taking the vaccinations that he pleaded others to be aware of in his blog and internet posts.

Dr. Blackstone worked with Oliver in the coming days and months. What he missed in formal education at the university, he gained in practical field experience in the outdoors connecting with nature.

"I hope you know by now that your oldest brother was not who they say he was Oliver."

Oliver nodded his head as a pupil sitting in one of the myriad of classes he had endured throughout his life.

"Be always questioning in science but also in people young man. Don't follow the herd mentality. Things aren't always what they seem."

"I never believed what people said or what was portrayed in the news about my brother. I know they were just doing their jobs. It's just hard when you're afraid to speak up or look into things because people say you're not patriotic if you do so."

"I'm a scientist as was your brother Oliver but I'll tell you this one crucial fact that many of my peers fail to recognize even with all their fancy degrees: sometimes the best conclusion is the simplest one. Always go with your gut instinct. It has saved primitive beings for the longest time and will save us as well- no matter how civilized or evolved we think we are."

Blackstone shared some of his major breakthroughs that were being developed up in the mountains, which he had written and preached about all those years ago. Much of the usable land and rivers were still tainted with the toxins dumped by humans and pests; however, weeds were always resistant to the chemicals and now were utilized as a staple of vegetation for consumption. Blackstone and his followers used natural herbs and organic compounds to make the once unused vegetation edible for humans. He also trained Oliver in the use of genuine recycling and pesticide-free farming. Steve and Tina didn't need any prodding to help Blackstone. They were loyal followers from the beginning.

Four years can seem like an eternity, especially when you are young and that time is high school. Four years can define a person and in the life of Oliver, it meant losing his entire family. He had a choice to be made: stay up in the mountains and live like a hermit or return to the city.

After nearly a year up in the mountain, Oliver took the knowledge he learned and returned to the city sharing his education with the Network in the hope that the next untainted generation would not follow in the footsteps of their predecessors.

THE END

ABOUT THE AUTHOR

Robert S. Azar is a lifelong educator and science enthusiast. He has worn many hats throughout his life including Senior Process Analyst, Chemistry Teacher and currently a High School Principal.

He lives in Allentown, PA with his wife, four children, and a cat.

Thank you so much for reading one of our **Sci-Fi** novels.
If you enjoyed our book, please check out our recommended title for your
next great read!

Culture-Z by Karl Andrew Marszalowicz

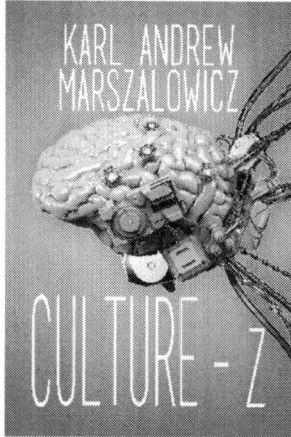

Made in the USA
Middletown, DE
07 December 2018